David Burnell is passionate a.
majestic cliffs but also its intri
tage gave him links with many
ries. No surprise, then, that l
a series of (so far) twelve Corn... Conundrums, each a tale of
crime today but with a long backstory. Merging the old and the
new is a special challenge, as are creating strong links between
female protagonist George Gilbert and the local police.

A Cornish Conundrum

Cornish Conundrum Author Reviews

Doom Watch: "Cornwall and its richly storied coast has a new writer to celebrate in David Burnell. His crafty plotting and engaging characters are sure to please crime fiction fans." Peter Lovesey

"A well-written novel, cleverly structured, with a nicely handled subplot . . ." Rebecca Tope

Slate Expectations: "an interesting view of an overlooked side of Cornish history with an engaging pair of sleuths, on the trail from past misdeeds to present murder." Carola Dunn

"An original atmospheric setting which is sure to put Delabole on the map. A many-stranded story keeps the reader guessing, with intriguing local history colouring events up to the present day." Rebecca Tope

Looe's Connections: "A super holiday read set in a super holiday location!" Judith Cutler

Tunnel Vision: "Enjoyable reading for all who love Cornwall and its dramatic history." Ann Granger

Twisted Limelight: "The plot twists will keep you guessing up to the last page. A thrilling Cornish mystery." Kim Fleet

"A clever, exciting story of modern-day skulduggery and romance on the beautiful north Cornish coast." Roger Higgs

Forever Mine: "An intriguing mystery set to the backdrop of a wedding in sleepy Cornwall, where all is not as it appears." Sarah Flint

Crown Dual: "A page-turning contemporary thriller with a deeply compelling narrative." Richard Drysdale

Unsettled Score: "A stack of mysteries to solve, including an unusual murder, all in a wonderful Cornish setting." Stephen Baird

Peter Lovesey holds multiple awards for his crime writing, including a Crime Writers' Cartier Diamond Dagger.

Carola Dunn pens Daisy Dalrymple and Cornish Mysteries.

Rebecca Tope writes the Cotswold and other Mysteries.

Judith Cutler created the DS Fran Harman crime series.

Ann Granger authors the Campbell and Carter Mysteries.

Dr Kim Fleet, poison expert, writes the Eden Grey Mysteries.

Dr Roger Higgs is a Bude geologist and local guide.

Sarah Flint authors the DC Charlotte Stafford series.

Richard Drysdale pens thrillers on Scottish Independence.

Stephen Baird, a Truro Cathedral Guide, is author of "Fire in the straw".

COSMIC

CALAMITY

A Cornish Conundrum

David Burnell

Skein Books

A Cornish Conundrum

COSMIC CALAMITY

Published by Skein Books, 88, Woodcote Rd, Caversham, Reading, UK

First edition: May 2024.

ISBN: 9798884176591

John Betjeman's poem, "Ireland with Emily", first appeared in "New Bats in Old Belfries" in 1945, published by John Murray (Publishers) Ltd. There is a limited extract in the Prologue.

The front cover shows Cornwall's Bedruthan Steps at high tide. The background is a commercial 747 jet, taken by a friendly plane spotter, Bill Gavin. Pictures inside include Cosmic Girl, the John Betjeman Centre at Wadebridge, Polruan from Fowey, the O'Connell Bridge in Dublin, St Enodoc's church and teddy-bear Archibald. Thanks to my wife, Marion, for the author cover photo; and to Dr Chris Scruby for refinements.

OUTLINE

PROLOGUE   September 1943

The hand-written invitation, unsigned, had been delivered just before he was due to leave the British Embassy for the day.

"Your presence is requested to a Gaelic exchange of views and poetry. Our representative will guide you once you leave the building."

That was a shock. He'd expected to be heading to the Maternity Wing to see his wife and their two-day old daughter. But he doubted if, right now, his wife even knew the time of day, let alone when to expect him. It had been a prolonged delivery, following twenty-four hours of sleepless labour. The whole thing had left him almost as exhausted as she was.

But he'd been warned on first arriving that, in this of all cities, and in these special times, such invitations were not to be turned down.

He gathered his coat, picked up his much-travelled wallet of material and left the building. As usual, he was one of the last to leave. His wasn't a job with fixed hours or well-defined routines.

He wondered, how would they know who he was? He wasn't going to hang about waiting. He mused on what sort of description they'd be given. "A rather battered man in his late thirties, looked more like he was hankering after a fading past than striving for a rosy future." That was what he might have said if he was crafting it himself. Except that he would have made it rhyme.

As he strode down the darkened street, a young woman detached herself from the building opposite and walked across the road to join him.

'Mr Betjeman, are you intending to come to exchange with us?'

He was tempted to reply, 'Or if not, how will you kill me?' But not many appreciated his oblique style of humour. It wasn't worth taking the risk.

'I am indeed. And you are to guide me there? Ought we to introduce ourselves? My name is John Betjeman. I was sent from London to build links with the Irish community.'

In the gloom, he tried to make out the woman who had joined him as they strode along. She had a strong Irish lilt – inevitably, this was a Dublin street; she was probably in her early twenties, with a round, cheerful face. It was too dark to assess the colour or style of her hair.

Whoever had sent the invitation had judged the chemistry of his personal tastes to perfection.

'They call me Niamh,' she replied. 'They tell me that you write poetry, John?'

'I try to. It's easier to write anything here than back in England. The wretched war blots out everything. Are you a poet, too, Niamh?'

She laughed. 'I wish. Perhaps one day, with proper tuition . . .'

Betjeman wondered, for an instant, if this was a subtle form of seduction. And, if so, just where he was now being taken. But he rebuked himself; this was just wishful thinking.

'Are we going far, Niamh?'

'Less than a mile. I was told to insist you put on a mask so you wouldn't see the exact location, but I refused. I feared you'd revolt and not come with me at all. That would be very bad for both of us.'

Betjeman considered her words and the implied threat.

3

'Niamh, I have no interest in knowing which house we're going to. On the other hand, I don't want to get you into trouble. What if you put a mask on me when we reach the street, so I won't know the house number? Then you can deliver me as specified.'

It was all bizarre, but these were bizarre times. When Britain had defeated the French Navy at Trafalgar, half Nelson's forces had been Irishmen. Ireland was then a part of the United Kingdom. Now, in the latest war, Ireland had declared itself neutral. But if it wasn't supporting Germany explicitly, there were plenty in Ireland with reason to distrust Britain. And the island would be a convenient place to launch an invasion.

Betjeman had been sent to "sell" Britain to the Irish and pour soothing oil on the troubled waters. No-one had ever said this would be easy, he told himself, as Niamh fixed on his mask.

She took John's arm and led him some way down the street. Someone must have been watching out for them for, as they stopped, he heard a front door being opened. Niamh took his poetry wallet from his arm, then led him up a few steps and inside what he presumed was a house.

Once in the hallway he had to take rather more steps down; he guessed that he was now in a cellar.

He was guided into a chair, but the mask remained on. Then he felt some rope being put around each arm and he found himself tied to a wooden armchair. There was no way of removing his mask now.

More ominously, he heard Niamh being dismissed. Was something going to happen to him that they didn't want the woman to witness? He braced himself for whatever was to come. Plenty of others had disappeared in this city over the years. And in the turmoil of war, he knew there wouldn't be a massive

4

search to find him. He wished he'd thought to leave the invitation to this event on his boss's desk.

There were a few minutes of uncomfortable silence. Then he heard someone else come into the room and sit themselves in front of him. An authoritative, male voice spoke. It wasn't one he recognised.

'Mr Betjeman, my colleagues and I have received many reports of you visiting Irish communities across Dublin over the past year. Can you explain yourself? You are a British citizen, I believe?'

A pause while Betjeman collected his thoughts.

'I have been sent here from London to improve the understanding between our two nations. I was chosen because I had spent many years holidaying in Ireland. I know many Irish poets and I find it much easier to write my poetry in Ireland than I do in England. That's why I have made it a priority to visit as many communities as I can identify. I hope that sharing my own poetry, and listening to poets here, can help build a bridge between us all.'

'Hm. And how have you identified these communities?'

'There is a personal network connecting them. Your citizens here are very sociable. Major poets are regularly invited to read some of their work, usually in one of the larger pubs. A few glasses of Guinness make a wonderful lubricant. I knew many of these bards in pre-war years; they also know and trust me.'

'Hm. All this "intelligence" is passed back to colleagues in the British Embassy?'

'I tell my boss what I'm doing, certainly. Tell him the names of both the sympathetic ones and the more hostile. But I don't make lists. I'm trying to make friends.'

Betjeman was about to add, 'That's why I'm here.' But he

recalled he was currently blindfolded and tied to a chair. It was not a purely voluntary visit.

There was a pause and then his interrogator spoke again. 'But we keep a list, Mr Betjeman. And your name appears on it – many times. In fact, too many times. You are far too curious for our tastes. You have the habits of a spy; and I have orders to eliminate you. I doubt you'll be greatly missed for some time. If at all.'

Suddenly, for Betjeman, the world started to turn upside down. He'd gone along with the invitation, thinking it would give him a broader perspective on life in Dublin, as seen from the other side. But by that he'd meant the Irish scene, not life beyond the grave. Now, it seemed, he was fighting for continuing life on planet earth.

As reality sank in, his voice became croakier. 'But I'm not a warmonger, sir, I'm not even a soldier. I'm just a poet. I'm no great enthusiast for the British establishment and their posh ways. Sure, I studied at Oxford, but they never gave me a degree. One of my poems was about bombs falling on Slough. And I've written plenty of appreciative poems about Ireland.'

He stopped for breath, but he was being given space to defend himself; there was no interruption so far. 'Let me share one with you.'

Betjeman was used to declaiming his own poems in the bustling pubs and clubs of Dublin. It didn't matter that he was blindfolded – he'd laboured for hours over the words, didn't need to see them before he spoke.

He took a deep breath. 'This one's called "Ireland with Emily":

Bells are booming down the bohreens,
White the mist along the grass.

6

Now the Julias, Maeves and Maureens
Move between the fields to Mass.
Twisted trees of small green apple
Guard the decent whitewashed chapel,
Gilded gates and doorway grained
Pointed windows richly stained
With many-coloured Munich glass.

The captive paused. 'Do you want to hear any more?'

There was a pause. It seemed he'd thrown his questioner. He wasn't used to hearing rhyming poetry from his prisoners.

'Mr Betjeman, that's beautiful. Could you start it again please?'

'It's all about what I saw on a long bike ride through Ireland one summer with a friend called Emily. Verse one is about the ladies we saw heading for Mass, in a small, whitewashed chapel.'

Betjeman paused then recited the verse again.

'Mr Betjeman, that's some of the sharpest verse I've ever heard. It's so evocative, I can picture the whole thing. Please could you give me the rest of the poem. I promise not to interrupt again.'

The poet saw a glimpse of redemption from his dire situation. Fortunately, "Emily" was quite a long poem and a hymn to the lonely beauty of the Irish countryside. It was also relatively intelligible, even to a non-poet.

He heard his questioner sighing with gentle appreciation as he recited all six verses. He felt he'd never voiced it so eloquently. But would it be eloquent enough?

It was as he was on the last verse that he heard a rustle of movement and the sound of the door being opened. Betjeman was an accomplished performer. He wasn't distracted and finished his recitation.

> *'There in pinnacled protection,*
> *One extinguished family waits*
> *A Church of Ireland resurrection*
> *By the broken, rusty gates.*
> *Sheepswool, straw and droppings cover,*
> *Graves of spinster, rake and lover,*
> *Whose fantastic mausoleum*
> *Sings its own seablown Te Deum,*
> *In and out the slipping slates.'*

To his amazement, after a few seconds pause, he heard the sound of clapping. Then a female voice spoke. It was Niamh.

'John, that was so special. You've moved my father to tears. And answered his many queries. He says I can take you away from here now. You've authenticated yourself, you won't be bothered again. You may not have been born in Ireland, but you've certainly taken us to your heart.'

PART ONE
THE CORPSE IN THE
CREVICE
APRIL 2023

Bedruthan Steps and (centre) the Queen Bess Rock

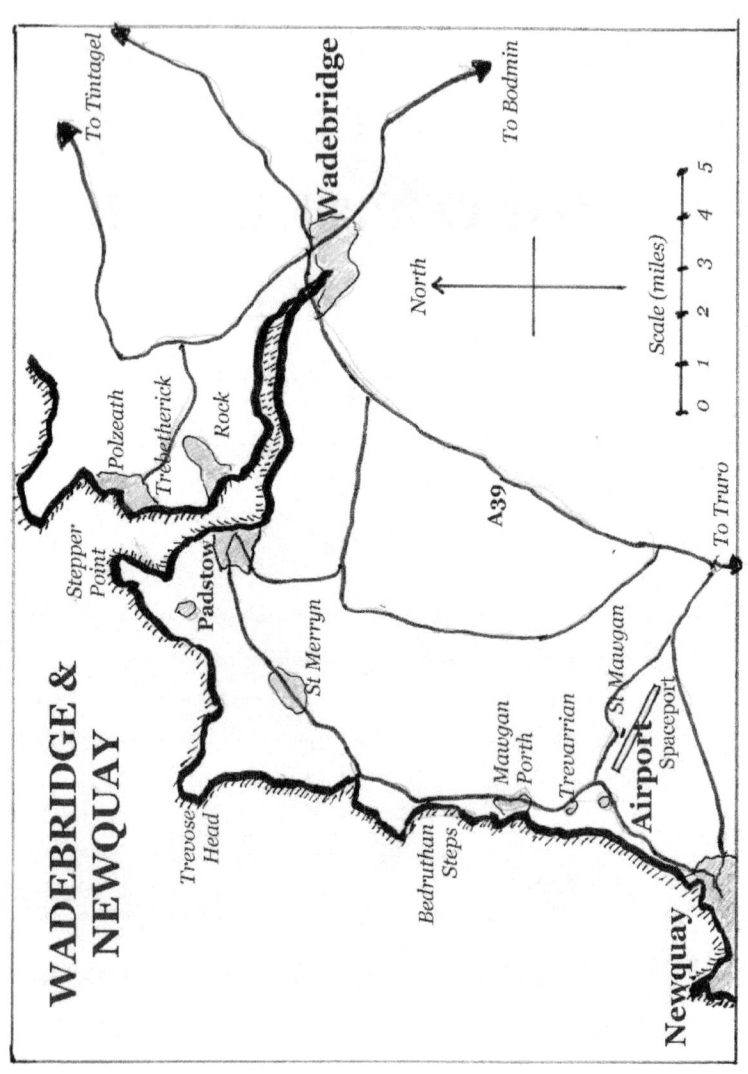

CHAPTER 1

Bedruthan Steps: Sat April 1st

The sharply pointed Queen Bess Rock was less than two hundred metres away, the lowest tier covered with slime and wet seaweed. Zac and Rosie looked slightly awed. There was no obvious route up and the cone got steeper as it neared the top.

It was the opening day of Newquay Climbing Club's summer season. The youngsters had asked to join; now Judith Stanley, the Club's President, had taken them in hand. This wasn't the Cuillins but the Bedruthan Steps were a useful starter.

The trio wandered round, looking for weaknesses in the Rock's defences. Judith was aware that she needed to protect her charges.

'We need to get onto the granite above the seaweed,' she observed. 'Zac, you're lighter than me. Could you manage to stand on my shoulders and scramble onto that ledge?'

It was tricky but eventually Zac was six feet above them, looking rather pleased with himself.

'Right, now Rosie. Zac, you reach down to give her a hand, I'll give her a heave.' The manoeuvre was slowly accomplished.

Finally, it was Judith's turn. She wasn't trusting herself to the novice hands offered from above. It was safer holding onto chunks of seaweed. Then she reached for a handhold on the ledge which she had only noticed as she helped the youngsters

11

to reach it.

The climb had begun.

An hour later the three had reached a narrow ledge just below the top. Only a tightrope specialist with a death wish could get any further. They could see where there had once been a head-stone and it had sheared off.

'It takes after Queen Bess's mother,' Judith observed. 'That was Anne Boleyn, you know. She lost her head too.'

The Queen Bess was the most northerly of the Bedruthan Steps. Judith suspected that this stack at least had been climbed before. There was a hint of a path that wound its way slowly round towards the summit. Only once had they needed to rope up; that had been a useful exercise in its own right.

'Well done, you two. Sit down and we'll have some choco-late.' Judith reached into her rucksack and pulled out a bar.

As they munched, feeling rather pleased with themselves, they glanced along to the other stacks. Progress of a sort was being made by club climbers on them all.

Then Rosie looked the other way, to Diggory's Island. It was higher than the Queen Bess. There was a similar undergirding of seaweed; above that, the rocky surface was heavily frag-mented. But the top itself was relatively level and covered with grass.

Judith followed her gaze. 'That's mostly granite. The main-land rocks that brought us along here are crumblier,' she told her. 'That was the problem with the footpath to the beach – lots of fallen rocks over the years. They daren't let the public use it anymore.'

Zac looked too and frowned. 'Hey. There's something odd over there. Look, Judith – on the seaward side, almost at sea level. Inside what looks like a small hollow.'

The youngster's eyesight was better than hers, Judith thought. She couldn't see anything unusual. But he was a keen lad, she'd better not dismiss it out of hand.

'What colour is it, Zac?'

'Sort of . . . well, sort of skin coloured. It might possibly be an arm. Over there.' He pointed downwards on the island.

Judith followed the angle. And then she saw it too. It looked horribly human. And then a gigantic wave broke over that part of the island. Once the water had seeped away the arm had disappeared.

They kept watching but there was no further sighting of the arm – or whatever it was. Judith made up her mind.

'Right, guys. View time over. We need to get back down to the beach.'

'Shouldn't we ring the Coastguard or something?' asked Zac.

Judith gave a short laugh. 'My phone doesn't work out here. There's no signal. We'll get down to the beach first. The tide's still on its way out. We'll be able to get closer to the island now. I don't want to worry anyone till we're sure of what we've seen.'

'The sea's still completely round the island,' observed Rosie gloomily. She hadn't seen anything at all.

'I'm afraid we're going to get our feet wet, guys. But maybe not much more.' They trudged back towards Diggory's Island. There was no idle chatter now.

Half an hour later they had repeated the earlier manoeuvre to clamber up over the seaweed and were on the uneven rocks of Diggory's Island. The challenge now was to maintain that level as they traversed round the island.

'We'd better rope up again,' asserted Judith. 'In all this spray these rocks are slippery. Then we'll move just one at a time.'

Slowly they made their way round, judging progress by the

line of the stacks and the top of Queen Bess, two hundred metres away.

And then they found it. On the seaward side of the island, now below them, rose a small promontory. It looked like an aspiring Queen Bess, but much smaller.

Between this and the main island was a dip, closed by fallen rocks at either end. And in the centre, half submerged and face down, completely naked, was the bloated body of a young woman.

As they watched, shaken, another wave came along and crashed over the boulders into the dip. The movement was enough to raise the woman's left arm for a few seconds. That must have been what they had seen from the top of Queen Bess.

'We're not going any further,' said Judith firmly. 'The poor woman's clearly been dead for some time. There's no point in adding more bodies down below.' She pulled out her phone and took a dozen pictures of the scene, then a few more looking across to the Queen Bess Rock and beyond.

It wasn't the kind of record she'd hoped to make. But it should convince the authorities that they'd seen something needing attention. First, though, they had to make their way back to a place where their phones would operate.

CHAPTER 2

Diggory's Island: Sat April 1st

If there'd been a video camera covering it, the retrieval of the dead woman from Diggory's Island could have made an epic human recovery presentation for years to come.

It was a good job Judith had taken so many photographs of the woman and the way she was trapped, or it might have been impossible to persuade the coastguards to take her seriously.

But Judith was a serious woman – her day job was Chief Librarian at Newquay – and she was used to dealing with authority. There was a dead body, it had been seen by visitors to Bedruthan Steps, and no-one knew when tourists would next be allowed on the beach. Apart from anything else, the body's discovery would do nothing for the local tourist industry. It could blight Newquay's reputation for years. And it was almost Easter; the spring season was about to begin.

Judith had finally got her phone to work once seated at Carnewas Café, run by the National Trust. She'd rung the coastguards in preference to the police, she'd seen nothing to suggest any criminal activity. The rest of the climbing club, out of phone contact, were still occupied on the main Bedruthan stacks.

The coastguards had sent someone straight away – Will Cosgrave, a sturdy man in his forties with piercing blue eyes and a rugged beard. He'd found Judith, Zac and Rosie having restorative mugs of coffee in the café. Quickly, with the aid of a large-scale map he'd brought with him, their story was recounted.

Will pointed at the map. 'So the body's stuck at the far side of Diggory's Island?'

Judith nodded. 'Yes, but there's no easy access. The island's covered in seaweed and is slippery from the recent rain. We had to rope up to get anywhere near it and we didn't go as far as the pool. The body's in a rocky crevice, trapped by boulders at either end. It's a young woman, I'd say, but the body is very bloated.'

'Mm. Would a boat get us anywhere near it?'

'Better a helicopter. If it let down a stretcher.'

Will considered her suggestion. 'You'd need at least a couple of guys to help move the body onto the stretcher. Judith, would you be prepared to help me? I'm a fairly experienced climber.'

Judith had feared it might come to this, but there was no alternative. Speed was important – they couldn't be sure what would happen to the body at the next high tide. 'Zac and Rosie shouldn't come with us, though,' she said. 'They're new to all this.'

'Couldn't we come and watch?' asked Zac. 'We could learn a lot. And explain to the rest of the club what's going on.'

Fifteen minutes later a rendezvous had been agreed by phone with a helicopter based at Newquay Airport and the four set off for Diggory's Island.

They'd allowed half an hour for Judith and Will to clamber over the Island and get poised to pull the body out of the foaming waves. By then the helicopter should be overhead. It was a calm day: the helicopter could easily maintain its position. And Judith felt confident with Will as her companion; he knew how to keep his balance on the slippery rocks.

Soon after they'd arrived at the pool the helicopter appeared, hovering fifty metres above. A hatch opened and a rope appeared, attached to a stretcher. It was lowered down to them and Will released it. Next, a crewman was lowered – Judith never found out his name.

Then the hard work began. They had to coax the woman's body out of the pool and onto the stretcher. The surging waves made this harder and soon they all were soaked to the waist. The victim was a slim woman, so the dead weight was manageable. But they couldn't grip too hard or they'd pull the body to pieces. It needed the three of them to move her, very gently, onto the stretcher.

Next the chopper crewman strapped her down, then looped the stretcher onto the still-dangling rope. He waved to his colleagues above and slowly, ever so slowly, it rose back up to the helicopter and was pulled inside.

A few minutes later, the rope came down again and the crewman was hauled up to join her. The hatch was closed. Then, with a roar, the craft swung round and disappeared in the direction of Newquay hospital.

There was nothing else to be done. Judith and Will made their way carefully back across the island and then up the cliffs. Zac and Rosie were taken on by other members of the climbing club. Fifteen minutes later the recovery pair were back in Carnewas Café with mugs of coffee. Not just tired physically, but highly stressed from the activity they'd just completed.

'I know I'm the Climbing Club president, but I don't feel like doing any more climbing today,' said Judith. 'I feel sort of tangled up inside. I'm a librarian, I'm not used to handling dead bodies.'

Will looked at her across the table and felt a wave of sympathy. 'Is anyone waiting for you at home?'

She gave a wry smile. 'I'm afraid not. The trouble is, tonight would be good to have someone to talk to.'

'I'm in much the same boat. Would you like to go out somewhere for a leisurely meal?'

Judith grinned, she hadn't been asked out for a long time. 'I'd really appreciate that, Will. But I don't want to muck up any plans of yours.'

He gave a hollow laugh. 'Plans? Me? I'm the least socially active man in Newquay. Which part of Newquay d'you live, Judith? Is there anywhere that's suitable for us to eat near to you?'

A quarter of an hour later it was all settled. The Copper Kettle had been chosen as a suitable place to eat, not far from either home. First, though, they'd each go back and get out of their climbing gear. Her trousers were soaking from where they'd had to step into the pool to recover the dead body.

Most of all, Judith relished the chance of a long, hot bath.

At six o'clock, Will was already waiting at the door of the Copper Kettle when it opened for the evening. He hoped he didn't look too keen. But it was alright, the restaurant catered for all tastes.

Judith turned up ten minutes later. She wanted to make the most of an unexpected meal out and had changed into a dark blue dress that Will found rather striking (though of course he said nothing). They decided to have a drink before their meal.

'D'you come here often?' he asked, as they sat down with their ciders.

She shook her head. 'Not that often. When I'm not working, my main relaxation is climbing. It's a complete contrast, you see. I enjoy the company of my fellow-climbers, but the meals we eat afterwards reflect the pubs we've been close to rather than anywhere posh. This is welcoming in a more subtle way. Thank you for suggesting it.'

'I've never been here before,' Will admitted. 'My work takes me all over Cornwall. By the time I'm back home I'm tired, can't be bothered to go out again. I guess I'm a bit like you: weekend coastguard duties make up most of my social life. I must say, it's really nice to come here.'

They'd booked a meal for seven and chatted amicably in the meantime. It turned out they had a lot in common. Time shot by until they were called.

They'd each ordered a standard tandoori and a second glass of cider. Judith forced herself to be less superficial. This was her opportunity. If she didn't share her thoughts and fears with Will, they would keep her awake all night – or much longer.

'Will, have you had much to do with dead bodies?'

'Hardly anything, actually, Judith. Most coastguard work is for safety or protection rather than body recovery. Today was far worse than anything I've had to deal with before.'

'For me, the problem was that it came out of the blue. One minute I was coaching a couple of youngsters, enjoying the day, the next I was looking at a dead body.' She shivered. 'D'you reckon that's as bad as being with a close relative, say, during a lingering death?'

Will considered. 'It's bound to take time to process. You're probably still in shock. Maybe if we talked around it, what might be behind it, that would help us to cope?'

There was a pause as they started their meals. 'D'you reckon she'd been there for some time?'

'I'd say several months,' said the coastguard. 'They'll have a postmortem; that might sharpen the estimate. But it'll only ever be a range. It'll depend on water temperature and other factors.'

Now they were into the subject, Judith had many more questions.

'Where might she have gone into the water?'

Will shrugged. 'It could be anywhere up from Newquay. There are rip tides running parallel to the coast here. Unless we know how long she's been in the water, we can't start to estimate where she went in.'

Judith paused for a mouthful of her curry. 'Poor kid. I wonder who she was?'

'That's a challenge for the police. I looked carefully but didn't see any marks on her body. No tattoos or anything. And remember, her body was bloated. I bet that's wiped out her fingerprints.'

'But Will, they can still get her DNA, can't they?'

'Oh yes. But unless she had a criminal record, there'd be no way to make much use of it.' He shook his head. 'And she didn't have any clothes the police could work with either.'

Judith nodded. 'That was odd, too. How could that happen?'

'Well. Either she voluntarily went into the water fully naked and then got into trouble while swimming; or else someone took all her clothes off her before dumping her in the water.' A pause then, 'It'll be the first. But no-one strips off outdoors at this time of year if they can avoid it.'

Suddenly Judith looked apprehensive – or was it embarrassed?

'Whatever's the matter?' he asked.

'I can think of one lot of people that do. On New Year's Day, anyway.'

Will looked at her. Why on earth did she look embarrassed? Another mouthful of his tandoori as he pondered. Then he had an idea. 'You're not talking about the New Year's Day swim out of Porth Beach, are you?' The Newquay Naturists had sprung up during Covid, though he'd never been up early enough to see them in action.

Then an even more shocking thought struck him. 'Judith, you weren't one of those brave women that stripped off and plunged into the icy-cold Atlantic? Were you?'

CHAPTER 3

Newquay Library: Thurs April 6th

It was almost a week before a police officer came to find Judith Stanley at the library. She had worked in Newquay for many years and recognised the man: Sergeant Charlie Higgins. He'd been around for years too.

Fortunately, her role meant she had access to a private office when required and she showed him in.

'Coffee?' she asked. Higgins nodded, this was going to be a low-key interview. Nothing more was said until two mugs of coffee were brought in to them. Then he produced a notebook.

'Can I have your account of last Saturday, please, Ms Stanley?'

Judith had thought about little else all week and was glad of the chance to unload.

'Saturday was the opening meet of the Newquay Climbing Club. We'd only decided to go to Bedruthan Steps three days before. The main path down to the beach is closed, but we got down a bit further along.

'I took a couple of newcomers up the Queen Bess Rock, that's the most northerly stack. Near the top, one of them spotted what might be some part of a body, right on the edge of Diggory's Island. So we climbed down and went over to have a look.

'Diggory was wet and slippery so that took us a while. Then we reached the point where we could look down; there was a body, trapped in a crevice on the seaward side. But it was certainly dead: it was face down in the water. Only piles of boulders were keeping it in.

'My phone didn't work on the beach, so we retreated to Carnewas Café and I called the coastguard. Will Cosgrave was on duty and came straight away. He called the Air Ambulance, then he and I climbed back over Diggory and down to the victim. The helicopter came and hovered overhead.'

She sighed. 'Between us, we got the body out of the water, onto a stretcher and up into the helicopter. It was a grim task. I'd never touched a dead body before, let alone help to fasten one onto a stretcher.'

There was silence. Higgins wrote diligently onto his notebook. Then he looked up.

'Had you ever seen the victim before?'

'Not to the best of my knowledge. Neither naked nor fully clothed. Have you identified her?'

'Not yet, Ms Stanley.' He paused for a moment. 'Why d'you say "neither naked nor clothed". It's an unusual turn of phrase.'

Tricky ground. Judith took a second to answer. 'Well, I've no idea how she dressed. As far as I know she never came into the library. But her face when I saw it was bruised and very puffed up. I've no idea what she really looked like.'

'I may be able to help with that,' smiled Higgins. 'We've got special software at the police station these days. It can reconstruct an original face from pictures of a battered visage. Very useful with the beaten-up corpses that we get here in summer months. Would you like to see?'

Judith nodded. The policeman opened a folder and pulled out an A4 image. It showed an attractive woman in her thirties, with blue eyes and the faint suggestion of a cheeky grin. Her hair was a shoulder-length honey blonde. 'Can you recognise that?'

Judith looked at it carefully from several angles. She was used to scrutinising documents. It certainly wasn't anyone she knew well. But it was possible that she'd seen the face before – and not too long ago.

'I've no idea who she is – or was. The face looks slightly familiar. But you can't be sure of her hair colour, can you?'

'How d'you mean?'

'Some women dye their hair all the time. If you're going to use this picture to track her identity, you also need to generate variants with different hair colours.'

'That's a helpful comment. Thank you. But if you think there's any chance you might have met her before, you can keep it. The only thing is, if you're showing it to anyone else, I'd really like you to keep quiet on where it came from.'

Judith was surprised. 'If you insist. But why aren't you using the local media? Someone must know her.'

'We're not going public until we have more information. Knowing where this came from – one of our most famous beaches - could cause widespread alarm. Or dent Newquay's reputation for years.'

It seemed there was nothing else to be said. Higgins gathered his material and left Judith to her library duties.

That evening Judith phoned Will. 'Hi. I saw the police this morning.'

'No problems?'

'None at all. But I wouldn't mind bouncing a few things off you.'

'Fine with me. D'you fancy another meal at the Copper Kettle on Saturday?' Details were quickly agreed.

This evening Judith was there first, this time in a splendid lemon outfit.

'You look very smart,' he told her, when they met.

'Thank you, Will. But don't expect something new every week. I don't have that many outfits.'

They ordered halves of cider and sat in the lounge. There were no crowds this early in the evening.

'The police came to see me yesterday afternoon,' Will began. 'It'd be good to swap notes.'

Judith smiled. They had something else in common. 'How was it for you?'

'Very straightforward. I'd met the officer before. I guess I had less to say than you would.'

'But did you learn anything on the state of the enquiry?'

Will frowned. 'It was disappointing, actually. As far as I could tell, they hadn't made much progress at all. All I gained was an aside or two from the victim's postmortem.'

'Better than nothing. Well done.' She looked at him questioningly.

'They narrowed down the time of death. Reckoned it was December or January. As you and I saw, the body was horribly smashed up from its time in the crevice. But no really suspicious findings. The woman had not been drinking heavily and there were no signs of her being on drugs.'

'What about the cuts and bruises on her head?'

'They thought these were most likely the result of being bashed about on Diggory. Nothing definite enough to prompt further inquiries, anyway. The police won't do any more till they are sure of her identity. She didn't match anyone recently reported missing in Newquay. But they asked me to keep it all quiet for the time being.'

'Same as me,' said Judith. 'But they did give me a computer-derived picture of the victim before her last swim.'

'And did you recognise her?'

'She did look faintly familiar. I may have seen her before - but if I did it would only be a chance encounter.'

'I don't suppose she was part of your Newquay Naturists?'

Judith sighed, she wished she'd never mentioned it. 'I only did it once, Will. I was shamed into it by two of my younger library colleagues, didn't want to appear fuddy-duddy.'

She didn't want to get into detail, but it did seem this was the nearest they'd got to a clue.

'The thing is, Will, when standing cold and completely naked on a wind-swept beach, my only thought was getting the dip over as fast as possible. I didn't take much notice of who else would be suffering with me. I'm pretty sure our victim was not there, but I can't be certain.'

'I don't suppose anyone took a group photograph before you went in?'

Judith looked horrified. 'Will, we made jolly sure no pictures were taken at all. I mean, three of us were librarians. We certainly didn't want to feature in the Newquay Gazette: "These girls are always ready to remove their covers."'

At that moment they were called to their meal; the table was ready. They had plenty more to say to one another. None of it, though, was relevant to the body on Bedruthan Steps.

PART TWO

COSMIC GIRL

JANUARY 2023

Cosmic Girl, the 747 Jumbo Jet that carried the rocket

CHAPTER 4

Newquay Spaceport: Tues Jan 10th

Suzanne Kennedy, the Spaceport Chair, was in full flow. It was the senior managers' review on the brave but calamitous attempt at putting satellites into orbit from the airport, the evening before. She was in no mood to take prisoners.

'So the bloody airliner took off without difficulty?'

'It did, Ms Kennedy. Even though it had 24 tons of rocket hanging under one wing.'

'That's the benefit of a long runway with the sea beyond,' added Ruth Fisher, the Operations Director. 'You'll recall, that's why Newquay was chosen for this project in the first place.' There were strong arguments for all that they'd tried to do, it was important they weren't lost in the sound and fury. But right now, it wasn't an easy battle to fight.

'How old was this plane?'

Ruth was tempted to say 1983, her year of birth, just to stoke the blaze - perhaps if she said it confidently, Suzanne would self-combust? - but she restrained herself. '2005, I believe. If we hadn't hired it to launch the rocket, it would still be in some form of commercial use.'

'And we're sure we didn't get an old banger by mistake? Or a 747 that had once been hijacked in Beirut? Bought back as part of some devious exchange scheme?'

Ruth shook her head. 'It only arrived here in December. It came from New York. Our technicians have checked and double-checked everything on it. As well as arranging for it to carry our 24-ton rocket underneath the left wing.'

'Left wing, eh? To appease Joe Biden, perhaps?'

Ruth sighed. 'It's a random choice, Suzanne, got nothing whatsoever to do with the American administration. I agree it's got some funding from the British government, but that's 'cos Boris Johnson, when he was flying high two years ago, thought Britain conquering space was a sellable alternative to leaving our European cousins.'

'Then he imploded himself instead. So now we've got the Sunny Spreadsheet. Is he as enthusiastic?'

The nickname made Ruth smile. 'That remains to be seen. Last night's abortive flight won't have done much to make the case for the Spaceport. Not with the UK economy this tight, anyway.'

'But somehow or other, the plane took off?'

'Yes. And reached almost 35,000 feet.'

Suzanne scowled. 'Do we know that for certain? Couldn't it just have been a dodgy altimeter?'

'Well, it was being tracked by Goonhilly Earth Station, over on the Lizard. They are recognised to be among the best trackers in the world. They had the plane covered for its whole flight.'

'So then, Ruth, what went wrong?'

'The rocket shot away from the plane exactly as planned. Then it was time for stage one to launch the second stage, holding all the satellites. Which is where it went wrong. Rocket Two just didn't fire.'

There was silence. Her last five words encapsulated the nub of their challenge.

Suzanne was about to launch another round of blistering

invective on the project when the phone on her desk rang.

She scowled at it. 'I thought I told Maggie "no calls under any circumstances". Gee, can't you guys do anything?'

'It must be really important, ma'am.' pleaded the do-all gofer, Mal.

'Unless it's Joe Biden himself they're going to get a bucketload of my anger and frustration. We're in a crucial meeting.'

But the ringing continued with a very shrill tone. Perhaps it was important. Suzanne picked up the phone and listened. Then she put her hand over the speaker and turned to the group.

'It's some guy called Wallace. Who the hell is he?'

'Greg Wallace?' asked Mal. 'He hosts a cookery programme on BBC2.'

For a second Ruth thought Mal might have succeeded where she'd failed, in igniting Suzanne to self-destruct. She held her breath. Then, when nothing happened, she had a better idea.

'It can't be him, Suzanne. It'll be Ben Wallace. He's the UK Defence Secretary. The longest-serving members of the current Cabinet. Please, please be polite to him.'

Suzanne was used to steamrolling remorselessly over those below her. But she also knew the need, occasionally, to submit graciously to those above. She turned back to her phone. 'Mr Wallace,' she began, 'how kind of you to call.'

The rest of the senior managers didn't know quite what to do: go to the outer office until called back in, or wait for some guidance from Suzanne? They couldn't overhear what Wallace was saying but they could infer quite a lot from their boss's response. Ruth thought Suzanne might say something that could later be used against her, if her dark mood continued.

'Of course, we're all very disappointed, Mr Wallace. The

staff here have worked very hard for months. It was all going so well until the final stage. But there were plenty of successful aspects and no-one was injured. I'm sure we'll succeed next time.'

It appeared the last observation was premature. Or, at least, it was not shared by Ben Wallace. They couldn't hear his exact response, but his tone seemed to grow harsher.

'Sabotage?' she said. 'Mr Wallace, there's been nothing whatsoever to point to that. It's just a technical fault on a highly complex project. Space is the new frontier, you know.'

There was silence at the Newquay end for a few minutes. Then Suzanne spoke again.

'I don't think we need help from British Security, thank you. They haven't been remotely helpful to me in the past . . . Oh, I see. You're not making an offer, it's an instruction. . . OK, an order. . . So when should we expect them. . . Of course we'll do everything we can to assist. But I'll be amazed if it produces anything at all. . . It's good to know the British Government is behind us. Thank you very much indeed. Good morning.'

It's never easy for a somewhat bullying, forceful Chair to recover his or her authority after being so publicly humiliated by a higher authority, especially in front of her own colleagues.

In retrospect it would have been better if her team had walked out as soon as the call had begun, and she could pretend afterwards that nothing had happened against her will. But life is full of might-have-beens: Suzanne was a woman of action, not a dreamer.

There was a moment's pause. No-one dared to speak. Then Suzanne glanced round the room and started to explain. Her voice was quieter now. Ruth perceived that an external enemy had replaced her own, failure-burdened subordinates. There was someone else to hate.

'The Ministry of Defence fear that the failure of the UK's first own rocket launch is such a triumph for our enemies that they might have had a hand in what's happened. Mr Wallace is sending someone from the British Security Services down here. They are to conduct an investigation into the Spaceport's external security. Would it be possible for an enemy agent to cause the failed rocket launch? Is there any evidence at all that someone has done so?'

It wasn't good news. In less than twenty-four hours, the Spaceport had gone from being a potential major success story for Brexit into an addition to its disasters. Politicians would support success; they would keep well away from failure.

'When will they arrive?' asked Ruth.

Suzanne shrugged. 'Apparently someone is already on their way. Wallace said that the sooner the investigation began, the better its chance of success.'

There was a pause as the news was considered. Then the comments began.

'They'll be coming from London,' said the Finance Director. 'That's a six-hour drive. We're safe for a bit.'

'Unless they fly down here by helicopter, or are parachuted onto the airfield, that does give us a little time.'

'It might be someone brought back specially from the battle-fields of Ukraine,' offered the Technical Director. 'If so, they'll probably still be in combat gear.'

'That's right. Steel helmet and a bullet-proof vest.'

'Heavy-duty boots.'

'Mud all over the carpets.'

Black humour was all very well but it was a miserable future to imagine. It was bad enough the staff trying to spot possible launch weaknesses for themselves. Even worse having an outsider foisted on them, someone with no understanding of local sensitivities.

They were still bickering when there was a knock at the door. Then Suzanne's secretary, Maggie, appeared.

'I'm really sorry to interrupt, guys. But there's someone here to see you all. It has something to do with the phone call you've had recently.'

Behind her, waiting to be invited in, was the promised Security Officer.

CHAPTER 5

Introducing Maxine Travers: Tues Jan 10th

The newcomer stepped into the Control Centre and introduced herself.

'Good morning, ladies and gentlemen. I'm Maxine Travers. I've been sent to help you check your external security.'

It wasn't a battle-hardened returning soldier, at any rate. Maxine was around fifty and dressed – but not overdressed – in a maroon business suit. She had a round face, fair hair and a cheerful grin. But there was certainly tension here. She could tell that she was not immediately welcome.

But they had been asked by the Defence Secretary to give her every assistance. They had at least to start off being civil.

The Chair stood to shake Maxine's hand, then returned to her desk. 'I'm Suzanne Kennedy. I'm the recently arrived Chair of the Newquay Spaceport Company.'

'And I'm Ruth Fisher. I'm the Operations Director, I've been here from the beginning, five years ago. I have overall responsibility for every piece of kit in the spaceport, how it's chosen and the way it's used. Also security. My staff handle the links with Newquay Airport. We share the same runway, you see.'

The rest of the group stood up to shake Maxine's hand then spoke in turn.

'I'm Tom Willoughby. I'm the Technical Director. Most of my work is managing the Unit where we take delivery of, and assemble, the rockets, their fuel and the way the larger one is attached to the aircraft. I also deal with the company that provides the plane. That's not our own, of course, it's hired from a commercial airline.'

Next came a smart-suited accountant, still clutching a briefcase. 'I'm Colman Carter, Finance Director. I deal with the accounts, keep the City happy and make sure we pay for everything we use.'

Finally came Helen Smithers, the Human Resources Manager.

Ruth was well-aware of the need for courtesy and saw to her horror that Maxine was still standing. She grabbed one of the spare chairs and pushed it forwards, allowing the newcomer to be made part of a wider circle.

'This is very much a Cornish-based project,' she began. 'There are lots of local sensitivities. Do you know Cornwall very well, Maxine?'

Maxine took a deep breath. The question was almost patronising, but taking ten minutes to introduce herself would pay off if it reduced some lines of opposition.

'Well, I was born in Helston, on the Lizard. I studied maths at Cambridge. For the last few years I've been working at the Bude Listening Station, up at Cleave Camp. That's an outpost of GCHQ. I'm married to a police officer who was born and bred just up the coast in Delabole. And we got married at St Just on Land's End. How about you?'

It was a good job she addressed the question to Ruth. The Operations Director was the only other one there with any sort of matching answer. 'I've not been as far as Cambridge. I was brought up in Truro, latterly at Truro College. I studied space science at Exeter and later at Leicester. After that I spent three years with NASA, in the United States. Then in 2018 I had the chance to start a UK launch facility at Newquay and I grabbed it with both hands.'

No-one else rushed to offer a Cornish autobiography. Maxine guessed they'd come from further afield. She made a mental note to learn their backgrounds in due course.

'Perhaps it would be best,' she said, 'if I explained what I've been told so far, which I admit is not a great deal. Then we can work out how we're going to make this happen.'

'Go ahead,' said Suzanne. Before she opened hostilities, she wanted to know what they'd be up against.

Maxine glanced at her, then continued. 'I'm on the senior management team at Cleave Camp, with responsibility for external contacts. Our Director was rung up by GCHQ Cheltenham earlier this morning. He'd just had a call from London. Security was in a panic about your space flight last night and they urgently needed someone to come and take a look. As someone with a Cornish background and a wide range of security experience, already based in Bude, I was the obvious choice.

'I've listened to Radio Five Live on the journey down here, so I know what Adrian Chiles thinks about last night's launch, but that's the limit of my knowledge. I'm starting from a long way back. But I think, if you let me, I can help you ask the right questions.'

There was a pause before Suzanne responded. 'So, on your own admission, Maxine, you don't know much about space exploration.'

'No more than Adrian Chiles, anyway. But I'm not here to comment on how you've been going about it, or where it might need enhancement. I'm simply looking for ways that an outside group could learn enough about what you are doing to mess it about.'

Suzanne frowned. 'And you think that's what happened?'

'No, I don't. As far as I can see, space travel is a complicated activity. Even with the best preparation it could go wrong in lots of ways. There are a host of unavoidable risks: space is a hostile environment. It doesn't always allow for belt and braces.

'All I can do, as a newcomer, is to think how an outsider could possibly make trouble. I don't guarantee I can find it, mind, but if, after say a month, I've found nothing, then the Government will be very relieved. And they do have a stake in this, don't they?'

The group were not yet welcoming her with open arms, but she sensed they'd become slightly less hostile.

'So how d'you plan to make this work?' asked Ruth. Maxine sensed she would be the easiest person to get alongside. They'd got a Cornish background in common, if nothing else. That would be fine with her.

'I don't want to get in your way, guys. Clearly you all have plenty to talk about, trying to make sense of what happened on last night's flight. It will probably work best if I talk to each of you – or your staff – individually.'

'Obviously,' said Ruth, 'what we're talking about here is highly confidential. We don't need you to contribute at all. But I'm sure we wouldn't mind if you stayed to listen.' She glanced round; Suzanne looked far from ecstatic at the idea, but no-one openly disagreed.

'As you say, space travel is complicated. There's a lot to learn, so that might be the fastest way of bringing you on board. Then, after we've had lunch, you can come back to my office, and we can work out what needs attention from a security point of view.'

CHAPTER 6

Lunch with the Ops Director: Tues Jan10[th]

'Maxine, let's go for lunch,' said Ruth. 'We have a works canteen for our staff upstairs, though the other Directors don't usually eat there. Perhaps they don't need to eat at all; or they take a lunchtime break off-site. If you're going to help us, you'll need to see how the place operates here on a day-to-day basis.'

Maxine dutifully followed her up the stairs. Her head was spinning from information overload. She hadn't deemed it wise to take notes in the fraught meeting she'd attended with Suzanne and her colleagues, so she had plenty of questions. But it seemed Ruth understood that and was wanting to help her.

Ruth stepped ahead of her in the canteen queue. A tall, determined woman in a bright yellow suit, with short-cropped blondish hair. She reminded Maxine slightly of a stretched-out Nicola Sturgeon. And she noted that Ruth was completely at home here – the same level as all the other diners.

There was a limited menu, but it was perfectly adequate. They loaded their meals onto trays, then Ruth led them to a table for two by the window. Maxine found herself looking out on a long runway, though she could see no planes flying at present. She could also see a single-storey flight terminal, with a Cornish flag waving in the breeze, on the far side.

'It's a great view.'

'Here is where most of us watched take-off from last night. Seeing a jumbo jet with a massive rocket underneath a wing was pretty spectacular.'

Maxine thought she'd better explain herself. 'When I go out to meet clients, I normally have a few days to familiarise myself with background material before I see them. I'm afraid I'm pitifully ignorant here. There wasn't much advance publicity, was there?'

Ruth chuckled as she started her chicken curry. 'There was none at all, Maxine. We'd hoped to fly last week, you see, but it was too windy. But we couldn't persist with the craft at high readiness for long. And we couldn't halt regular traffic to and from the airport. Each day we asked them not to fly was costing us an arm and a leg. Yesterday the forecast was better, so we decided at lunchtime that this was our best chance.'

'Whew. So there wasn't advanced publicity that passed me by. That's a relief. Ruth, would you mind sketching out the basics. Why is this major trial happening down here, in the depths of Cornwall? Is it usual to be launching a space rocket from a high-flying aircraft?' She spooned some mango chutney onto her plate and started on her curry.

Ruth nodded. 'It's rare to try and launch from a plane, actually. But if it can be done reliably it will reduce costs and environmental impact. And if you're going to do it, you need a long runway, preferably one pointing straight out to sea. As we have here.'

She ate some of her curry before she continued. 'So in one sense last night was a big success because, as far as we know, that part of the operation succeeded perfectly. The 747 took off, reached a great height, then launched its rocket and returned to earth. But trying to explain that to an impatient media, when the final stage fell limply into the sea, is a tough ask.'

'Even a master salesman like Boris Johnson might have struggled.'

Her hostess grinned. 'Oh, he intended to be here for the launch in person. But then he was fired instead. Anyway, Boris doesn't have much interest in complicated detail. And whatever his strengths, he's no scientist.'

There was silence for a few moments as they continued their meal.

But Maxine had been thinking. 'So the fact that the flight happened at night wasn't pre-planned? Have you got pictures of the plane racing down the runway with its big rocket hanging off one wing?'

Ruth grimaced. 'Not planned. It all came from uncertainty about the weather. Taking off in a gusty wind with a lopsided aircraft would be dangerous – not worth the risk. And it was a dark night, there are the landing lights along the runway, but they don't have many floodlights at Newquay Airport. They don't usually receive or send flights at night, you see.

'There might be a few amateur videos, but no official pictures for the media. In fact, I was tempted to tell no-one and pretend it never happened. But Suzanne wouldn't let me. And we'd still incurred plenty of costs.'

They finished their curries and started on the fruit salad. 'I've got coffee back in my office,' said Ruth. 'You can have as many mugs as you like. I'm sure you'd prefer that.'

But Maxine was not distracted, she still had her teeth into the case. 'So, if you didn't know it was happening till twenty-four hours ago, Ruth, nobody else would know either?' She paused. 'That's important, you see. If foreigners wanted to do anything at all, they'd need to learn about it from lunchtime onwards. That's not very long at all. And any leak, whether accidental or deliberate, must come from a very tight circle.'

Back in her own office, which was on the floor below, also

overlooking the runway, Ruth invited Maxine to take one of the easy chairs and ordered coffee from Chloe, her personal assistant. While that was being brought and Ruth dealt with a few urgent emails – the failed flight had many repercussions – Maxine opened her laptop and started tapping in as much as she could remember from the earlier conversations.

Once Ruth had joined her, Maxine tried to plug some of the gaps.

'You've explained the final timing. But there must have been a local expectation it would happen, even if the exact date was uncertain. You said Newquay Airports cancelled regular flights from yesterday afternoon?' Ruth nodded. 'But they must have known that the spaceflight was going to happen sometime soon. And the local grapevine would transmit that as far as Newquay.'

Ruth nodded again. 'Of course. We only had a short list of invited guests inside this building, Chloe can give you details. There were also onlookers in the main airport reception. I've no idea who they were. But they wouldn't see much. It was very dark.'

Maxine decided to leave this topic for the time being and ask some wider questions. 'You mentioned this morning that your remit included security. How is that handled?'

Ruth considered for a moment. 'Our main concern has been protecting the Spaceport site from intruders. We have some very valuable kit in here that we wouldn't want damaged.

'Now, the Spaceport area is what used to be the military part of the airfield. Until quite recently that was occupied by the American air force, and as you can imagine, security was tight. There are still cameras on top of high wired fences. Each of those is linked to a separate security unit which has a twenty-four-hour presence. I'll introduce you to the staff later. Nothing untoward has been reported from there for years.'

Maxine smiled. 'Yes. I had to get through that to reach the Control Centre. Even with my GCHQ documents that was hard work. As a security professional I was quite impressed.'

Ruth frowned. 'It shouldn't be that hard. If you're going to be here for more than a couple of days, I'll get you an entry pass.'

'That would be useful. I've been told to give it two weeks, more if I uncover anything. We have to convince the Government that there's nothing to worry about.'

'Where are you staying?'

'To be honest, Ruth, I came here in such a rush I've not given it any thought.'

'Well. The Spaceport has a set of reserved rooms in the Molesworth Arms in Wadebridge. It's not the Ritz, but it's good for Wadebridge. Traditional comfort, you might say. And unless you fancy an early morning dip, you wouldn't really want to stay in Newquay.'

Maxine shivered at the thought of the cold Atlantic. 'Not this time of year, anyway.'

'Right. There's no-one there at present, shall I book you in?'

Maxine considered. 'I'd need to go home at weekends. I have a three-year-old daughter who's at nursery. My husband takes and fetches her on his way to work and we have friends who'll cover for us. I may even be able to do some of the cross checking from home.'

Ruth was silent for a moment, reflecting.

'Look, Maxine, your expertise is really vital here. If there is anything wrong, then between us we need to find it. Right now, you're the key visitor to the Spaceport. If the Prime Minister comes down I might need to throw you out, but in the meantime you can use the accommodation as you wish.

'Right now, you see, our whole existence is hanging by a thread. We really need you.'

The Operations Director paused to assemble her thoughts.

'If it's just some technical malfunction within the rocket, then finding that is Tom Willoughby's remit, our technical expert. That might lead to an improved design, or backup facilities that will fire the rocket if the main routine fails.

'But if it's not an accident, then it's even more important we accept that, take steps to sort it and make sure it doesn't happen again.'

They were on the same side. But Maxine challenged her.

'The trouble is, Ruth, that also could happen in two ways. Either home-grown sabotage or external interference. I'm only here to look at the second. If that can be ruled out, as I expect and hope, then you might need to have someone else check on your staff here. I mean, do any of them have reason to cause trouble? More critically, have any others been laid off? And if mischief is afoot, how might they progress it?'

Ruth looked gloomy as she considered the options. It wasn't the best day to be Operations Director. But she reckoned that, with Maxine's help, she'd as good a chance of sorting it as anyone she had ever met.

CHAPTER 7

Molesworth Arms, Wadebridge: Tues Jan 10th

Maxine had never stayed in the Molesworth Arms before, though she'd passed it once or twice – had drunk in the bar on occasion. But this was, to her, free accommodation!

It would be helpful to keep GCHQ's expenses down. She could see the Spaceport inquiry might take some time. Her head was already spinning with the detail, and she'd barely started. But there was no doubt it was an interesting location. And Ruth seemed a good person to be working with – intelligent, well-informed, committed. If there was something to be found, she believed the pair of them would find it.

She had left the Spaceport just before five. 'Remember, everyone here has been up half the night,' Ruth had told her. 'The 747 didn't get back till two in the morning. At that point we didn't realise it had all gone so wrong. It would be much better for you to speak to everyone fresh tomorrow.'

The pair had drafted out a list of the key people Maxine should speak to and made appointments to see them over the next few days. Then Ruth had handed over various documents to start her off, making some sense of the whole enterprise. Those had kept her busy for the rest of the afternoon.

'I'm Maxine Travers,' she told the lady on reception. 'I've got a booking as a guest of Newquay Spaceport.'

The receptionist glanced at her list and nodded. 'Yes. You're

44

welcome, Mrs Travers. That's Room 14. Sign in, please, and then come with me.' She led her guest to the rear of the hotel and up a flight of dark-wood panelled stairs. Room 14 was a comfortable double suite: a small lounge plus two bedrooms, each with an ensuite bathroom. Maxine smiled to herself: this was luxury, compared to her home in Bude – or to lodgings provided by many other clients.

She slipped into jeans and a thick jumper – she was off duty now. Then made herself a pot of tea. She would make more notes on what she had learned so far before sampling the hotel's restaurant.

Two hours later, work done for the day, Maxine phoned home to say goodnight to her young daughter, then made her way downstairs to the restaurant.

Room 14 was on a spur from the rest of the guestrooms: there was no-one else staying up this flight of stairs. She wondered if the Spaceport had requested this isolation for security reasons; or conversely, if this room had been chosen for them by the hotel, as one that wouldn't otherwise get much use.

Then, as she reached the ground floor, she saw a discreet security camera, high over the foot of the stairs. The Molesworth Arms had some security. As long as the camera was not switched permanently off.

The restaurant was not busy, but this was a mid-week evening in mid-January: that was to be expected. She found a small table in an alcove, sat comfortably on her own and had a light meal: she'd already had curry for lunch.

It was as she enjoyed a concluding mug of hot chocolate in the hotel's lounge that she had another thought about Molesworth security in connection with Room 14.

Since the room was permanently reserved for Spaceport's

official visitors, would it not be sensible to find out who else had stayed there recently? Say, since the start of the year. For Ruth had implied that the launch could have happened at any time in the past week, if only the weather had allowed. So there might have been visitors staying here who had come for the launch but then gone away disappointed. Could she identify them from the Molesworth guest list?

When she'd finished her chocolate, Maxine went back to her room via the hotel reception. The woman who had been behind the desk when she arrived was still on duty.

'You keep long hours,' she began sympathetically.

'I'm the deputy manager,' the woman replied. 'The hours go with the job, I'm afraid.'

'I'm Maxine. You showed me to Room 14.'

'Oh, I remember you, Maxine. I'm Laura. Is everything OK?'

'All fine so far, Laura. I've enjoyed the restaurant and am about to have an early night. I spent most of the day at the Space-port and I've got information overload. D'you have many visitors to Room 14?'

'Not many, I'm afraid. Only three before you since Christmas.'

'Ooh. I wonder if I knew any of them.'

'I couldn't possibly say. It would be against the law for me to tell you their names or contact details. Data protection and all that.'

'Of course. But isn't that the visitors' book over here?'

'It is.'

Just that moment the reception phone rang and Laura moved away to answer it. It was obviously a friend making a private call and she moved away from the desk to gain some privacy.

This was her chance. Maxine seized the visitors' book and scoured the last few pages. Fortunately, guests entered their room along with other details. And there they were: three separate entries for Room 14 since Christmas. Maxine had taken a shot of each of them on her phone and put the device away again before Laura had finished her call.

'Anyone special?' asked Maxine politely.

'Just my friend from the Swan. They're as quiet as we are.'

'OK then. Right, I'll go for my early night.'

Maxine felt only slightly guilty at her minor deception as she climbed the stairs. Presumably she could have got the same information from Ruth or someone on her staff, but it was always good to find out things for herself.

Back in her room, Maxine peered at her new images.

None of the three names were known to her. Two men and one woman. It was a pity guests weren't invited to leave their pictures, so she had no idea how old they were.

There was a column for guests to enter the name of their employer. None of the three had filled this in. Were they all simply private citizens?

The nationality information was a bit more revealing. The two men were from different parts of the United States, while the woman was from the Shetlands. She would have to ask Ruth about them tomorrow. Probably the Director would know the reason for each of their visits.

It would be interesting, though, to learn a little more about the woman from Shetland. It would take her longer to travel here than the men from the States. Whatever was she after?

CHAPTER 8

Spaceport Technical Unit: Wed Jan 11th

Maxine's first task next morning was to talk to the technical staff who had designed the rocket – or, at least, had put all the pieces together.

She wasn't here to critique the design. But she couldn't hope to pick out anything out of place in what had happened until she had some idea of what the expected pattern was.

Ruth took her over to the Technical Unit. It was a short distance from the Control Centre, where she'd been for most of yesterday. It had a separate security system, right now she needed Ruth to help her navigate it.

'I'll get you special keys so you can go where you like,' said Ruth. 'But it'll take a week to get them delivered.' She smiled ruefully. 'Some aspects of security are taken seriously.'

Once inside the Unit, a revamp of an old aircraft hangar, Ruth took her to the office of Technical Director Tom Willoughby. It was a functional space – plain carpet, with a view only as far as the concrete forecourt – but quite sizeable. There was a whiteboard, and a dozen chairs: they must use it for staff meetings. Ruth handed her over to Tom and then left them to it.

This was Tom's home turf. He was obviously more comfortable here than he'd been in Suzanne's stronghold. 'Welcome,' he said, shaking Maxine's hand. 'One more top-class brain to work on this is welcome.'

'I'm starting from a low base,' Maxine began. 'But I need to understand how most of this works if I'm to be any use at all.'

'I understand that, Maxine. Better than pretending you know more than you do – like the idiot in charge of the country last year.' It wasn't clear which one he meant. He drew breath. 'Actually, I've a meeting at half past ten for all my managers, to take stock of what happened. We were too dysfunctional to do much yesterday. You'd be welcome to join us – and to ask questions where necessary. I promise we won't shoot you down.'

As good as Maxine could hope for. While they waited for the others, Tom blended some coffee and then quizzed her about her background in GCHQ. She sensed her particular skill set – mathematics and computing – was better matched to the problems found here than anything she'd touched on yesterday.

But soon she dragged the conversation back to the Spaceport. Her low-profile career was not important today.

'Let's see how much I know,' she began, as she sipped her coffee. 'Your staff had to build the facilities and design the whole operation. What size of rocket was needed? How big was your satellite load – how many satellites, what size? What speed did the stage two rocket have to achieve? With all these parts interacting, the whole process must have taken years.'

Tom nodded encouragingly. His visitor had some grasp of the work involved.

'Once all that was done,' she continued, 'you had to obtain, assemble and, on the day of the launch, fuel up both rocket stages.'

Maxine paused, then thought some more. 'And to fasten the stage one rocket securely to the jet airliner, under its left wing, so it could take off without falling off, but later be released at great height.'

There was another question here. 'Hey . . . were any of your guys piloting the plane, two nights ago?'

'No,' Tom replied. 'She was called Cosmic Girl, by the way. Came with a fully-trained aircrew. Flew in a month ago. We had to work like crazy to refine the attachment to the wing and the release mechanism in the cockpit. But the design's been used since the Iraq war, seemed to work fine on the night.'

Maxine wondered if the enormity of Tom's tasks was appreciated by the other senior managers. This was pioneering work and it had almost come off.

But there was no more time to chat further. Tom's team had arrived and were helping themselves to coffee.

'Welcome to the postmortem, everyone,' Tom began. 'We have a special visitor here today. Maxine is from UK Security. They are worried there might have been some sort of external interference to cause the rocket to fail. She'll be asking us slightly different questions to the ones we've asked already. But if there is anything amiss, it's important for us all that we find it.

Maxine took the chance to set out her stall. 'Thank you for letting me join you. Ruth Fisher tells me that the decision to fly on Monday was only taken by her at the last minute - lunchtime.

'So if anything was done by forces beyond our shores, it would either need to be built beforehand into one of the rockets; or to use information that was only a few hours old. It's not likely, but we need to have a good look.'

Maxine's opening comments caused an immediate response. A sturdy-looking bearded man in his forties was ready to argue.

'Hi Maxine. My name's Rory. Could we take each option in turn? Starting with the second. Suppose that, somehow, word got out that Monday was to be the day. You're a Russian in a warship in mid-Atlantic who plans to shoot the flight down. How on earth would you manage to do it?'

'And I'm Jimbo,' began a rotund character from the corner. 'How could you know the route beforehand? Not just "out over the Atlantic", but a specific course with actual coordinates. That's unknowable. It's affected by wind speed and all sorts of other factors. And you'd need to know the height as well as the sea coordinates.'

'But could a weapon be launched that latched onto the rocket – some heat-seeking missile, perhaps?' This was Maxine, stoking the discussion.

'It's a hell of a problem,' observed Tom. 'I mean, these days the Royal Navy can usually shoot down a drone before it can damage their vessel. They use clever tracking to predict the exact line it's on. But that's only a few hundred metres.

'By the time it fell out of the sky, our rocket was fifteen miles up and moving at 10,000 miles an hour. The odds of hitting it, with any weapon I've ever heard of, are negligible.'

'How long was the intended flight of the first stage?' asked Maxine.

'Reuben here,' answered a smaller technician with owl-like features. 'About twenty minutes. How does that help us?'

Maxine marshalled her thoughts. 'Well. One person who did know the intended route and its timing would be the Cosmic Girl pilot. If he'd been corrupted, he could message the enemy warship. But if stage one flew on for twenty minutes after it left the plane, that still wouldn't fix its final location.'

There was silence in the room as they all sought gaps in Maxine's logic.

'Let's call a halt for coffee,' declared Tom. 'After that we can move on to Maxine's other probe.

'My other question,' said Maxine, once they'd started again, 'is whether there is any chance the rocket technology itself could be corrupted, so it would cause stage two to fail to ignite.'

This was a hard question, took a while to extract an answer.

'That's an uncomfortable line of enquiry,' admitted Tom. He turned to his team. 'But you guys are the only ones that can give the question a proper appraisal.'

Maxine amplified the thought. 'And if you won't grapple with it, others will. You're not the only space experts in the UK. Any hesitation will make others more suspicious. You have to show them you've nailed down the options.'

There was a long silence. Then one of the other managers, a serious woman in her thirties, started the debate. 'I'm Debbie. Why don't we start with the rocket for stage one?'

'It's a standard piece of kit that's been used for years by NASA, at Cape Canaveral in the United States,' she declared. 'It came in pieces and we assembled it ourselves. So we know exactly what's is in it.

'But nothing at all went wrong with stage one,' protested Reuben. 'It took off from Cosmic Girl and got the second stage rocket to the edge of space.'

'The separation of the jet and the rocket was tricky, mind,' reflected Rory. 'The jet had to release the rocket, then cause it to ignite as it dropped away. Cosmic Girl might have been scorched in the flames. But it didn't: I would say that's the best part of what we've achieved.'

There was a pause.

'OK,' said Maxine. 'That sounds pretty watertight. How about stage two?'

'That's also been developed by others,' recalled Sandra. 'In this case the French. They've a launch pad in French Guyana, right on the equator. It too was shipped here in pieces and assembled in this unit.'

'So how was it supposed to be ignited from stage one?' This

was a key question.

'That's been where space rockets often fail,' admitted Jimbo. 'And not just in the early days.'

'How d'you mean?'

'Well, we know of 137 attempts to launch satellites into space around the world last year. Guess how many failed.'

Maxine considered. 'Two?'

Jimbo gave her a scornful grin. 'Seven of them failed – in four cases where stage two didn't take over properly from stage one. This is a pioneering activity: failures happen all the time.

'Some mechanism must link the two parts. It can't be a radio signal. Only the stage one rocket knows when its fuel's running out and it's time to hand on the baton. It's bound to fail occasionally.'

There was a melancholy silence around the room. His last five words seemed to sum up their morning.

'Why don't we stop there?' suggested Tom. 'We've had an intense couple of days. We all need a break. Let's come back here at, say, two thirty.'

He turned to Maxine. 'Why don't you and I go offsite for lunch?'

'Wherever you fancy,' she smiled. 'I'm here to learn.'

CHAPTER 9

The Trevarrian Inn: Wed Jan 11th

Tom Willoughby's choice of an out-of-the-way pub was the Trevarrian Inn. He drove Maxine along some minor roads, ending on the coast road from Newquay to Padstow.

'This is the nearest inn to the airfield,' he told her, 'only half a mile from the end of the runway. A bit awkward to get to from the Spaceport. But it's good to have the separation.'

From the carpark Maxine could see down onto Mawgan Porth and its beach.

'You won't see Bedruthan Steps from here, Maxine,' he said, 'they're in the cove beyond. But not that far.'

'I've been to this area lots of times,' said Maxine. 'I was brought up in Cornwall, remember.'

Tom nodded approvingly and turned toward the inn. 'Let's go in. They do a special toasted cheese sandwich here – at least, they did last year. I come out here whenever I need to clear my head.'

Maxine said nothing until they had been led to a table in the window, well away from the handful of other customers. 'That was quite an intense session,' she agreed. 'But then, you're under strong pressure, Tom, to identify what went wrong. The rocket that failed is thousands of feet underwater, somewhere in mid-Atlantic – that's lost for ever.'

There was a pause then she added, 'But I doubt you'll be able to launch any more, until you can come up with a plausible idea of what went wrong last time – plus some change to stop it happening again.'

Gloomily, Tom agreed. Monday could have been a day of triumph, for the Spaceport, for Cornwall and for the UK. Instead, it had turned into a major calamity.

'First things first. I'll go and order. You sit here and enjoy the view. Toasted sandwich ok? And a half of cider?'

Maxine used the few minutes he was gone to work out what she needed to learn while they were away from the Spaceport. She mustn't be too pushy. But she must make the most of this privileged access to a senior manager. How concerned was he?

Tom returned shortly with a glass in each hand. 'They'll bring the sandwiches shortly.'

'It was an interesting discussion,' she said. 'My background's mathematics but that overlaps with technology, including space flight. You've got a really bright bunch there.'

Tom responded with some background of his own.

'I did engineering at Bristol. My gap gear was at Filton, the GEC factory where they'd designed Concorde. They still recalled working with the French – it was more cooperative in those days.'

'Is that why you were using a French rocket for stage two?'

'Huh. It wasn't my choice. We could have got one from NASA. Trouble was, that would be a lot more expensive. The Finance Director blocked it.'

Maxine smiled sympathetically, though she lodged the fact away for later scrutiny.

'Were there many battles between the senior managers?'

'No more than other big organisations, I expect. We each had our goals to fulfil – sometimes they were in conflict. Mind, Suzanne, our Chair, was the worst. She'd worked in NASA in her younger days, felt she knew more than the rest of us. I'm not sure if that was true – space science is evolving so rapidly – but she certainly didn't know much about getting the best out of us. Ruth Fisher was a much more empathetic character. It was her that really held us together.'

Their toasted sandwiches arrived, causing a break in the conversation. They looked and tasted delicious.

'Given the quality of the food, this pub seems rather quiet,' mused Maxine, as she started to eat.

'It is mid-January. It was busier over New Year and last week. There'd probably be a few sightseers, hoping to see our rocket. The jet would be almost above them for a few seconds as it took off. Course, my staff weren't in here. We were all working like crazy over in the Spaceport.'

Maxine pondered, was there any chance of getting names of those present two days ago? Then she realised it would be impossible. She couldn't see any CCTV cameras. And customers here could hardly be the cause of the rocket failure, even if its path was right overhead.

'D'you like it round here, Tom?'

'On fine days it's magnificent. I've got my family settled at St Merryn.' He grinned. 'I've got two kids, both now at the local school. My partner works part-time in Padstow. We're very happy here.'

Maxine munched for a moment. 'So it'd be a big blow for you if the space project were to fold?'

'Certainly would. I'm a well-qualified engineer with bags of experience, I'd get another job easily enough. But probably not around here.' He looked hard at her. 'Why, d'you think there's a real chance of that happening?'

'I've no idea, Tom. Won't it all depend on if there are still customers out there who want to launch satellites into space? You don't have to convince me: they hold all the cards.'

There was a subdued silence as they finished their toasties.

'Fancy another drink?' asked Tom.

The honest answer was no; Maxine didn't usually drink at lunchtime – her responsibilities wouldn't allow it. However, she didn't think this depth of conversation would take place inside the Spaceport and they weren't due back for another forty minutes.

'Why not? I'll get them.' She returned from the bar a few minutes later, carrying a half of Cornish cider and a Britvic orange.

'So what's the agenda this afternoon, Tom?'

'There's still half your challenge to be wrestled with. Is there any way flight failure could have been built into the rockets themselves, regardless of when it happened? We talked about the link between the two but there's more to a rocket than that. That would at least get round the problem of the launch itself being a last-minute surprise.'

'Though it would raise much bigger questions on security within your Unit.'

Tom sighed. 'I know. But it's a personal challenge for me now. And I reckon for most of my team.'

A few minutes later they had finished their drinks and were walking back to the car.

CHAPTER 10

Spaceport Technical Unit: Wed Jan 11th

The middle managers were waiting outside Tom's office when he and Maxine returned. The debate had already started.

'Right, guys,' said Tom, as he ushered them in, 'you keep talking. Maxine will listen and I'll brew us more coffee. The wackier ideas the better for the next twenty minutes – but get them jotted onto the whiteboard. That'll help me construct our afternoon agenda.'

The team was obviously used to brainstorming and arguing strongly but respectfully with one another. Much shorthand was invoked. Maxine did her best to note down the more obscure phrases, to ask about later.

'OK,' said Tom, studying the board. 'I think we've enough ideas there – for one afternoon, anyway. Help yourselves to coffee and Maxine and I will finalise the order for discussion.

'D'you want me to have that much say?' she asked him quietly.

'As an outsider, you've got more chance of moving us away from what we've already thought about,' he explained. 'You can stimulate some fresh thinking.'

When they'd all got their drinks and settled down, Maxine started them off.

'I'd like to know more about how the stage one rocket is fired from Cosmic Girl,' she began. 'I'm no expert but I'm comparing that with the vertical take-offs I've seen on television.'

She went on, 'The rocket there starts inside a huge tower that is slowly pulled away during the launch. You'll have complete control on the direction the rocket will start off. Whereas it's pretty hit and miss what the trajectory of flight is, surely – and especially the climbing rate – when it's launched from a plane?'

'Exactly, Maxine. That's precisely why launching a rocket from a plane isn't often done,' replied Tom. 'And why we were so pleased when it worked.'

'One major challenge is to make sure the rocket doesn't fry the plane in its exhaust gases as it moves away,' observed Jimbo. 'The timing of the whole thing is critical.'

'The rocket-holding mechanism under the wing has to be released a second before the rocket fires,' explained Reuben. 'Simultaneously the plane has to turn away. Obviously it worked this time, 'cos the plane got back here.' He glanced out the window. 'But I've always thought the process was slightly hairy. Makes me glad I'm not an airline pilot.'

There was a pause and then Maxine persisted.

'So it's down to the pilot to set the broad direction of the rocket's travel? I'm still trying to unpack how an unhinged pilot could throw things off course. I mean, you had no say over who arrived with the plane. They just came over here last month.'

'The pilot is only one of the crew, Maxine,' protested Rory. 'They all work together. If he tried to sabotage the flight on his own, the others would move in to stop him. But nothing like that happened two nights ago.'

'So if anything was to be done,' she retorted, 'the whole crew would need to be replaced. That's not impossible. It's broadly what happened when the Twin Towers were destroyed in New York, twenty years ago.'

There was silence. They were all old enough to remember

that. It was seared into their memories.

Tom wasn't convinced. 'The aim of the 9/11 terrorism was to expose American weakness and Arab strength. Publicity was the whole point of the exercise. But in our case the second rocket simply fell out of the sky in the dead of night and the middle of nowhere, never to be seen again. It was hardly spectacular. If it was a rebel crew with freedom to do as they liked, wouldn't they prefer, say, to crash into Newquay? Or even somewhere more important.'

'The RAF would shoot them out the sky before they reached London,' said Reuben.

There was another pause. They were covering a great deal of ground.

'Have you interviewed the Cosmic Girl crew since they came back?' asked Maxine.

Tom nodded. 'I had a brief chat with the whole crew in the middle of the night, on their return. Mainly to check they were alright. I don't think anyone's given them a hard interview yet. Or even checked that their stories hang together.'

Mugs were refreshed, then they started again. Maxine was again given the chance to ask the first question.

'You've explained that both stages of rocket you used arrived here in pieces and you put them together yourselves. Sounds convincing. But presumably only from smaller pieces? Would you be able to tell if there was anything wrong with those? After all, you can hardly give either rocket a test flight, if you want to use them for real.' She mused for a second. 'Unless, I suppose, you'd done that with a previous version?'

Jimbo smiled. 'Yes. But that's true of every space rocket that's ever been launched. You can test some of the parts – the control computer, for example – but you can't test the whole thing. Your best hope is to order one from a regular production line, with a track-record of reliable service.'

'That worked fine for stage one,' said Debbie. 'That type of rocket has powered dozens of flights, mostly in the United States. There were problems in the early days, but now it hardly ever goes wrong. And it worked fine for us.'

'Could you say the same thing for stage two?' asked Maxine. There was a moment's silence.

'There's a shorter track record for stage two,' admitted Jimbo. 'It wasn't our first choice of supplier, but we were blocked. But the French had used them over the years. We checked everything we could.'

'The thing that I'm worried about,' said Maxine, 'is that it came from France. Don't get me wrong, I'm not anti-French. But that would give a completely different motivation for some-one to sabotage the flight – not just terrorism.'

'How d'you mean?' asked Rory.

'Well, as I understand it, your goal here is to be the first place on the Continent of Europe that can launch space satellites. Right now the French can do so but only from a very long way away – French Guyana. They might be nervous about local com-petition. Nervous enough, perhaps, to make sure your flight was unsuccessful? I'm not saying it's likely. But is it at all possible?'

By the end of the afternoon, Maxine felt she'd a reasonable grasp of the launch mechanics. She'd got confidence in the tech-nical team. But she'd not yet spotted any launch discrepancies.

Maybe she needed to visit Goonhilly Earth Station? After all, they were the only outsiders she'd heard mentioned so far, who had access to live data on what was happening.

CHAPTER 11

Goonhilly Earth Station, Lizard: Thurs Jan 12th

Maxine returned to Wadebridge on Wednesday evening feeling tired. She was used to long hours wrestling with complicated problems. But the current atmosphere at the Spaceport was hardly peaceful. Monday's launch failure had not been expected. There was an undercurrent of anxiety and fear.

Maxine could see that her own role, arriving out of the blue, had not helped. She'd had friendly conversations with Ruth Fisher and Tom Willoughby. But she was still a newcomer, beholden to outside authority. That required her to fear the worst, assume that there was something wrong until she was unable to find it.

If Maxine had been a police officer, that would have been a regular part of her job. But the thrust of her normal work in Bude was unpacking the intricacies of obscure messages from unwanted sources, not dealing directly with their human consequences.

She badly wanted to share the load with her husband, Peter Travers, a police inspector in Bude. Preferably face to face over a quiet supper. Today was only Wednesday, but it would certainly be worth going back home for the weekend. She must arrange that on her nightly call home.

Before Saturday, though, she wanted to spend time at

Goonhilly Earth Station, over on the Lizard. That had been mentioned several times in the last two days. The Station was linked to Spaceport flight activity: could there have been any leak here?

Goonhilly had featured before in Maxine's work, but not for some years. It would be good to go there next morning, while the trail – if there was a trail – was still warm.

It was as she was having her evening meal in the Molesworth restaurant that Maxine had an idea. Her long-standing friend, George Gilbert, had told her about her adventures at Goonhilly. It was worth a phone call to recap the details.

It transpired George was away on project work; it wouldn't be convenient to meet for a while. But George did pass over a few details of her recent investigations at Goonhilly. And mentioned one person that it would be worth talking to – Dr Jim Harvey, a station manager.

'He was very brusque with me when I started,' George admitted. 'Refused to accept that there could be anything wrong with security at Goonhilly. But in the end, he was the one that saved my life. It's a good story, Maxine, I'll tell you when we next share a meal. Harvey's basically a good egg: mentioning my name might help you.'

Maxine made two calls early next morning, one to Ruth at the Spaceport to tell her what she was doing and another to Goonhilly to prepare the way for her visit. Then she drove across Cornwall, down to Truro and onto Helston, before she reached the Lizard.

Goonhilly was on the road beyond. She could tell she was there by the huge satellite dishes which dominated the site.

She was battling with the Goonhilly entrance security by half past ten and had made it into reception ten minutes later.

She presented her GCHQ security ID to the receptionist. 'I rang earlier. My name is Maxine Travers. I'm working with the team at Newquay Spaceport. Their latest spaceflight was tracked here. Could I speak to the manager in charge, please?'

Clearly communications had been exchanged, following her phone call.

'Yes, certainly Ms Travers. The overseeing senior manager is Dr Harvey. He's expecting you. You'll find his office down that corridor.'

That was a relief, she'd be talking to the person that George had commended. A moment later she was in his office.

'Good morning, Ms Travers,' he began. She was being greeted by a tall, trim figure with dashing dark hair. 'I'm Dr Harvey – Jim. Do come in and sit down.'

'Please, call me Maxine,' she urged as they sat in two comfortable chairs, away from Jim's desk. Satellite dishes dominated their view.

'I've heard very good things about your work at Cleave Camp,' he noted. Maxine smiled in acknowledgement. It was good to have a reputation, even if the applauding circle was extremely small.

'I'm also a friend of George Gilbert,' she added. 'A long time ago we were maths students together at Cambridge. She spoke very highly of you, Jim, told me you'd saved her life.'

He shrugged the accolade aside. 'That was years ago. Not usually part of my job to rescue young ladies, but there was a reason.' He was silent, remembering. Then he shook himself, 'Right. Let's move on to Monday's space flight.'

Maxine hastened to explain her remit. 'I've been sent to Newquay by UK Security, to see if there's any reason to suspect the flight was sabotaged. The failure to launch is good news for

Russia, of course – or the UK's many other enemies. But it would be an incredibly long shot for them to do any damage. And Newquay were relying on Goonhilly to do their tracking?'

'That's right. That's been part of our long-term remit – and hope – for years. A distinct role for Cornwall, conquering space. It's something, really, that only Goonhilly can do. Space rockets move incredibly quickly, compared, say, with a commercial airliner. But we have huge dishes here, as you can see.' He waved out of the window. 'We can choose which part of the sky to focus on. Newquay gave us guidance on where the plane was meant to fly, at least until it launched the rocket.'

'Right. But there was uncertainty over its timing, wasn't there? Flights the week before had been prevented by bad weather. When did you hear that Monday evening was lift-off?'

Jim considered for a moment. 'It was half part two on Monday afternoon that I got the call: from Ruth Fisher, using our agreed codeword, so I knew it was her. That was when we started to finalise our arrangements.'

There was a pause. Maxine was glad this was a face-to-face conversation. She considered which issue to tackle next.

'I'm not wanting to be critical, Jim, but I've got to ask. Wasn't a direct phone call rather risky? After all, it was generally known that a space flight was happening in Newquay and people could guess you'd be part of the process. Couldn't someone with the right equipment have eavesdropped?'

Jim nodded. 'You'd be right, Maxine, if it was a simple phone call. But we have a special relationship and we've got protective protocols. Spoken messages are encoded at one end then decoded at the other. If there was some sort of information leak, I'm sure it didn't happen on that.'

Maxine nodded. That seemed unchallengeable. She sipped her coffee and considered the next issue.

'So what was the procedure, once Cosmic Girl took off?'

'My team leader was phoned by Newquay as the plane went down the runway. Our dishes picked it up at take-off and we followed it out over the Atlantic, gaining height all the time.'

'Right. Could you compute its speed and rate of climb?'

'Not in real time, I'm afraid, but we've computed it since.'

Jim went over to his desk, found the page of values he'd been sent and handed it to Maxine. 'I guess the technical guys at Newquay will want to check if that kind of performance was expected?'

Maxine glanced at the page: there was plenty to go on. But that would be for Tom's technical staff to pursue.

'OK, now let's turn to stage one. That was moving much faster – 10,000 miles an hour, I was told. Could you also follow that with your dishes?'

'We could, but only because we had it pinpointed as it left the 747. It's a tiny object. You'd struggle to pick it up without that.'

'And was its flight path steadily ascending? Or were there any wobbles as the rocket left the plane?'

Jim considered for a moment, not quite sure where she was going. 'You're thinking. perhaps, that launching a space rocket from a plane is novel and needs post-flight validation? I hadn't thought of that but it's worth examining.'

'No. Jim, it was more than that. Could the rocket, falling from the plane, be set off on the wrong trajectory – even downwards – so the second stage never had a chance?'

Jim reconsidered. 'Yes, that's a fair question. And one that you need to ask. Well, how about I show you the flight path?'

He stood once more and adjusted a large monitor on the wall behind him, linked to the laptop on his desk. Then he chose one flight image from the computer's drive and presented it on the monitor.

'There's some fiendish mathematics needed to take out the curvature of the earth. But this is our best estimate.'

The image he showed comprised two small circles on either side of a dark screen, with a gently curving white line between them.

'I've clipped it to the flight of the rocket, of course.'

Maxine studied it for a few moments.

'Can we zoom in on the plane end?'

'Of course.' A zoomed second picture showed just this component.

'Hey, look!' Maxine pointed excitedly. 'There's a small dip before the rocket starts climbing upwards. I'm sure the technical team would like to examine that more carefully.'

She continued to stare at it.

'It's almost level. Is the rate of climb as high as was expected? You know, the problem might not be with the second rocket at all. It could stem from the way stage one was launched from the plane.'

There was more study, but no further revelations emerged.

Maxine spent the day at Goonhilly. She spent even longer looking at the opening seconds of stage two. But it was impossible to comment any further without knowing what had been expected.

After lunch she met the team who had taken the raw data from the dishes on Monday evening and converted it to the images she had found so intriguing. She got the general thrust of their methods, enough to explain them to the team in Newquay. The full data set was being sent over that afternoon.

CHAPTER 12

Newquay Spaceport: Friday Jan 12th

Maxine was eager to get into the Spaceport on Friday morning. By now the Technical Department should have started to process all the flight data collected by Goonhilly Earth Station.

The crucial thing was what would come out of the comparison between what did happen and what had been expected.

Tom Willoughby was entrenched in his office and greeted her warmly.

'We got all the data from Goonhilly yesterday afternoon. Your visit probably hastened its arrival: we weren't expecting it till late next week. Thank you.'

Maxine suspected the fast response had come out of her good working relationship with Dr Jim Harvey.

'Have you made much of them yet?'

'It's a rich data source – locations every few seconds, for almost two hours. In three dimensions. It'll take a while to process, and we'll need a heavyweight computer to display it.'

This sounded less enthusiastic than she would have liked.

'Tom, what were your predictions of what should happen? Can you show me what the flight path should have looked like?'

'Oh, we've got those,' he replied confidently. 'We put them on the big monitor downstairs. Would you like to see?'

Maxine sighed quietly. But she wasn't the one in charge here. She just had to hustle everybody on as best she could.

Downstairs, the engineering staff were busy checking every detail of the rocket construction, line by line and delivery by delivery. Each detail subject to two independent reviews. The task could drag on for months.

Maxine feared their goal was more geared to defending their previous actions, less to finding where something unexpected might have caused a problem.

Tom looked around at all the effort that was going on, then called Jimbo over to help them.

'Maxine would like to see for herself our predicted flight paths for Cosmic Girl and the two rockets. We'll need them when we come to compare them with what actually happened, according to Goonhilly.'

Jimbo looked glad to comply. Routine checks were soul-destroying. 'Right, Maxine. Come over here, please.'

Tom left them to it. Jimbo led Maxine into a small office with subdued lighting and no outside window. There were a dozen chairs and a massive screen on one wall.

'This is our viewing area,' he explained, as he shut the door. 'It's also where staff do presentations.'

Jimbo fiddled with a laptop. 'I think that's it,' he claimed eventually. 'We were using this a lot in the early days, but we haven't needed it so much recently.'

The software was more primitive than that at Goonhilly, but it could display the results of their modelling.

'Right,' said Jimbo. 'What'd you like to see first?'

'Can we start with the flight of Cosmic Girl from Newquay? Presumably that's a standard trajectory?'

Jimbo shook his head. 'Nothing is standard here, Maxine. Remember the plane has a 24-ton payload under one wing. It needs a long runway like Newquay's to take off at all. It'll fly more slowly and climb at a slower rate than a conventional jet.'

He turned to his laptop and projected the anticipated flight plan onto the screen. The x-axis measured distance from Newquay and the y-axis the plane's elevation. This was predicted to reach 35,000 feet.

'So, when the time came to release the rocket, it was hardly climbing at all – on this projection?'

'That's right. Here's another graph, this one plotting height against time.' This one showed a steady rise, though it slowed as the plane's operating ceiling was reached.

Maxine looked at it carefully. So the stage two launch should be reached after just under an hour?' Jimbo nodded. Good, that was in line with what she'd seen at Goonhilly.

'OK,' she said, after a few moments study. 'I'm hoping you'll have a similar set of graphs for both rocket flights as well?'

'I certainly will.' Jimbo fiddled on the laptop, then brought up a second profile. This one was entitled "Stage One".

Maxine stared at it carefully for a few minutes. Especially the start.

'So stage one should continue to gain elevation as soon as it left the plane?' Jimbo nodded. 'So how was that to be achieved?'

'The rocket was given an upward trajectory, propelled by the gases from the rocket.' Jimbo sounded confident. But he was not talking to an ordinary member of the general public.

'But how was that achieved, Jimbo? Was the mechanism holding it to the wing pointing slightly upwards? Or was it something else?'

For a moment there was silence.

'To be honest, Maxine, I'm not sure. When these profiles were being developed, a year ago, we were more interested in the broad shape of the whole flight. Our questions were like, how big a satellite load can we cope with?'

Maxine saw she wasn't going to get much further.

'Right, then. Now can we see stage two?'

Much the same conversation ensued. Stage two was shown as rising at a steep angle and great velocity. There was no attempt to be precise over the separation from stage one.

Maxine saw that the planned trajectories were far less detailed than the ones observed from Goonhilly. A straight comparison would not be useful. But she would have to be very careful how she presented this finding to Tom Willoughby.

Later in the day, Maxine went back to see Ruth Fisher. She gave the Operations Director a brief résumé of her encounters so far, including Goonhilly, but refrained from offering conclusions. She was after a solid answer, not enticing fragments.

Maxine was about to leave for the weekend when she remembered her query about recent visitors to Newquay Spaceport that had been staying at the Molesworth Arms.

'Presumably, Ruth, you have the names of all the Spaceport visitors who stay at the Molesworth Arms?'

'I don't, but Chloe will. She can give you them if it would help.'

'It's a shot in the dark. I was wondering who was here on Monday evening, to watch the start of the historic flight.'

Ruth nodded. 'I see. Well, there weren't many, and I knew most of them. A few were friends of one or other Director. But if they weren't local, they might well be staying at the Molesworth Arms. That's the only place where we have an accommodation deal. I'll get Chloe to look out the names.'

She grabbed her phone and gave the instruction. A few minutes later, the list in her briefcase, Maxine was on her way. A weekend with her husband and young daughter beckoned.

CHAPTER 13

A Policeman's Perspective: Jan 12th – 13th

Maxine left the Spaceport early and headed straight back to Bude. She wanted a weekend completely away from it all. And to catch up with her family.

She was in Bude soon after four and in good time to pick up Rosanna from the local nursery. The three-year-old was over-joyed to see her mummy again. She talked non-stop. So much seemed to have happened to her since Tuesday morning. For-tunately, she wasn't seeking an explanation for everything.

They had reached their home in Poughill by five and Ro-sanna was eager to play with the toys she had received over Christmas. Her new marble run was a particular favourite.

Maxine's husband, Peter, was home from the police station by six and the three had a light tea together before bathing the little one. There was an armada of ducks and frogs eager to share her bath. Rosanna was in bed by seven, had two stories from mummy and three more from daddy, then was solidly asleep half an hour later.

'Right, my love,' said Peter, giving his wife a comprehensive hug downstairs in the kitchen. 'It's good to have you home again.'

'It's so good to be here, Peter. Gosh, I'm tired.'

There was a pause and then, 'Look, darling, it's Friday

evening. Why don't I slip into Stratton and buy us some fish and chips? We don't need to cook. You can chill for twenty minutes – though it'd be good to have the oven warm, ready for when I come back.

'Once I'm home again,' he continued, 'we can have a leisurely evening, doing nothing much at all. And don't you worry about tomorrow. I'm going to cook a banquet for us both.'

Maxine laughed, it was good to be home. 'You know, Peter, there'll be a queue in the shop. I might just have time for a quick bath.'

Forty minutes later Peter was back. The fish and chips had been given a boost in the oven and were now on heated plates before them.

Maxine had emerged from the bathroom much refreshed. She'd changed out of her business gear into lounge pants and a thick winter sweater. She hoped the homely combination sent the message: she was not up for much this evening. Except casual chatter.

Both Peter and Maxine had jobs where it was important not to say too much about what they were doing. Especially, in Peter's case, the early stage of a crime investigation. He was an inspector, the lynch pin of the small police department in Bude, and he'd been there for some years – with no desire to move away from the area he loved. The proverbial round peg in the smooth round hole.

So, although each of them had had a busy week, there was an unspoken embargo on sharing much about it.

'We don't need to wash up tonight,' he murmured. 'In any case, I got us some cake. Why don't we eat it in the lounge?'

He had certainly recognised that his wife would come home wrung out, thought Maxine. She felt so grateful for a wise and sensitive husband. Many folk wouldn't be that lucky.

Tonight she wouldn't even mention Newquay Spaceport or its personnel. But tomorrow was a fresh day.

She would love to bounce some of her own ideas off Peter and also to hear his response.

The details of her three-day stay in Wadebridge were inconsequential enough to share with her family over breakfast. Rosanna didn't know what a hotel was, but Maxine made it sound very exciting, especially the winding stairs with their dark wooden panels.

Later, as they set out with their daughter for the local playpark, Maxine remembered she had obtained the names of earlier visitors to Room 14 from two different sources. She took the chance to look at the names as she sat on the park bench, with Peter pushing their daughter on the swing.

She gasped in surprise. The dates of the visits coincided; but the names of the visitors, from the Molesworth Arms reception and from Spaceport admin, weren't the same at all.

No time to do anything about it right now. Rosanna was gleefully running everywhere, making the most of having both parents with her. It was two hours before they all returned home, and she retired for her late-morning nap.

'I've just discovered an oddity,' she told Peter as they took their mugs of coffee into the lounge for an hour's calm.

'Oh yes?' Peter was a master of the open question.

Maxine explained how Room 14 was reserved for Spaceport visitors. She had obtained the most recent names yesterday from Spaceport admin. But on Wednesday evening she'd also seen, and photographed, the names of recent residents staying in Room 14, as listed in the official visitors' book.

'But the thing is, Peter, the names aren't the same.'

The off-duty police inspector took a moment to make sure he had understood his wife's story. 'Can I see the lists, please?'

'Sure.' Maxine opened her phone to the relevant images and handed it over. Then she rescued the hard copy list she'd been given by Chloe the previous afternoon. And waited for the verdict.

'All the dates match,' he began. 'Let's assume they were the same people. So either they each made up a name when they arrived at the pub, or they gave a false one to the Spaceport.'

'Or both.'

Peter wrinkled his nose. Then he asked, 'But who were these people, Maxine? They all came just after Christmas and before the launch. They weren't there for the blast off. So what were they after?'

'The admin lady gave me them from her desk diary. She couldn't recall who'd booked them in. It's been a very hectic week, remember. All the attention was on the crucial first flight. The visitors had gone before the weekend; the launch came last Monday.'

'Right.' He thought for a moment.

'I expect security at the Molesworth Arms is patchy?'

'Well, they didn't ask to see my passport or anything. But they had been warned by the Spaceport to expect a visitor. If I'd made up a name, I would probably have got away with it.'

Peter looked again at the phone pictures. 'They've each given an address, I see. Would you like me to check both sets of names on HOLMES, our National Computer Database?'

'It wouldn't do any harm, would it?'

They were interrupted at that point by a crying sound from upstairs. Rosanna had had her nap and was wanting attention.

Newquay Spaceport did not feature again in their conversation until the evening.

Peter's "banquet" turned out to be less ambitious than the name suggested. It was a multi-course Chinese meal for two from Morrisons, with a bottle of Sauvignon now cooling in the fridge. But Maxine didn't mind. They couldn't go out anywhere for the evening without effort to arrange a babysitter for Rosanna. A leisurely meal at home was fine.

Peter wouldn't be able to check names until he was in the police station on Monday. But he had been intrigued by the morning conversation. At least some of the topic was in the public domain. He'd seen the overall space flight failure on the BBC's evening news. Especially in Cornwall it was a subject of considerable interest.

As they began their meal, with slices of aromatic duck and spring onion, enriched by hoisin sauce and wrapped in small pancakes, Peter voiced a question.

'Maxine, this is a private conversation. I don't want you to give me names or anything confidential,' he began. 'But can you give me an outline of the problem at Newquay, and how far you've got with the solution? Or to put it another way, m'dear, will I be on my own here for weeks and weeks?'

Maxine had been secretly hoping to share her ideas with Peter and was glad he'd given her the chance to do so.

'It's the UK government that's called me in. They want to be sure that the flight failure was not caused by international interference. It's bad enough for our reputation that the UK's first attempt at reaching space failed – it'd be even worse if it was the result of sabotage.'

Peter helped himself to another duck pancake as he considered.

'Isn't the best way to do that to start with the flight itself?

Asking, what might have gone wrong? I mean, starting with the least likely explanation of all and trying to show it didn't happen is madness, isn't it? How can you ever disprove a negative? Not in the real world, anyway.'

Maxine prepared her second duck and hoisin pancake as she wrestled with an answer. The trouble was, Peter was putting her own worries into sharp focus.

'There are a few aspects I can study. For example, the flight last Monday was only finalised by the Operations Manager on Monday lunch time. Before that it was too windy. Even if there was an information leak on Monday afternoon, there'd hardly be time to put a sabotage plan into action. The trajectory started with a one-hour airflight, so was not exactly known. And I've been told, by several sources, that firing successfully at a fast-moving space rocket, as it travelled fifteen miles high over the Atlantic, is logistically impossible.'

Peter smiled. 'That sounds to me like a good place to pause. Shall I fetch the main course?'

He stood up and returned with two full hot plates. 'That's everything, I think. Would you care for some wine?'

'You could start with a technical investigation,' Maxine began, once their meal was well under way. 'I've sat in on two days of that. But space travel is wildly complicated, and it could take months and months to unpack. At the end of which you still wouldn't be certain.'

Peter frowned in concentration. 'Could you haul the failed rocket out of mid Atlantic?'

'Maybe. If you were prepared to spend billions on the search. But the rocket's much smaller than the Titanic and has sunk much deeper. So I'd say that's impossible.'

Maxine sighed as she took another mouthful of her meal.

'For diplomatic reasons the government want an answer quickly. That's what my report is meant to provide.'

Peter gave a smile. 'So all you've got to do, Maxine, is write up an amplified version of what you've just told me. No sign whatsoever of foreign interference. Case closed.'

'Which would be true. Apart from this discrepancy over the names of occupants of Room 14. It's probably nothing, but I find it hard to ignore.'

CHAPTER 14

Molesworth Arms: Sun January 15th

Maxine left Rosanna and Peter enjoying their boiled eggs. It was late on Sunday afternoon as she headed back for Wadebridge. The forecast was for an icy night ahead. On Sunday evening the gritter lorries for the A39 might not be working. She'd prefer to be back in the traditional Molesworth, ensconced in Room 14, rather than face the same journey on Monday morning.

But as she made her way past reception, Maxine noticed that the regular receptionist she'd first encountered, Laura, wasn't on duty. No-one can work all the time, she told herself – not even hotel staff. She'd had the whole weekend off herself.

The stand-in receptionist looked like a student in her early twenties. Cheerful and friendly. More malleable than Laura, anyway. An idea started to bubble into her mind.

Maxine went back up the stairs to Room 14, unlocked the door and settled herself in. Nothing had changed. Was there any way she could make good use of the stand-in receptionist? She built up the key elements of her story.

Half an hour later she returned to reception. The young woman was still behind the counter, looking rather bored.

'Hi,' the analyst began, giving her a smile. 'I'm working at Newquay Spaceport, staying for a few nights in Room 14. My name's Maxine . . . Maxine Travers.'

'I'm Billie,' the woman responded. 'I'm afraid Laura isn't here this evening. It's her night off.'

'I'm sure you'll do just as well,' Maxine declared. 'I'm trying to solve a puzzle, you see, over who was staying in Room 14 before me. They had the recent visitor names at the Spaceport, of course, and gave them to me, but they couldn't tell me what any of them looked like. I'd like to jog my memory, see if I know any of them.'

Billie looked doubtful. 'It's very old fashioned here. Too trusting by far. They don't ask for passport photos or anything.'

'No, I noticed that. You haven't got mine, for example. But don't you have CCTV cameras?'

Billie gave a cry of recognition. 'Of course! I'd completely forgotten them. I was given a whole morning's tuition on the system when I started.'

Maxine grinned. 'That's useful. Shows the place is security conscious. Presumably the recordings are classified by date?'

Billie nodded. 'And also by the corridor or staircase where they're located. Now, d'you happen to know the dates when your Spaceport visitors were here?'

This was terrific. Maxine had hoped the question might be asked. She'd memorised the dates – there were only three since Christmas – and also the names attached to them on the visitors' book. (There was no point in giving Billie the names from Newquay, they didn't agree.)

Suddenly they encountered a snag. Billie remembered more of her training.

She looked apologetic. 'I wouldn't be able to lend you the recordings I'm afraid, Ms Travers. There's privacy legislation covering that sort of thing these days.'

Maxine hardly missed a beat. 'But could I at least look at them?'

This was the crucial question: the analyst held her breath.

'Sure. You'll need to come with me into the Security Room. I'm afraid it's a bit dingy. They don't decorate it very often.'

So saying, she invited her guest behind the counter and into the room beyond. For the second time in three days Maxine found herself in a dimly lit room facing a large screen. She sat down on a seat in front of it and waited for Billie to operate the machine.

'Let me see . . . it's one of these . . . that's it. We're on.'

The screen offered a brusque title in large letters: "Stairs to Room 14. Wednesday December 29th." It ran on.

'Presumably the camera will only record when it senses movement?'

Billie didn't know all the technical details. 'I guess so. Otherwise we'll be waiting here a long time.'

The footage ran on. There was a man – swarthy and with a beard, aged, probably, in his thirties – coming slowly, carefully, down the stairs. The caption in the corner told them that this was the Room 14 stairs at five fifteen in the morning. To Maxine the man looked shifty, almost sinister.

'Can you pause it for me?' asked Maxine.

'I think so.' There was the noise of buttons being pressed on the machine, somewhat randomly; and Billie was muttering to herself. Maxine took the chance to take her phone out of her bag.

Suddenly the screen froze. Billie had achieved a pause. Even the man on the screen looked shocked. Maxine had captured it on her phone before Billie realised what she was doing.

What would happen now? The snapper gambled that the chemistry was on her side: an established guest with part-time staff. And it worked. The young Billie decided that discretion was the better part of valour and pretended she'd seen nothing untoward.

'So that's Terry Baldwin,' declared Maxine. 'He's about to do something odd, I fear. Did he stay here for long?'

'Dunno.' Billie was feeling guilty now, wanted the whole event over as soon as possible. 'D'you want to see another day?'

Over the next twenty minutes the two caught up on all three recent Room 14 guests. Janice Macdonald had come on Dec 29th and Sam Chamberlain on Jan 3rd. Each time Billie halted the run as requested, for Maxine to take a proper look. And every time the analyst not only looked but captured the appearance on her phone.

Billie had obviously decided to roll with the tide and turn a blind eye to what the guest was doing. She wouldn't be reporting all the details to Laura. For now, it would be their little secret.

CHAPTER 15

The Cosmic Girl Aircrew: Mon Jan 16th

On Monday morning Maxine saw her first task as trying to resolve the identities and roles of the three recent Molesworth visitors. At least she now had clear photographs of all three on her
phone. She would begin with Ruth Fisher.

The Operations Director had plenty on her plate, but she
knew Maxine had the government behind her.

'Right now, I can give you fifteen minutes,' she offered, 'then
I've got meetings for the rest of the morning. After that we could
have lunch together if you'd like?'

Maxine came straight to the point. 'The Molesworth Arms
had three visitors staying in your reservation, Room 14, for odd
nights since Christmas. But their booking names in the hotel
register don't match the ones Chloe gave me on Friday. Last
night, with a bit of help, I managed to get each of their pictures
out of the security system. Have you seen any of them before?'

This was not the line of questioning Ruth had been expecting. Maxine was certainly ploughing her own furrow. But why
not? She took the phone and looked at the images in turn.

'I'm very sorry, Maxine. I'm pretty sure I've never seen any
of them before – certainly not in the past three weeks.'

Maxine had half expected that. 'In that case, Ruth, can you
tell me anything about the three whose names came to me via
Chloe? Who did they come to see, for example? More

importantly, why were they here at all at such a critical time?'

Ruth remembered that Maxine was specifically here to look for hard evidence of external involvement in the flight disaster. No wonder she was bothered.

'Let's talk to Chloe.' Her secretary came in, clutching her diary.

'Chloe, can you remember who gave you the names of the three most recent guests we booked in to the Molesworth Arms? You gave them to Maxine on Friday.'

Chloe pondered. 'Any senior manager could have booked it.' She paused, then 'I'm sorry, Ruth, I can't recall who. I was just given the names. I never saw any of them personally.'

There was no point, then, in showing Chloe her pictures.

'Right,' said Maxine, 'I'll take this up this afternoon with Tom Willoughby. And all being well, Ruth, I'll see you for lunch later. Same time as last week?'

Maxine's next appointment was with the aircrew who had flown Cosmic Girl to 35,000 feet to launch the satellite rocket.

She wasn't sure how much there was to be gleaned from them but her investigation had to cover everything. In any case, she'd been told the crew would be flying out of Newquay airport next morning – back home, no doubt, for the plane to be reused on commercial flights.

Maxine reminded herself they had arrived not long before Christmas, weren't Spaceport regulars. They'd flown in from the United States, might not have the same sense of loyalty. Also, they wouldn't know the basis for her inquiries, or their high-level provenance. She mustn't take too much for granted.

It turned out the aircrew had a small unit of their own, including accommodation, behind the Technical Department. There was the usual tussle with security, then Maxine was allowed in. She found herself in a comfortable rest area.

'Hi guys,' she began, 'Thank you for seeing me at such short notice. My name's Maxine Travers.'

Four crew members were in the room but not in uniform. She was introduced to them in turn.

'I'm Greg, the captain and chief pilot. This is my backup, Harry.' He nodded to the table where the other two were playing chess. 'Wally's on radio, and Cynthia is our navigator. There were a couple of flight engineers but they're back now with the Engineering Department. A couple of flight attendants came with us. But they weren't on Monday's flight.'

'Rockets don't need flight attendants,' commented Harry. 'We haven't seen them for days.'

'Last minute shopping in Newquay,' muttered Wally.

'More chance they're in Truro,' added Cynthia.

Maxine smiled. 'That's OK. You four are the ones I need to talk to. I usually work in British security, up at Bude. I've been sent here to check there's no reason to suspect any foreign interference. I'm having a brief chat with everyone.'

The crew nodded. They knew security was a world of its own.

'I'm surprised you're leaving so soon,' she began.

'It's only a short contract,' said Cynthia. 'We've been here for five weeks, right over Christmas, we want to be flying properly by next week. Frankly, Maxine, we're bored. There's not much going on here in the depths of winter.'

'Have you ever launched a space rocket before?' There was a shaking of heads. 'I presume you've had masses of training?'

Greg smiled. 'Oh, plenty. The main problem is taking off with 24 tons of rocket hanging off one wing. The plane's unbalanced, you see. We didn't want to skid off the runway – or to crash alongside a rocket full of space fuel.'

'So how was that tackled?'

'Well, the fuel on a jet is mostly stored in the wings. We loaded the fuel unevenly, with more in the right wing, offsetting the rocket under the left at take-off.'

Harry took over. 'The Engineering guys made a mock-up rocket, the same size and weight, but filled with sand and water. We practiced taking off with that, with different mixes of fuel: it took a while to get it right. Of course, we didn't have as much fuel with us in practice as we did on the real launch.'

'Right,' said Maxine. 'That's a lot more work close to the time of flight than I'd realised.' She paused for a moment. 'The other tricky point, I guess, happens when you launch the rocket from the plane.'

'How d'you mean?' asked Greg.

'Well, the timing's got to be spot on. The rocket can't be ignited too early, or the exhaust gases will burn up the plane. But if it's dropped too far before it fires, there'll be uncertainty on the rocket's trajectory.'

Greg smiled. 'Not many people dig that deep, Maxine. But there's one clever thing we do that helps a lot.'

'Oh yes?'

'We don't try to launch the rocket while travelling in a straight line. We move into a tight circle – well, as tight as you can get with a jumbo jet. Then we fire the rocket at the exact point on the circle where it'll be heading in the right direction.'

Harry took over. 'Releasing the rocket makes the plane lighter on that side. So its turn is even sharper. That also helps to prevent us from being fried.'

It was quite complicated. Maxine took a few moments to make sure she understood what they were saying.

'But guy, there's still a problem. It's one thing to fire, say, due south. With Cynthia's navigation you can control that. But if you drop the rocket, how do you know how fast it'll climb? It might even point downwards.'

'Ah. There's one more thing we do. We don't fly in a level circle. Nothing so simple. As we turn, we also start to climb – as steeply as we can. So when we drop the rocket, it will also be pointing upwards. Heading for deep space, exactly as we want.'

Maxine decided she'd got as much as she could cope with. Maybe she needed to go back to the Engineering team.

But there were still a few questions needing an answer.

She turned to the radio operator. 'Wally. I've nearly finished but can I ask you about communications during the flight?'

He nodded.

'Did you receive any unexpected messages during the flight?'

'Nothing at all. We were in touch with the Spaceport all the time, reassuring them that everything was fine. Once we'd re-leased the rocket we headed back for Newquay. It wasn't till after we'd landed that we realised the final stage had gone wrong.'

That fitted in with what she'd learned at Goonhilly. Now she turned to Cynthia. 'Was there any trouble keeping to the planned route?'

'There were a few wobbles when we left the runway, but I'd say we were on track, both flying out and coming back.'

Maxine would like to have spent longer with them. There were good vibes here, in a world she knew so little about.

But it was already nearly one o'clock. She needed to be back for lunch with Ruth.

CHAPTER 16

Lunch in Quintrell Downs: Mon Jan 16th

Chloe had already gone for lunch when Maxine arrived back in Ruth's office suite. She took a chair and waited. The aircrew had given her plenty to ponder on.

A few moments later the tornado swept in. It was Ruth – but not the calm, systematic woman that she'd dealt with earlier. This was a very angry lady indeed. Practically simmering with fury. As Maxine told her husband later, the steam coming out of her ears looked superheated.

'I'm too upset to go into the canteen right now,' she muttered, through clenched teeth. 'I might swear too often. Trouble is, if I drive out onto the road, I might kill someone instead.'

Maxine suspected the person Ruth wouldn't mind knocking over, was whoever she had just been meeting. But identifying the source of the anger was for later.

'I've got my car here, Ruth. Let's find somewhere off-site for lunch – somewhere you're really off the record.'

'That might be for the best. Thank you.'

They made their way out to the Visitors' Car Park. Nothing was said until they reached Maxine's Polo, which was covered in the mud of a winter in Cornwall.

'I doubt it's as grand as yours.'

'I don't care, Maxine, as long as it goes and doesn't stall. I've had enough of that for one week. There's said to be a fine country pub in Quintrell Downs.'

Mercifully, Ruth simmered silently as they made their way over to the Royal Oak. Maxine always struggled to drive when her Rosanna was howling in the back. The silence, on almost empty roads, was balm. It also gave Ruth a chance to calm down.

'It's my shout,' said Maxine, once they'd reached the bar of the Oak. 'What'll you have?'

Ruth settled on a half of the local brew; Maxine tried a half of Healey's cider – that was local, too, she realised. They found themselves an isolated table in the far corner and seized the menu.

'I feel like something substantial,' confessed Ruth. 'I'm shattered; I need all my tender pieces pulling together again.' After a few minutes deliberation they each settled on sirloin steak and chips and placed the order when the waitress came.

Maxine knew enough not to press, but soon Ruth was pouring out all the details of her morning's humiliation.

'It's that bloody Suzanne. She's only been in Cornwall for six months and she thinks she controls everything. Whereas it's me that keeps the place on an even keel. I'm usually here long before dawn and I'll still be here well after dusk. The spaceport's my baby, not hers.'

She stopped for breath. Maxine thought it safe to venture a question. 'Something must presumably have unsettled her, to make her take it all out on you?'

'Oh, she'd been unsettled alright. By our latest Prime Minister. Or at least, his staff in Downing Street.' She gave a long sigh that might have been a muffled sob.

'Last week's failure to launch the satellites had hit them hard – harder than we'd realised. "UK reaches into Space" was a headline they'd been banking on. So now, it seems, they want to blot us out altogether.'

An unplanned break arose as their meals arrived. But it gave Maxine time to think.

'Ruth, no government operates on spite. This site's been an investment for years. Boris's pipe dream. Cornwall Council's seeding of the new local economy. As well as lots of backing from its citizens.'

Ruth took a mouthful of her steak before venturing a reply.

'I'm sure spite isn't far away, Maxine, but there's also raw political logic. If the Spaceport can't deliver – I don't mean satellites in orbit but winning back Cornish votes – then isn't it best done away with?'

There was silence for a few moments as they tucked into their meals. Maxine thought Ruth was calming down a little. But the analyst realised she'd not yet got the whole story.

'So how had Suzanne learned of this change of heart? What triggered the explosion?'

Ruth gave a rueful grin. 'There was no warning. It was over the phone. By some nameless minion in Downing Street, who's probably never run anything successfully in their life. Not on this scale, anyway. The backroom mafia had given it twenty minutes thought and made an executive decision.'

Maxine started to feel upset now. 'But they can't do that. Look, I was sent down here on the orders of the UK Defence Secretary. HQ Security had convinced him that the rocket failure was probably down to foreign interference – they could think of half a dozen candidates. And if there's that many people out there wanting us to fail, surely its diplomatic madness to let them succeed?'

She had more of her steak and sliced a fragment of fried tomato to go with it. The Royal Oak was an excellent eating place: they'd done well to eat there.

'OK, that's why Suzanne was angry. Justifiably, I'd say. But why did she take it out on you?'

They ate in silence for a few minutes. Ruth was getting her thoughts in order.

'She asked to see our business plan. Wanted something to send back to them, to show we could account for the money already spent.'

'You'd have something like that, surely?'

'Of course. But the plan was written in 2018, when we first started – before Covid and long before Suzanne had joined us. A huge amount has changed since. Both out in the world of space and here on site.

'Boris might have been happy with our plan – he was never a man for detail – but our latest Prime Minister exults in numbers. If it was shown to him in its present form, it wouldn't just be the minions after our blood, it would be the whole wretched Treasury.'

'But you'd be able to explain that, wouldn't you? This was an early draft, you were intending to update it, using data from the real launch. I mean, it's not exactly how you'd hoped to play it, but it's not as though you've been spending money like water.'

Ruth took a moment to frame her answer.

'Maxine, the Spaceport is a large operation that requires lots of money. But we don't spend much of that on people. We don't have dozens of background workers in an office somewhere, checking every fact and poring over every detail. All our effort – the whole Technical Department – has been spent on hiring good staff, working them hard and making the thing work.

'This is pioneering technology. As far as I know, no-one else tries launching their rockets from a commercial airliner. It'd be far more expensive for us to build a full launch pad.' She ate ferociously for a few minutes until she saw her plate was empty.

Maxine had almost finished as well. But the conversation wasn't over. They'd not yet considered any possible solution. 'Why don't we treat ourselves to a dessert?'

Ten minutes later they had called the waitress and ordered desserts: one chocolate brownie and one blackberry crumble with cream. Followed by coffees. It wasn't the day for anything cold. Ruth was unwinding well now – all Maxine had to do was to come up with a feasible, constructive plan.

This was way beyond her original remit, but there'd be no point in reporting that security at the Spaceport was sound, if the whole place was about to be wound down.

'I can't help you produce a business plan, I'm afraid. It's not my skillset. But I know someone who could. Mind, she'll probably be busy on something else: her home's in Tintagel but she does work all around Cornwall. In fact, her name came up when I was talking to the senior manager at Goonhilly that was covering last week's flight: she had done work for him a few years ago. She's a Cambridge mathematician like me.'

'I'd never thought of getting outside help,' Ruth admitted. 'But won't that be hugely expensive?'

'George is flexible. It could be arranged in all sorts of ways. Pay by the day. Or you could take her onto the Spaceport books for a couple of months. She's used to making things work.'

Their desserts arrived at that point, giving them both the chance to consider.

Ruth was the first to speak. 'The trouble is, for something as big as this, I'd need Suzanne's approval. Reducing our costs is her driving ambition. She and I battle over it all the time.'

'But Ruth, if Suzanne were to organise some outside help, wouldn't that cost a lot more?'

'Oh, a huge amount. She's half American, I expect she'd

want to bring in an American consultancy. They hunt in packs, give glossy presentations and charge the earth to do so.'

'Well, why don't you let Suzanne start to look. Get hold of the price she's considering. Then throw up your hands in horror and say that you'll find someone local. My friend George is bound to be cheaper; she works on her own, you see. And I know the senior manager at Goonhilly would give her a top reference. You could probably get four months of her time for four weeks from American consultants.'

Later, as they enjoyed their coffees and compared memories of Cornwall, Ruth came back to the suggestion.

'So first, Maxine, if you wouldn't mind, I'd like you to have a private conversation with this George. See how she'd feel about it and how much time she could give us. Then, if that could be made to fit, I'd like to meet her myself: unofficially, of course, off the record.'

She mused for a moment. 'Maybe I could offer her lunch? I'd be happy to come here again, the food's excellent, I can get here easily and it's out of the way. Of course, Maxine, I'd be happy for you to be here as well: make the introductions between us.'

CHAPTER 17

Handing on the Baton: Tues Jan 17th

Maxine Travers' catch-up meeting with her old buddy George Gilbert took place in the Molesworth Arms snug the following evening.

She had rung her friend when she'd got back to Wadebridge after Quintrell Downs. By coincidence George had plans that took her to Truro the next day, so she'd be passing Wadebridge on her return. It was too good an opportunity to miss.

'I can offer you a meal if you like,' Maxine began, once they'd exchanged opening pleasantries. 'I'm here as a guest of the Newquay Spaceport, and they've told me they'll cover all my expenses.'

George had learned over many years not to turn down a free meal. 'Oh yes, please. D'you know, I was so busy today I didn't have time for lunch. So perhaps you can tell me, what are you doing for the Spaceport? It's a wider role for you, isn't it? Sounds intriguing.'

There was currently no-one else in the snug, so Maxine seized the opportunity. She'd thought hard about what level of detail it would be sensible to share: she was, after all, here on a high-level security mission. But her own views on what was going on were private. She knew George would be scrupulous in not passing anything on.

'I've been sent down here by British Security. You know the

space rocket they launched last week that plopped into the sea? Well, the government want reassurance that it was an accident and not the result of foreign interference. I've been down here for a week, meeting people and checking everything I can.'

'Sounds better than supervising decoders in Bude, anyway. More fun than most of the things I get up to. Is that what you wanted to talk to me about? Or is there something even more enticing on the agenda?'

Maxine hesitated. 'Well, there might be. Why don't I tell you what I've learned about the Spaceport first? I've booked dinner for seven, by the way, so that gives me about forty minutes. Then, if you're not bored stiff and want us to carry on, we can try to imagine a possible complementary role for someone like you.'

'Sounds good to me,' grinned her friend. 'You could think of me as an independent sounding board if you like. See if your interim conclusions sound remotely plausible.'

They settled themselves for the exchange. 'If anyone comes in here, George, we'll have to switch over to something else. My three-year-old, Rosanna, for example. Ask what you like about her. But we'll probably be alright. The place doesn't get very busy at this time of year.'

George prepared to be a friendly critic and Maxine began.

'These days, a key part of the battle for space is putting up satellites. To help with weather prediction and telecommunication. They can also tell us more about climate change. A dozen countries already have ways to launch satellites; right now, not one of them has a launch site inside Europe.'

George looked surprised but said nothing.

'Satellites are getting smaller and smarter. Designing them is a separate branch of the space industry. Would you believe it,

George, the rocket sent up from Newquay last week was carrying no less than nine small satellites and they came from eight different sources.'

Maxine paused for breath then pressed on.

'The distinctive feature of Newquay's operation is that the rocket is carried up to 35,000 feet under one wing of a large commercial aeroplane. A 747 in fact, commonly known as a jumbo jet. I was talking to the crew yesterday.'

'Why not start with a vertical rocket like everyone else?'

'That's an interesting question. The answer seems to be that Newquay has a long runway, almost two miles. It was extended by the Americans in World War Two.

'Launching with a plane may conceivably be cheaper,' she continued. 'I haven't checked that – but it also gives some interesting problems, both at the launch and later, when the rocket is released. Anyway, it's the way Newquay has chosen to go.'

'What went wrong?'

'That's the $64,000 question. The plane took off and the first rocket was released and ignited. But the second stage, which contained the satellite load, didn't fire at all. It just dropped like a stone into mid Atlantic, never to be seen again.'

'Wow. All they said on the news was a brief comment that it had failed. Almost like the authorities would prefer to skip the story altogether. But the staff on site must be devastated. How long's it been in preparation?'

'I think they started in 2018.'

'Hey, that's when I was refining security links between Newquay and Goonhilly. But that was about tourist flights into space – something else altogether. Anyway, Maxine, why don't you tell me what you've found on security for the latest space flight. Have the Russians found a way in?'

Her friend grinned. 'Well, if they have, I haven't found any trace so far. The key thing, you see, is that the plane can't set out in a gale. So the launch was postponed for nearly a week till they had a calm day. The decision to fly was only made on Monday lunchtime. After that, everyone on site was getting the rockets fuelled and fastened on. Not much time for news to travel out to where it's not wanted.

'And secondly, I can't find a single method for anyone to shoot down a rocket as it's about to go into space. So I don't see how it can be deliberate sabotage. The thing they need to worry about is some mischance in the design.'

Maxine had timed her summary well, they were called for their meal a few minutes later. Once again they had Maxine's isolated table.

'I'd better not have anything alcoholic,' said George, as they pored over their menus.

'Hey, you could stay here if you wanted. My suite has two bedroom. Won't cost you anything.'

George considered. 'That'd be jolly convenient, actually. I'm back to Truro tomorrow morning. Right, which wine would you prefer?'

A few minutes later they'd placed their orders and could re-lax till their meals were brought.

'You were hinting at the Spaceport having something for me?' asked George quizzically.

'Oh yes. But tell me first, how busy are you over the next few months?'

George smiled: this sounded promising. 'Well, I expect to be very busy down in Fowey for most of February. The Council wants a study of the town's traffic problems. But it should be done by March. After that I've got plenty of ideas but nothing as yet committed. What did you have in mind?'

'Well. The Spaceport has a piece of work they need doing, over the next few months probably, which someone of your skills might undertake.'

'Tell me more. Longer term projects are always more satisfying. As long as you're not offering me to work out why that rocket didn't fire.'

Maxine grinned. 'They've a whole Technical Department working on that. But what they seem weaker on is strategic planning. Does that ring any bells?'

George pondered for a moment. 'Well, it's certainly work for months rather than weeks. I've done some in the past. But they must have done some themselves. I mean, it's had public funding, hasn't it?'

'My reading is that they had a business plan when they started. Then all their energies went into making it happen. So there is a plan, but it's four years behind the times. Which, in the world of space travel, is an age. It might not have mattered if the flight last week had succeeded. But now that it hasn't, everyone is being far more critical.'

Two lamb shanks with dauphinoise potatoes arrived at that point. The pause gave George a chance to give the idea some thought. She sipped her Rioja before returning to the discussion.

'The thing is, Maxine, I'm not someone to produce a token document – however glossy. If I'm asked to work on something, for months rather than weeks, I'll do it properly. In other words, I don't want to be told the answer. Who would the client be for this work – if it happened?'

Maxine was unsurprised at her response. 'Well, the Company Chair's a bit of a fireball. But this project would be for the Operations Director – a woman called Ruth Fisher. She's been there from the beginning. She's holding the Spaceport together, and it's not an excessively big crew. The biggest team is the Technical Department. They've done all the design work and put the pieces together.'

'But there must be some sort of finance capability?'

'Oh yes, there's a Director. I haven't had time to meet him yet, but I've no reason to think he would be awkward.'

'The key thing, from my point of view, is the relation with the client. Would you say Ruth Fisher is my kind of woman?'

'She's Cornish born and bred: does that help? And she's authentic – studied space at university and spent time in NASA with the Americans. As far as I can see, from a week on the site, she's also good with people.'

'That's reassuring. Is there any chance I could meet her before we get into any contracts?'

'D'you know, George, that's exactly what Ruth said, when I floated the idea to her yesterday. I'll see what I can do.'

That evening, during her regular call home, Maxine asked her husband what his office computer had made of the mysterious visitors to Room 14 in the Molesworth Arms.

'I'm afraid I can't tell you anything, my dear. None of the names matched up on the UK Police database – even with your pictures. So they're not well-known criminals – in Britain, at any rate.

'The thing is, people obscure their names for all sorts of reasons. Authors do it all the time. It's not necessarily illegal. You'd need a stronger reason to worry before we took it any further.'

The Molesworth Three trail seemed to have reached a dead end. For the time being, at least.

CHAPTER 18

Rendezvous in Quintrell Downs: Tues Jan 24th

Over the next week Maxine interviewed the rest of the senior management team and a few of their key subordinates.

If it was certain there'd been a leak of confidential information from the site and the question was how had it happened, fiercer interviews would be needed. But her remit was looser: was there any evidence of a leak at all?

For years, Whitehall had been awash with leaks. Indeed, it was stories about parties in Downing Street, when the rest of the country was in Lockdown, which had led, eventually, to Johnson's downfall.

But in this case, Maxine's higher-level bosses were more interested in reassurance that nothing was seriously amiss.

The trickiest chat would be with Suzanne Kennedy, the Spaceport Chair. She'd seemed so tense: was there something difficult buried in her past? Maxine had no idea but had left her till last. She wanted to be as well-informed as possible on Spaceport activity before they met. It would be their first encounter since that fierce opening clash.

Suzanne remained seated as Maxine arrived. It occurred to her that the Chair was much shorter than Ruth Fisher. Was that was why she'd sat down so rapidly after they'd first met? Strutting around like a pocket battleship was hard work if you were not that large. But today she was on more of an even keel.

Maxine reintroduced herself. Then, 'I'm asking everyone, Ms Kennedy, did you communicate the exact time of the launch to anyone, between that being decided on Monday lunchtime and when Cosmic Girl returned in the dead of night?'

'Why ever should I do that?' the woman bristled.

Maxine shrugged. 'I wasn't sure of your exact role. Aren't you the external-facing part of the leadership team?'

'Huh. I try to keep abreast of everything, not just publicity. Some people in an organisation don't respond to anything less than tough love. But the afternoon of the launch wasn't the time for that. The morning after, with a successful mission behind us, was when I should have had the key role – except that it never happened.' Quickly, she turned the question. 'So have you found the culprit yet?'

'I've found no evidence that there is a "culprit". No foreign government, anyway. I've been to Goonhilly Earth Station and spent a day with the staff monitoring the flight – of course they'd been told when it was to happen, but nothing suggests that any information leaked there. And I've talked to security experts. Even with advance information, they tell me, there's no way that the second stage could have been shot down, flying that high and moving that fast.'

A short while later the interview ended. Suzanne seemed satisfied with the foretaste of the forthcoming security report, but a lack of animosity was the most encouragement she could provide.

Maxine had agreed a date for Ruth Fisher to meet George Gilbert informally. It would be over lunch at Quintrell Downs, a week after her own supportive meal. Maxine had been away from the Spaceport, pulling her final report together in the Molesworth Arms, so all three had to come in different cars.

But they arrived within a couple of minutes of the agreed time: for businesswomen, punctuality was a cardinal virtue.

Maxine went to fetch drinks – three lemon and limes – while the other two introduced themselves and made their choices from the menu. A positive chemistry between the two was a major goal of this encounter. So she didn't hasten placing her order, but when she got back to their table she saw that a shared love of Cornwall was providing a promising starting point.

'What are you currently working on?' asked Ruth.

'I'm helping with a business plan for Truro Council,' George replied, 'but it's nearly finished now.' She sketched out the key ingredients in a manner which Ruth found comfortable – just the right level of detail. She could see similarities here with what was needed for the Spaceport.

'I was brought up in Truro,' Ruth admitted. 'I was in the Cathedral choir as a teenager. It's a reassuring place, actually, good acoustics and not nearly as old as you might think.'

'I have a couple of girlfriends in Truro,' responded George, smiling. 'One of 'em, Frances Cober, is a police officer I met on an earlier visit; the other one's a vicar – Joy Tregorran. She currently runs the church on the Lizard at Church Cove – fifty yards from the sea.'

'No! Joy Tregorran? I was in sixth form with her, in Truro College. We were both doing A-level sciences. Our lives went different ways after that – she into teaching and eventually into theology, me into space science - but for those two years she and I were best buddies. It's a while since I've seen her, mind.'

Maxine could imagine the lunch unravelling into a long chase down memory lane and sought to bring the conversation back on track.

'When you were on the Lizard, George, weren't you doing something with Goonhilly? I was over there last week, met one of your contacts.'

George quickly picked up the prompt. 'Jim Harvey? He was head of security at that time. A bit of a rough exterior, but we ended up good friends. We swap cards at Christmas.'

'What a coincidence, I know Jim too,' said Ruth. 'He's a key contact in tracking our own space rocket. He's extremely capable – maybe too serious for his own good. He was always fine with me, mind.'

'My project was on enhanced security for links to Newquay,' said George. 'When I started, he didn't think the security there needed enhancing at all. But we eventually found common ground.'

Their meals were brought and broke the flow for a few minutes. But George's summary had raised a bigger question.

'George, don't you find it frustrating to be always the advisor and never the final decision-maker?'

It was a good question. George considered for a moment as she started on her biryani.

'I think my answer to that comes in two parts. First of all, like Maxine, I'm a mathematician. I've always loved solving problems, especially ones based on the complexities of the real world. And I know that statistics, computer simulation and hard logic are key elements in that.'

She took another mouthful of the curry.

'But secondly, I'm probably not ruthless enough to be a top manager. I mean, you get a long way by being kind and considerate to your staff, setting them a good example, going the extra mile and so on. But it's a competitive world. Someone, somewhere, will have funded what you're working on, and they'll want their return. That may sometimes mean taking options that are unpopular or divisive. It's not an easy balance to maintain.'

She paused for another mouthful.

'So, temperamentally, I'm better earning a living as a clear-thinking advisor than being the final decision maker.' She suddenly realised how long an answer she'd given. 'I'm sorry, Ruth, I've talked too much. But does that make any sense?'

The two had never met before. For an opening encounter this was getting rather deep. But Ruth appreciated being told a fragment of the truth. Better than a polished, oft-repeated slogan. And it made a lot of sense.

There was silence for a few minutes as they ate their meals. But Maxine in particular was aware that time was precious here, it mustn't be frittered away.

'Ruth, if possible, could you share a little of the reason an updated business plan might be useful for the Spaceport.'

Ruth wrinkled her nose. 'I could. And I will. But things are moving fast at the Spaceport, I'm not sure if that's the most urgent priority.'

The other two ate a little more, waited for her to continue.

'We had a business plan, but now it's largely out of date and easy to rubbish. We've got our own data on how much it costs to do things. And the world of space exploration is moving at an incredible pace. What seemed obvious four years ago is often overtaken by new science or new pressures.'

'Give us an example,' pleaded George.

'Launching a rocket via a commercial jet is not just cheaper – I still believe – but is better for the environment. If we had a conventional vertical launch here, the residents of Newquay would be regularly deafened. That sort of factor will matter even more in the future.'

Maxine could imagine the ingredients of a business plan and would share those with George later. But she was disturbed by Ruth's opening words.

'What did you mean, Ruth, that priorities might have

104

changed?'

Ruth sighed. 'Well, I don't often mention our Chair, Suzanne. She was inflicted on us a few months ago by our shareholders. You've seen her at full throttle, Maxine, she likes to think she knows more than she does.

'But given the attention now on us from Downing Street, she's become conscious that her own experience of space, in the United States, is older than mine. Today's journalists are far better informed. So now she's pressing me for an up-to-date review of space experience around the world, as shown on the internet. She's even willing to pay for an independent consultant to provide it.'

Ruth was looking despondent. It was exactly the sort of interference from above that she hated.

But George could see a silver lining. 'Hey, Ruth, internet surveys are the sort of thing I do. I can't do it for a few weeks, mind, but I can give it my full attention from the beginning of March. And what's even better, it would be a great way for me to prepare to produce a business plan. It's win-win all round.'

CHAPTER 19

Developments in February

During the entire month of February neither Maxine Travers nor George Gilbert visited Newquay or its Spaceport.

Maxine had submitted and presented her report to HQ Security. There was no evidence of external interference in the flight of Cosmic Girl – though she had a few suggestions in the appendix of what might have gone wrong.

George had moved on to a project in and around Fowey, on Cornwall's south coast. But a keen bean like George couldn't be satisfied with a single project. She had been drawn into helping trace the story of one of Cornwall's least well-known captains of mining, working around Par. She had also met, and become friendly with, the head of mathematics at Fowey's Fimbarras Academy. His name was Peter Jakes.

The Technical Department at the Spaceport had been a hive of intense activity. Maxine had written privately to Tom Willoughby, with suggestions for where things might have gone wrong. That had prompted his team to look outwards as well as inwards.

Tom had sent his most multilingual manager, Reuben, to cross-examine the French-based team in French Guyana. 'Get to know them. Reuben. Make friends. Take as long as you need.'

The circumstances warranted the long journey. There were

questions needing answers. Had the French had similar problems? What proportion of their second-stage rockets (as used at Newquay) had failed and was the failure rate increasing or declining over time?

More subtly, at Maxine's suggestion, what was the altitude and the angle of flight when ignition had been applied? Was that different to what had been tried from Newquay? Could that, should that, make any difference?

Reuben was sent with a digital copy of all the flight data from the Spaceport. 'It's not public domain, mind,' Tom told him. 'Keep it safe. But we need to work cooperatively. There's room for all of us in the space race.'

Tom was trying to be outwardly positive. Inwardly, he feared the worst. There might be room but would Newquay still be in the race? Or had its fall at the first fence destroyed their chances for ever?

The Spaceport's shareholders, too, were anxious.

Up to now they had been happy to invest their money and leave the experts at the airport to get on with making it all happen. They'd never expected the project would become a financial legend – space was a frontier where risks were taken and anything could happen. But if it made a profit and they also came away with a little associated kudos, that would be more than they'd get from many other investments.

Now, though, the terms of investment had changed. Before the launch, hope had triumphed over limited experience. Now experience at home had started with a whimper and it wasn't welcome.

The shareholders' appointment Suzanne Kennedy, in post only since last summer, was summoned to a special meeting in London to explain what had happened. She elected to take Ruth

Fisher with her. She hated to admit it, but Ruth was far more on top of the plethora of events than she was. They even agreed, to keep down Spaceport costs, to share a car.

Suzanne knew it would be a tricky meeting, but she hadn't reckoned it would be that difficult. After all, shareholders didn't know that much. She could leave Ruth to handle the detail. That was what an Operations Director was for, wasn't it?

The meeting started in a conventional manner. Suzanne gave a fluid overview of the events of the last month. But she couldn't help slipping into being over-positive – a tone which riled many of the shareholders.

A florid man in a check suit stuck up his hand. 'OK, Ms Kennedy. We all know the first one failed. Not an overwhelming disaster, I agree. This is space, not a new shopping precinct. We've nothing against you personally, Ms Kennedy. Your American references were excellent. But now we shareholders want to know your plans: what happens next?'

Similar sentiments followed from other shareholders. Some response was required, or the mood would quickly turn ugly. In desperation, Suzanne turned to the Operations Director beside her.

'Ruth Fisher will now explain what will happen next.'

It was a hospital pass of an introduction, but Ruth had feared the worst and prepared accordingly. If she played this well, she realised this could change the balance of power between her and Suzanne. She took half a minute to stand, gather a few papers and wait for total silence.

'As Operations Director since this whole project began, in 2018, I was as upset as anyone by what happened on Jan 9th. Since then various things have happened. Firstly, we have had an immediate review, by a senior Security Officer from the GCHQ Listening Station, of security at the Spaceport. Her conclusion is that there is no sign at all of foreign involvement. To put it another way, there's no-one else to blame.

'Secondly, our technical staff are putting everything into trying to understand what could have gone wrong. A senior member of their staff is currently talking to French space experts over in French Guyana, who sold us the second-stage rocket that failed. What are the statistical odds of that happening, or more to the point, happening again? And what can we do to the design that might improve our chances? Obviously, I can't give a deadline on this: it will take as long as it takes. But we know that time is against us.

'Thirdly, we want to set what happened to us into a wider context. Today there's a huge amount going on around space exploration, particularly with respect to satellites. A surprising amount of that makes it onto the internet. So we are commissioning an independent study of the latest state of play around the world. That will be illuminating for us all.

'Fourthly, we are planning an update of our own business plan. We have a better understanding of costs than we did four years ago. But we need to learn more about the alternatives. And we need an honest answer: is a plane-based rocket launch good value for money? And you shareholders need that answer too.

'We're not in position yet to say when we will try again – or even if. It's less than a month since we failed. We need to take a bit of time to rake over the ashes. But the Newquay team are still keen to make it work. And with your support, I'm sure we can.'

A round of applause greeted this effort. More relief than anything else. These shareholders wanted them to succeed. They just wanted to be sure that they weren't frittering away their investments. Ruth had given them that confidence. For the time being, at any rate.

A Cornish Conundrum

There was an interesting drive back to Cornwall ahead for the two Spaceport Executives.

Eagle-eyed readers may have wondered what, if anything, has happened to the bloated body off Bedruthan Steps. But a scrutiny of dates will confirm that, before April, it had not yet been discovered. It was still tossing about in the ocean. The rip tides had not yet got it as far as Diggory's Island.

But one day soon they would.

PART THREE

NO LONGER A HERMIT

March 2023

The end of the Hall Walk, Polruan, seen from Fowey

CHAPTER 20

Abandoned in Polkerris: Sat March 4th

It was the weekend – there was no hurry to get up. No reason to, for that matter. For it would be another day on my own.

'Peter Jakes, you're an idiot,' I told myself. 'You take an attractive, unattached woman out for dinner – not just once but twice – and you tell yourself that shows her you're interested. Things have progressed since your courting days with Annie. You've got to tell her, in words and deeds, not just look beseechingly at her across the dinner table. Make her hear your lips, not simply struggle to read your mind.'

I sighed. George hadn't even come round to say goodbye. Just a phone message, wishing me well in my teaching. I'd sent her a brief WhatsApp but she'd replied she was working on something confidential, over in Newquay. So I hadn't persisted, didn't want to look pathetic. But when would I see her again?

Before George had come to the town I'd thought I was content. Living on my own on the outskirts of Fowey, in charge of sixth form maths at Fimbarras Academy. It was five years since my beloved Annie had finally lost the fight with liver cancer. I'd found satisfaction, after a fashion, helping able youngsters in the Academy to move on. Thought that would do.

Then, without warning, I'd met George Gilbert.

It was a sign that, for me, there could be more. Life wasn't over. I couldn't be a hermit for ever.

But that was true, surely, with or without George.

I hauled myself out of bed and looked for my walking gear. I'd take a good long walk, down the coast to Gribbin Head, then back around into Fowey. Maybe, as a special treat, I could try the shop behind the jetty that sold those special croissants? Expensive but delicious. Why not?

Breakfast was over quickly. I'd had a solid walk along the coast – it was a fine morning and there was a view right over to Charlestown. Then I'd tramped past Readymoney Cove. Only a century ago that was the home of Daphne du Maurier. Then on through Fowey, till I reached the jetty. There were plenty of people about, locals and tourists, they all looked more cheerful than me.

There were a few spaces left to sit in the coffee shop. I ordered my coffee and croissant and sat down for a break.

A woman came down the aisle with a tray of coffee, looking for a seat. I realised I knew her: it was Liz Wild, a former colleague at the Academy. 'There's a space here,' I murmured.

'Thank you, Peter. Not got that gorgeous young lady with you this week?'

I shook my head. 'She's working in Newquay now.' To be honest, I was surprised she knew about us, but it's hard to keep even the smallest items secret in a little town.

'So you're on your own for a while? Tell me, what do you do with yourself, in the few hours you're not working?'

I was about to protest that teaching was a full-time job then I realised she knew that: she was making a joke. She'd been an English teacher; it's a lot more time-consuming marking essays than it is checking maths homework, where everything's mostly right or wrong.

'Go on then, Liz. What do you do with all your time, now you're retired?'

She took a sip of her coffee before answering. 'Fowey's a busy place. There's plenty to do here to keep anyone active. Even in the evenings, for those unlucky enough to still be working.'

'Like what?' I didn't really care, to be honest, but I recalled my morning's resolution to stop being a hermit.

'Well, how about a writers' circle?'

There was a pause as I recoiled in horror.

'Liz, I'm a maths teacher, not a writer. I haven't written a story for years and years.'

'But you make up tales to liven up your mathematics lessons, Peter. Sometimes your students would tell me about them. Occasionally they were very funny. You could start with one of them.'

'Piffle. The topic the leader would set us to work on would never match what I do, surely.'

Liz smiled. 'On the contrary. I agree, we do have competitions from time to time, usually with a set subject. Most of our meetings consist of members reading out something, then their colleagues suggesting ways it could be improved. Almost like teaching, without the hassle of a teacher. I'm sure you'd like it.'

She sounded so enthusiastic. I could feel my resolve weakening. 'I couldn't manage every week, Liz.'

'Don't be silly, it's not as often as that. Once a fortnight, with gaps in the school holidays. Thursday evenings. 7:30 to 9:30, with a break for tea or coffee at half time. Why not come along next Thursday? Just give it a trial, Peter. Make some new friends. You can't hide away in despair for ever. Annie wouldn't have liked you doing that.'

There was a shuttle minibus running to the top of the town from just outside the coffee shop and I took it to avoid the steep hill. Then it was an easy trek across the headland to Polkerris, back in time for lunch.

I was glad I'd had some company over my coffee break. I realised as I walked back that I'd more or less agreed to come to at least one of Liz Wild's writers' circle meetings.

But I didn't have too much marking on Thursday evenings. It wouldn't harm to go once, surely?

CHAPTER 21

Fowey Writers' Circle: Thurs Mar 9th

Fowey Writers' Circle was to meet in the Fimbarras church hall. I found myself ridiculously caught up in the minutiae of what to wear: what was the accepted dress-code for this sort of group? How formal was it?

It all shows how you ought to get out more, I told myself.

And when I got there, I realised it was stupid to be so apprehensive. This wasn't some highbrow bunch of academics, wanting to explore the subtle rhythms of Shakespeare's early poetry. Nor was it a meeting of well-known authors, each with a dozen books to their name, vying for pre-eminence.

This was merely a dozen local Fowey citizens, half of whom I already knew. Their ages spanned the decades, I was somewhere in the middle. An even mix of genders. Their only common ingredient was a love of writing.

It was a relief to see that Liz was not the chairman of the meeting. She knew far too much about me, might make me do too much. Instead it was someone called Les Williams, who turned out to be a retired finance officer from the local water supplier. I could imagine having something in common with him: he must have a passing interest in numbers, surely?

I was the only newcomer to the Circle that night but they all made me welcome. I explained that I was here just to see what sort of things went on, as well as to widen my own social circle. No, I hadn't written anything in recent years, apart from thousands of school reports.

'D'you consider those fact or fiction?'

'Would you consider bringing any of them to our next meeting?'

'What's the worst howler you've ever made?'

I wobbled through the friendly banter – this wasn't a formal interview, I reminded myself – and set myself to listen to the various offerings being read out.

The most surprising thing, I thought, was the range of subjects being tackled and the styles brought into play. A couple of short stories seemed fairly accomplished: one was a romance, the other a fantasy. At the other end of the scale, one of the others, trying to update Enid Blyton, was clearly starting from a low base.

But Les cajoled some lively discussion from us on each of them. He always had a comment of his own; sometimes these were controversial and prompted fierce counter argument.

It was a different sort of fun. I'd certainly be happy to come here again.

After a sociable tea-break there was a change in the pattern.

'There's something the committee have been arguing over for the past few weeks,' Les began. 'I thought it was time to bring it to the whole group.'

I could see from their reactions that this was news to most of those present. Were we about to disband? Had the church ended our lease, or trebled the fees? Was I attending the last ever Fowey Writers' Circle? I hoped not; and started to listen more carefully.

'Taking a wider view of the kind of things we each bring,' said the chairman, 'I reckon that over recent months we've fallen into a rut. I take a brief note, you see, on what's brought here each fortnight. There's plenty of variety; but there's one category of writing that is missing altogether.'

'Edgy material?' suggested someone. 'No,' he replied.

'Potential newspaper articles?' Les shook his head again. 'No.'

'A history of how we came to have our regular regattas here in Fowey?'

He shook his head once more. 'They've already got something like that in the town museum.'

A pause and then, 'Intense full-bodied romance, no detail spared?'

'A few of us might quite like that,' admitted Les, 'but it might drive others of us away.'

There was silence for a moment. Brows were furrowed. Then Liz spoke. 'You're not by any chance thinking of poetry?'

Afterwards, thinking about it as I drove home, I could see it had hardly been a humdinger of an idea. First reactions were distinctly muted.

But they were a group gathered to consider new ideas and wrestle constructively with them. They all had respect for Les; he didn't often try to steer them anywhere. He at least deserved a hearing.

'We used to have poetry quite often,' reflected one of the older members. 'We even had an annual poetry competition, with an outside judge. Whatever happened to that?'

'The judge died. Probably worn down by reading our modest efforts.'

'No, it wasn't that. Or not entirely. Didn't he go on to become Poet Laureate? Rose above mere writers' circles. Had to write lofty poems about the Queen and her mates instead, for every royal occasion.'

The debate went on for some time and then Les asked, 'So

what should we do about it?'

No doubt he had some sort of idea but was wanting to tease more out of us. I considered: how would I handle this if it was a sixth form lesson? I took my courage in my hands and spoke up.

'What if each of us were to choose a poet – living or dead, but we'd need to make sure they weren't all the same – and then tried to produce a profile of their life, illustrated with one or two of their poems. Then we'd do our best to write something in the same idiom.'

'That sounds different,' admitted Liz. 'It'd be a real challenge for all of us. But we're not that brilliant, we couldn't just do it in a fortnight. We'd need to set a deadline, say the end of May?'

I'd managed to stir up the group, anyway. I'd never taken the slightest interest in poetry, didn't know what I was letting myself in for. But the project would take me out of myself. Well out.

Stop me being a hermit, anyway.

CHAPTER 22

Encouragement from George: Sat Mar 18th

It was over a week later that I had a phone call from George Gilbert. She hadn't abandoned me after all!

'I'm so sorry I didn't ring earlier,' she began. 'Thing is, it's been absolutely hectic here in Newquay.'

I wanted to tell her how much I'd been missing her but somehow that seemed too heavy to share over the phone. 'It's term-time here, of course,' I replied. 'I've been busy too.'

'Peter, I'd so much like to see you again. And I've been thinking about how it might be done. They've given me solid accommodation in Wadebridge, but I've had to be in Newquay Spaceport virtually every day since I started. There's so much to learn about space flight. But I've reached a point where most of what I've got to do next is based on systematically scouring the internet. That doesn't have to be done in Wadebridge at all.'

Hey, what was she saying? Was there a chance I'd see her after all?

'Well, George, you know you're always welcome here in Polkerris. I've got a second bedroom that could be used as a study if you like. Would it work for you to come here?'

'It would be really good to have a change of location, Peter. Perhaps just for a week. But you're sure that wouldn't be a nuisance?'

'When can you come?' I was eager now.

'Well. How about this afternoon?'

That gave me just three hours to catch up on the housework; it always got behind in term time. There wasn't much time to think about what we would eat, I never planned that far ahead.

Then I remembered the Fisherman's Arms, upstream from Fowey, in the village of Golant. Perhaps if we ate there it would help us carry on where we'd left off a month ago? Feeling slightly daring I rang and booked us a table for seven pm.

Last time we'd eaten there, I recalled, we'd agreed a prohibition on mentioning the word "survey". That was what had initially thrown us together, using my students to study Fowey traffic. Would there be any restrictions this evening? Not from my side, obviously, but from hers? I had little idea what she was working on, or how much she'd be able to share.

George turned up in her yellow Mini-Cooper, just after three. We gave one another a polite hug then I helped her unload. I'd been worried we'd be sharing the same computer but there was no problem. She had a special kind of laptop that allowed her to load up internet articles and extract items of interest. It all looked very swish.

I noted that she hadn't dressed up for the journey, she was simply in a sweater and jeans. 'Have you got any walking gear with you?'

'Course,' she replied. 'I love the south coast. Let me unpack, then we could we go for a stroll. I could do with some fresh air.'

We headed off on my favourite walk, along the coast to Gribbin Head. The conversation flowed, exactly as I remembered from a month ago; better than I'd dared to expect. Later, refreshed, we came back along the road to Polkerris.

Once we'd got in I put the question. 'I wondered if you'd like to go out for a meal this evening?'

She smiled. 'Peter, I'm your guest. I'd love to. Take me wherever you want. But on the same basis as we had last month, please.'

'Oh. You mean, we'll split the bill? I'm happy with that.'

'I was more thinking of key words for us to avoid – like "survey". With the clothes-removing penalty you suggested if we failed.'

I blushed. Had I really said something like that? To a woman I barely knew? 'I doubt we'll be talking about surveys this evening.'

'We'll have to find some other word instead, then.'

I saw that she was grinning. She'd obviously relished the detail, even a month later. Perhaps my behaviour had worked in my favour. Was this going to be a more animated week than I'd bargained on?

'We'll take my car, I think, George. You've driven over here and I know the route.'

'Fine by me. Means I can drink without any worry for a change.'

It was still light when we got to Golant, though starting to get dark. The Fisherman's Arms, beside the swollen River Fowey, looked as welcoming as ever.

They had plenty of guests but we'd been given a table close to the window; we could share intimacies without being overheard. We both chose steak and chips and I ordered a bottle of Merlot. As the driver I wouldn't be drinking more than one glassful, but we could take the bottle home if necessary. I'd no idea how much George would want to drink.

'OK,' she said. 'I'd like us to ban the word "Spaceport". We can talk about it during the week, maybe, but tonight I'd like an evening off.'

'With the same forfeit?' I asked mischievously. After all, it was good to be clear. I warned myself sternly not to ask George anything about her work. I didn't want to be the one taking items of clothing off – not this early in our relationship, anyway.

'If our friendship is going to blossom, we need to know more about one another. Tell me, Peter, what do you do in Fowey that's nothing to do with your Academy?'

I felt so relieved for the writers' circle that I'd joined the week before. That would be a fresh thing to talk about which wouldn't go anywhere near spaceports.

I launched into it with gusto. Described the other circle members and the way it operated. Then I got to the second half.

'We've been set a different kind of project for the next couple of months,' I revealed. 'I need to find a poet I can make sense of, to work up an outline of their life.'

George blinked. 'That sounds pretty ambitious, Peter. Was that the chairman's idea?'

'To be honest, it was mine. The sort of thing I'd do with my sixth form. So I've got no option but to tackle it. Trouble is, I'm a mathematician, I've never taken the slightest interest in any poet or their poetry. D'you know much about the topic?'

Our meals were brought at that point, which gave George a few minutes to ponder.

'I'm no poetry fanatic, either. Too busy with my calculations. But do you recall Sir John Betjeman?'

I enjoyed my next mouthful of steak before answering, 'Just about,' I said. 'It came up in school English lessons. Wasn't he the one that wrote poems that actually rhymed? Is he still alive?'

George shook her head. 'I don't think so. But he was Poet Laureate in his final years – someone must have thought he was special. He was buried in Cornwall. I have the feeling it was at St Enodoc, a tiny church near Rock, close to the sea. But I've no idea why. Why don't you plump for him? Then at least you wouldn't have to grapple with old-fashioned English.'

We enjoyed our meals for a while. 'If Betjeman spent his closing years in Cornwall,' I said, 'there'd be some chance of visiting key locations. I could even take pictures. That'd go down well with the other members. Hey, I need to make sure no-one else nabs him before I do.'

When we'd both finished our steaks, and George was onto her second glass of Merlot, there was a pause before we started to consider desserts.

When the dessert menu board was brought, George was amazed to recognise the waitress. It was Izzie, the Academy's top maths student, who'd given her help in completing her traffic studies a month ago.

'Gosh ma'am, you're here again – with sir. I really like your chunky necklace.'

George hadn't brought many changes of clothing to Fowey, she was in her best going-out dress. She was happy that Peter had given her a chance to wear it.

'Hi, Izzie. Still working hard?'

'Like crazy, ma'am. I'm sure you were like that, back in the day.'

Whatever her academic strengths, the girl's diplomatic skills still needed sharpening.

'Are you still analysing traffic flows, ma'am?'

'For my pains I'm onto space rockets. Or, at least, the one that failed recently at Newquay.'

This conversation could rapidly destroy any chance for George to keep off work topics. I'd better intervene.

'Izzie,' I asked, 'will you be on duty here next Saturday?'

'I'm here every Saturday, sir. It's a good way to boost my

pocket money.'

I gave her a grin. 'Well, I'll do you a deal. If you get on with the dessert menu, I'll make sure George and I come again next Saturday. Then, once you're off duty, we'll have our coffees with you in the lounge. There you can ask George all you want. Is that alright, George?'

George nodded gratefully. It would be hard to explain her work without using the forfeit word Spaceport. For now any clothing removal would have to wait.

CHAPTER 23

The Hall Walk, Fowey: Sun Mar 19th

Neither Geoge nor I woke early on Sunday morning.

We'd brought the Merlot back with us and finished it off in my lounge, sharing all sorts of things from our backstories. I even got a second bottle from my wine "cellar", though some of that was left for this evening.

I told George about my long and happy marriage to Annie and how that had come to a painful end five years ago. Somehow, though, it was in the past now, no longer had the same hold on me. With George's help I was starting to move on.

She unpacked some of her own checkered romantic history and outlined how she'd come to own a cottage on the edge of Tintagel, overlooking Trebarwith Strand. From where she now did independent consultancy work around Cornwall.

'What's your usual Sunday routine?' asked George, as we tucked into toast and marmalade and swigged our first mugs of coffee.

 'I try and keep it a work-free day – unless it's the exam marking season or the like. I regard it as my day for exercise.'

'I've worked pretty hard over the last month,' she replied. 'I'd be happy to take today off, too. So where should we go?'

I didn't have to ponder long. 'The classic saunter for Fowey is the Hall Walk. That's across the ferry at Bossiney, then along the far side of the Fowey, looking down, as far as Polruan. Then back over the passenger ferry.'

'Great. I've done it before but I'd love to do it again.'

'The only thing is, we'd best do it this morning. It gets quite busy in the afternoons – though it's not the tourist season yet.'

We took my car to the Academy carpark, then walked down through the town to the Bossiney crossing. The vehicle ferry was just making its way back across. I recalled, this had been one location for the traffic survey which my sixth formers had carried out under our joint supervision.

We walked onto the ferry and sat in the side cabin as cars were slowly loaded on board.

'Annie and I used to do this walk regularly,' I told her. 'Till the last years, when she was too weak to manage it. She'd been brought up in Polruan, her parents still lived there. It was our regular stop-off point for a cup of tea.'

'Are they still alive? D'you want to drop in today?'

'Her dad passed away three years ago,' I said. 'But her mum's still alive. In her late seventies now, I guess.' I hesitated for a moment. 'Would you like to meet her?'

'I'd love to Peter. I mean, if it's not too complicated. After all, she's part of your past. I want to know as much of your history as I can.'

There was a crunching noise as the ferry reached the Bossiney side and its drop-down bow scraped along the slipway. We let all the cars drive off before we disembarked.

'I'm afraid we start with a rather steep hill,' I warned her. But then we'll be high up for ages, with lovely views across the estuary.'

No problem, George was fit enough. No doubt she did plenty of exercise around Tintagel. We hauled ourselves steadily up the road then through the snicket and onto the start of the walk. It was a good path, with occasional views down through the trees. At those points Fowey was laid out before us.

Like all Cornish footpaths, it meandered up and down. But there were benches allowing the occasional stop. An hour later it started to go down steadily; we found ourselves, not at Polruan, but at a Fowey inlet with a stone jetty. It was a chance to stop for a rest and a drink, I showed George where we were on the map.

We weren't alone, there were a few more people here. Not walkers, they were doing something else – measuring distances and comparing angles. Also taking pictures. It was intriguing.

'What are you doing?' asked George, of a cheery-looking man with curly fair hair who seemed in overall charge.

'We're refining a new television series. Based in Looe but we daren't admit that. We need a few extra locations for later episodes or the next series, more anonymous and quiet. This looks ideal.'

'The Cornish coast is pretty well walked,' observed George. 'If you really don't want crowds you'd be better off, say, in the West Indies.'

'Oh, I've done that,' he said nonchalantly. 'Lots and lots. This is a sequel.'

'What's it called?' I asked.

'"Beyond Paradise",' he replied. 'D'you reckon it's a good title?'

I laughed. 'I'm a maths teacher. 'Numbers not titles. Not yet anyway.' I could see the man looked puzzled.

'Peter's in a writers' circle, you see,' said George. He has to research a local poet. Trouble is, we're both mathematicians.'

'Not sure I can help,' the man grinned. 'I studied history, you see. Cambridge 1990. Gosh, that was a long time ago,'

'Hey, I started there then,' declared George. 'Which college?'

This was a conversation that I sensed could go on and on. 'George, I think we'd best leave him to it.' I offered him my hand. 'Very nice to meet you. My name's Peter Jakes, by the way.'

'And I'm George Gilbert. George Goode in those days.'

He shook both our hands.

'My name's Robert Thorogood. Very nice to meet you. Hope your poetry hunt goes well. John Betjeman wrote high-class doggerel. At least it rhymes. I'd go for him.'

We found the footpath, which led up the other side of the inlet and, eventually, along to the main river. Another hour and we'd reached the outskirts of Polruan.

'My mum-in-law lives down this street here,' I said. 'Sure about dropping in?'

'I'd love to,' my companion replied.

Polruan developed on the side of a hill and Annie's mother lived in a cottage halfway up. It had a splendid view across the estuary and over to Fowey. When we reached the cottage I knocked firmly.

'Hi Angela,' I said, as she came to the door. 'My friend and I are doing the Hall Walk. Would it be a good time for her to meet you?'

'Peter. How nice to see you. And who is this?'

George responded. 'My name is George . . . George Gilbert. I'm from Tintagel. Peter and I only met recently.'

'Well, you're very welcome, m'dear. Would you both like a cup of coffee to help you on your way?'

'Yes, please,' I said, 'and can we come in?'

We followed Angela into a small lounge and sat on the settee. It was certainly a cosy cottage. Pictures on every wall. Most were well-known locations in Cornwall but there were a few I didn't recognise. Angela returned with the coffees a few minutes later.

'So you're from the north coast, George?' Angela began.

'But I do work all over Cornwall,' George explained. 'That's how I met Peter, here in Fowey. But I understand you've lived in Polruan for most of your life? It's a lovely spot.'

'My husband – Annie's dad – was born and bred here. I've only been here for half a century. You might not think so but I came originally from Ireland. My sister still lives there, in fact. Nesta. D'you remember her, Peter? She was here for your wedding.'

A distant bell tinkled in my mind. 'Ah. That's who she was. I recall Nesta. But I never understood where she fitted into the family. There were so many people to meet on that day.'

Angela stood up and took down one of the pictures. 'This is where she's always lived. Dublin. She's very hospitable, I'm sure she'd love to see you – see you both, if you liked.'

I suppose it was Angela's way of encouraging our friendship. The conversation blossomed; we didn't leave for another hour.

The final stage of the Hall Walk meant crossing back over to Fowey on the passenger ferry, which ran every twenty minutes. I knew the ferryman and several of the other passengers on the boat and introduced George to them. I was inordinately proud of my newly endorsed friendship.

Once we'd crossed over, we made our way back through the streets to the centre of Fowey.

'How about a bite of lunch before we head back to Polkerris? There's that café outside Fimbarras Church.'

George started to play the cautious housewife. 'Mm. Have you got anything back home for our meal this evening?'

'We'll manage,' I said, trying to remember what was left in the freezer. And for some reason she trusted me. We went inside and ordered some toasted cheese sandwiches.

The café was located opposite Fowey's independent bookshop, "Shrew Books". George spotted it as we came out.

'Peter, if you're going to turn yourself into an authority on Sir John Betjeman, you need at least one book of his poems. You'll like them. Let me buy you something.'

Fowey had few visitors this early in the year – Easter was still three weeks away – and the beautifully laid out shop was far from crowded. The owner, a woman in a light blue jumpsuit, in her late thirties, was quietly reading behind the till.

'Good afternoon,' George greeted her. 'Do you have a poetry section?' We were directed to some shelves in the corner. I saw a dozen books with Betjeman's name on them. But which one to choose?

George made her way back to the counter. 'Can you advise us? We're late developers, I'm afraid, wanting to read some of John Betjeman's poems. Is there anything you'd specially recommend?'

The owner stood up and joined us, smiling. 'And this is for the pair of you, not just your children?' I nodded, smiling at the notion, but it was a fair question.

'Why don't you start with this one?' She pulled out an anthology of poems with a Cornish theme, by John Betjeman. 'It's got an introduction about his connections down here. His dad owned a cottage in Trebetherick, next to Polzeath; he was always here for his school holidays. And he came back in his later years – he's even buried in the nearby churchyard. He wasn't Cornish, strictly speaking, but he was Cornish in taste and outlook. I'm sure you'll enjoy it.'

Other customers came in at that point and she returned to her till.

'Sounds a good one to start with,' said George. 'Please can I get it for you? A souvenir of my first stay in your cottage. Perhaps, in the evenings, after we've stopped work, we can read it together?'

CHAPTER 24

The Fisherman's Arms, Golant: Sat Mar 25th

For me, at least, the following week passed in a delirious blur. I was as busy as ever at the Academy, while George scoured the internet remorselessly for the latest information on space activity and satellites.

In the evenings, after some discussion (was George here as guest or housemate?), we took it in turns to cook supper and to talk. We'd committed to eating out again on Saturday, I couldn't justify any more meals out in the meantime. Not in term-time, anyway.

After supper, we also spent some time exploring John Betjeman's poems. To my surprise I found them delightful – and not just because of George's lyrical recitations.

One was written from the viewpoint of a church mouse – there was no clue if that was at St Enodoc, where the poet would end his days. Another was the "Ballad of Joan Hunter Dunn", set during a tennis tournament. There was even one about Betjeman's teddy. And a soliloquy which started "Come friendly bombs, fall on Slough." We decided that this was some sort of black humour, which we didn't find very funny.

There was also a poem about a bike ride with Emily in Ireland, with the poet delighting in the local landscape. The lady didn't seem to be his wife. He obviously got about, I thought.

On Friday I was approached by Izzy after a maths lesson. Was there any chance, she asked, that her friend Wilson could join us at the Fisherman's Arms on Saturday evening? He would also love to hear what George was doing. I recalled he had also helped her in February and said I was sure it would be OK. But no-one else, please. I left it to Izzy to fix the arrangements.

George and I didn't spend much time talking about work. We had plenty of other things to share. But on Thursday came the bombshell. She would have to go back to Newquay on Sunday. 'The deadline on this phase of my work has been moved to the week before Easter.'

We set out in my car on Saturday evening for the Fisherman's Arms. I was wearing my best jacket and George sparkled in a dark green dress. It was a privilege to be with her.

We were led to a quiet table by the window and placed our orders. A lamb shank each, with a rich gravy and vegetables including broccoli and dauphinoise potatoes. I also ordered a carafe of water and another bottle of wine, this time a Shiraz.

'What's our banned word to be this week?' asked George, smiling coquettishly.

I'd quietly been hoping she might play the game again and had made my choice beforehand.

'Why not "spaceport" again? It'll stop you talking about work.'

'No doubt with the same forfeit? Fine with me.' Was she trying to shock me – or simply to make life more exciting for us both?

'I've been doing some internet research of my own,' I said. 'On dear old Betjeman. He was made Poet Laureate when we were kids, though I sense it was done a bit reluctantly. Perhaps he wasn't taken seriously enough?'

'I don't think he was a signed-up member of the establishment,' she responded. 'Too idiosyncratic, perhaps? Risked rocking the boat? Though he was at Oxford. I read that in the foreword to your book.'

'But he didn't complete his degree,' I retorted. 'Perhaps he was too much of an outsider? And as we've seen, he tackled a wide range of subjects – over a very long career.'

Our meals were brought at that point, disrupting the flow. Once again the food looked, and tasted, delicious.

'I was thinking about his connections with Trebetherick,' I said. 'At both ends of his life. D'you think there's much there to see?'

'We could go to St Enodoc's one day, if you liked, Peter. He has a big gravestone in a tiny church. I've been there but never taken much notice of it.'

Her words made me conscious that we'd soon be apart.

I sighed. 'I'm sorry, George. I can't get away easily in term time.'

George looked equally glum. 'And I've got to present my Space report in less than two weeks. I promised them it by Easter.'

Suddenly an idea struck me. 'Just a minute. Our last week of term is coming up. We stop a full week before Easter.'

George paused in mid mouthful as my words sank in. 'So you'd be free to come to see me next weekend – if you wanted. For two weeks?' She saw me nod and smiled. 'Peter, that would be wonderful.'

We both ate contentedly for a while.

'I don't know North Cornwall very well,' I admitted. 'I'd have to explore on my own till your report was handed in.'

'But Peter, while I'm at the Spaceport I'm staying in Wadebridge. They've reserved a room for me at the Moles-worth Arms. You could stay with me if you liked. Betjeman must have spent some time in the town. You could see what they've got in the town's museum, for example. And I could certainly take off the week after Easter. Hey, you could come and stay in my cottage Does that grab you?'

I was so excited I didn't like to point out that she'd used the banned word. But it didn't matter now, we'd be eating out again soon enough.

After we'd finished the bulk of our meal, Izzy came to join us and showed us the lounge annexe that she'd reserved for George to retire to. It was a separate room, very relaxed, the easy chairs were comfortable and we wouldn't be overheard.

We moved through and were served with coffee; then Wilson joined us – George was surprised but delighted. My two brightest students had obviously made a big impression.

'This is useful timing for me,' she began. 'I'm driving to Wadebridge tomorrow morning and I'm back to Newquay Spaceport on Monday, so this will get me focussed. I can't share much of what I will be doing because it's confidential; but what I've been doing over the past month is from the internet, so it's not confidential at all.' She looked at each of them in turn. 'But I'm taking this as a private conversation between a few friends. I'm trusting that it will go no further.'

Izzy and Wilson nodded wholeheartedly.

'What I'd like to do is briefly to outline the opening project and the questions needing answers; then tell you what I've learnt about space in general and satellites in particular. It's a fast-moving area but really interesting. Please barge in with questions where I'm not clear. This isn't a well-rehearsed presentation, though it might foreshadow one in the future.'

George had a sip of her coffee and took a deep breath.

'No doubt you both heard about the Newquay space flight in January that didn't make it to space? This project stems from that. It didn't get much publicity but the consensus was that something unforeseen had happened in space, which meant the second stage rocket didn't ignite.

'But one thing that it did for the Newquay Spaceport was to make it tougher to justify the investment for the next attempt – if there was one. The Technology Department is desperately trying to work out what went wrong, but the key piece of evidence – the second rocket – is deep under the ocean.'

She looked around us. 'And now the government are also asking hard questions.

'Three years ago Boris Johnson signed off a White Paper about space flight with typical Johnson panache and optimism. You can find it on the internet. Several Greek heroes but no numbers at all.

'Our latest Prime Minister is fond of numbers and wants them to add up, to justify every item of expenditure. The world of space has changed radically in recent years. My remit is to summarise where it all now stands, then help generate a new business plan.'

There was a stunned silence. This was big-league stuff. 'You can see how mathematics is fundamental to the way things are done,' I said. 'But you two asked to be here. Your young brains will cope. Take in all that you can.'

George grinned at the advice then resumed. 'The thing that's surprised me most since I started, I think, is what's been happening to new satellites. They've shrunk. Guess how big the ones were in the latest Newquay rocket?'

'Weighing twenty kilos each?' suggested Izzy.

'Nah, it's got to be at least fifty,' amended her friend.

George corrected them both. 'The total load was well under a hundred kilograms. That was made up of nine satellites, each with a weight of between five and ten kilograms.'

137

'Hardly worth putting them up there,' said Wilson disparagingly. 'Is it?'

'Computer chips are getting smaller,' I contributed. 'Tell us what they might be doing.'

I could see their minds were buzzing. This was beyond A-level, hard work for a Saturday evening.

'How about collecting the latest weather data – temperatures and so on?' suggested Izzy. 'Oh, regularly,' George agreed.

'Helping with tele-communication and mobile phones?' said Wilson. Again George nodded.

The youngsters were into their strides now. 'Surveying every square kilometre of the planet and monitoring every vehicle on the road – the whole basis for the growth of Sat Navs?'

We unpacked this for some time. We'd all appreciated our navigation systems – though, of course, that needed a lot more besides satellites.

'There's one more area of science where satellites are vital,' said George. 'That's climate change. Measuring the coverage of arctic ice, for example, and how it's decreasing year by year. That sort of thing is only really possible from space.'

There was a pause. George finished her coffee as her audience mused on what they'd heard.

'So where do these satellites come from?' asked Wilson. 'Are they developed in some converted hanger at Newquay?'

'Oh no. Each one's built away from Newquay by a different company, with a particular task in mind. Which could be any of the ones we've talked about.'

She considered for a moment. 'Most are developed by university departments or small start-up companies. They'll pay significantly for the chance to be put into orbit. Part of the next stage of my work, I think, will be to talk to a few of these companies and make some sense of the market.'

'There's one more thing I should mention. Everything I've read suggests that around the world, the demand for more satellites and their data exceeds current capacity. There are launch points in many countries – but not yet anywhere in mainland Europe. Newquay would love to be first in the field.'

There was a pause. Then Wilson put the killer question. 'But if these satellites are provided by external companies, George, couldn't one of them contain the reason why the Newquay rocket didn't fire?'

George had never considered the problem from that angle. She'd need to check whether Maxine had considered it.

CHAPTER 25

Peter in Wadebridge: Sun April 2nd

It wasn't clear, I thought, as I drove over to Wadebridge a week later, what George's invitation to "share her room" might mean, it had been said so casually. It would be enough, for now, to share more time with her: our friendship was rewarding.

When I got to the Molesworth Arms I saw at once that her accommodation comprised two bedrooms and a small sitting room. All reserved by Newquay Spaceport. I guess they must have the occasional big-wig visitor – maybe Boris in an earlier incarnation? But fortunately not at the moment.

'How well d'you know Wadebridge?' asked George, after we'd greeted one another and dumped my case in the room.

'Hardly at all. There's plenty to keep me happy on the south coast.'

'Right. Let's go for a stroll before the evening meal.'

We left the hotel and walked down to the river. 'This is the River Camel,' she said. 'It flows on down past Padstow. After that there's Rock and Betjeman's grave on one side, and lastly Polzeath beach and Stepper Point. The lookout on the cliffs there was where my Uncle Bill was a watcher in his later years. I used his legacy to buy my cottage. That was what brought me to Cornwall.'

There'd be more to learn there, maybe over supper. But the bridge before us was very old. 'How long's that been here?'

'It was built at the insistence of the local vicar in the fourteen

140

hundreds. So many people had drowned as they tried to ford the Camel. It's been widened and extended over the years. They built a bypass in the nineties – that high bridge over there. That takes most of the traffic these days – fortunately.'

We walked on, past a variety of intriguing shops and cafes, ending at several bike shops. 'Too many?' I ventured.

'Ah,' she smiled, 'this is the start of the Camel Trail. Wadebridge's biggest attraction. It's a cycle way that runs beside the river, all the way down to Padstow and up to Bodmin. Following the track of the old railway line, which was closed in the 1960s. It's very popular, you can use it all through the year.'

Now I was better informed, I saw dozens of people of all ages cycling back along the track beyond. Plenty had children in trailers behind them. They weren't selling bikes at all here, they were hiring them.

'Did Betjeman write any poems about this? Seems the sort of subject he'd go for – or even enjoy himself.'

George frowned. 'I think he died in 1984. That's before the Cycle Trail started. So he'd never have had the chance. But he'd have travelled on the railway in his younger days, I'm sure. He was very fond of trains.'

George was off to the Spaceport early on Monday morning and I had the day to myself. Maybe I should start with the museum?

Wadebridge isn't a big place and it didn't take me long to find it. There were pictures of all kinds – the railway had made a big impression here in the last century. I saw there'd been two lines reaching here: one from Bodmin and the other, the North Atlantic Railway, coming down through Launceston and Delabole.

Also a spur onto Padstow that I'd seen part of yesterday, that later became the Camel Trail. There was even a black and white photograph of an armoured engine and tender, manned by Polish refugees. The contraption had defended the Camel estuary in wartime.

The place was run by local volunteers, mostly older than me.

After browsing the shelves for some time, I approached one of them.

'Do you have any information on Sir John Betjeman?'

'I'm not sure we have much,' the lady replied. 'Frank, can you remember anything about him?'

'He was buried over in St Enodoc,' he replied. 'I'm not aware of any connections this far up the Camel.'

'I'm hoping to go over there next week,' I explained. 'I've read that he used to come down to Trebetherick and Polzeath as a child. Was he here during World War Two?'

'If he was here at all, I'm sure he'd stay at the Molesworth Arms. That's the poshest hotel in Wadebridge. It's been here for ages, was certainly open for business during the war.'

But his colleague had a different idea. 'Have you been to the John Betjeman Centre? Down in the old station, just past the Library. If anyone can help you at all, it must be them.'

I felt an idiot, not even having heard of the Centre. But I was here to explore and soon tracked it down.

It was less helpful to me than the name suggested: a recreation centre for older people, from table tennis to dominoes, bearing the poet's name. But Betjeman wasn't that local. Maybe he'd left a bequest in his will?

Those in charge were friendly. I had a mug of coffee while I worked out my strategy. I just needed a good opening question.

'I came here at the recommendation of the museum,' I began. 'They thought you'd have more than they did on John Betjeman.'

'We're primarily a social centre,' the receptionist responded. 'But we have a small room holding some of Betjeman's personal belongings. Shall I show you?'

I followed her to the far end of a dining area, which was currently unoccupied. She pointed to a glass-fronted cupboard in the corner. 'We're not a museum. But we're well known around Cornwall and we'll accept anything we're given that comes from Sir John.'

To me it all looked a bit random. 'Do you have a list?'

'One of our staff keeps track of it all. She'd love to talk to you, but I'm afraid she's not here on Mondays.'

I'd come all this way, what else might I ask for? 'Would you mind me taking a few pictures of the items in the cupboard?' She nodded, they weren't fussy about copyright, anyway.

There were all sorts of items and I captured as many as I could. Betjeman's first typewriter. Hand-written versions of a few of his shorter poems. A very battered looking teddy bear. A few bottles of expensive-looking wine and spirit.

I personally thought it was rather a shallow history for a man who, after all, had been the UK's Poet Laureate for over a decade. It seemed he'd ploughed his own furrow, right to the end. He hadn't even been buried in Truro Cathedral.

I roamed around Wadebridge for the afternoon. Spent some time looking at bike hire – might it work for George and me to take bikes to Padstow and then go on to St Enodoc? I'd need to check the map. And also confirm it with George.

On Tuesday, still on my own, I decided I'd follow George's example and take some time to follow John Betjeman's life on the internet.

I'd never used the resource for this kind of purpose and found it addictive. My most surprising find was that John

143

Betjeman had spent two years of World War Two based in Dublin. Ireland had declared itself neutral in this war. Betjeman had been an attaché to the British Embassy, with a remit to make friendly relations with the local population. The goal was to try and offset some of the hostility towards the UK, and the underlying support for Germany.

I could see this was an important strategic objective. Enemy troops over in Europe was one thing, having them settled right next door would be something else.

There wasn't much published about how he operated, but I was starting to build a picture. John was a genial fellow, enjoying a drink or three with anybody. And he'd spent time in Ireland in the 1930s. "Ireland with Emily" had come from that time, he obviously enjoyed the countryside immensely. Moreover, his poetry would provide a natural bridge between communities. There were plenty of Irish writers and poets to get alongside.

I learned that John came back from Ireland in 1943. I could find nothing recorded, though, on what he did afterwards.

By now it was lunch time and, following in Betjeman's footsteps, I headed down to the Molesworth bar. I wondered if there was any trace of time he'd spent here. Had this been a place he'd retreated to?

The saloon wasn't busy and the hotel's main receptionist, Laura, was serving behind the bar. There was no queue. I'd gathered from George that she'd worked here for most of her adult life. That wouldn't cover the last war, of course, but still . . .

'Half of Doom Bar, please,' I requested. When she handed it over, I went on, 'Laura, does the hotel keep a long-term record of its guests? If it does, I'd love to see it. You must have had some interesting people staying here over the years.'

Laura smiled. 'D'you know, Peter, I was asking much the

same question myself only recently. It turns out we do. We couldn't let you take it away, of course, or even take notes, but you could look for any names you recognised. I'll take you to see it after lunch if you like. As long as you're happy to research in a dingy cellar.'

Half an hour later, quarter past two, the bar was practically empty. Laura declared it closed and gave me a nod. I was ready.

I followed her along a couple of corridors, then we came to a locked door. But Laura had the key. When opened there were uneven steps down to a dry but dusty-looking cellar. Fortunately, with lighting available.

This must be where the Molesworth Arms stored its wine for special occasions – I could see why the place was kept locked. It was cool, anyway. There were hundreds of bottles, all laid on their side, they must be worth a fortune. At the far end was a table, on which were a collection of thick, leather-bound ledgers.

Laura looked at me inquisitively. 'How far back d'you want to go, Mr Jakes?'

'I'm interested in the World War Two years, actually. I'm studying John Betjeman, you see, trying to fill in what he was doing from 1943 onwards. A guide at the local museum thought it was possible he'd been staying here.'

Laura nodded. It was a plausible scenario. She picked her way through the ledgers, which were in some sort of date order. Then she gave a whoop. 'Hey! This is the one you're after.'

I hesitated. It looked very old, did I need gloves to handle it? But Laura hadn't got any, it was hardly medieval. Fortunately, whoever had transcribed the names and dates had a steady hand.

I turned the pages rapidly till I reached 1943, then examined each page line by line. I only had one chance. Laura was being supportive enough, but she wouldn't wait for ever.

Each page covered a month's visits. I got as far as November 1943 and was starting to feel it was a dead end when, to my joy, the name Betjeman appeared. He'd stayed in this hotel from November 25th to the 29th.

The outlandish theory was correct. The poet had stayed here at least once. 'Found him,' I yelled.

Laura looked for herself and was equally excited. She was old enough to remember Betjeman in his heyday, had even enjoyed his verse.

But was this a solitary visit? I turned over to December. His name came up repeatedly. I didn't know why, but I thought it might be useful to know exactly when he was here. I looked across to my companion.

'I won't write down any names, Laura, but could I possibly make a note of the dates he was here?'

'Best if I record it, Mr Jakes,' she replied. 'I'll slip you an unofficial copy afterwards.'

Which was how we continued. It was a weekly pattern: five-days of occupancy, followed by a two-day gap. Right through till June 1944. Why was that significant?

Then I realised that the hotel had been Betjeman's weekday residence for each of the seven months preceding D-day.

It was quite a find. But I'd no idea where the trail would lead.

CHAPTER 26

Betjeman Scenarios: Wed April 5th

There was lots to talk about with George over supper next evening. But she had plenty to share too.

It had been the day of her presentation to the Spaceport Chair, Suzanne Kennedy. The apex of her recent endeavours and the cusp of what happened next. What could she say on where Newquay Airport stood in the wider scheme of things?

'There's a strategic case for Newquay,' she began, '– or if not, somewhere else in the UK – to have its own satellite launch capability. Satellites will be even more important in the future.' She listed some threads to build on.

'It's a bit like the start of the railways in the 1830s,' George had argued. 'No-one knew, least of all the political leaders, how that fumbling idea, with its huge wheels and rickety carriages and noisy cranking pistons, would turn out. Which was arguably the core reason for continuing. And, of course, in the end it was the entrepreneurs who led the way through the later industrial revolution.'

Suzanne had known much of this. But it had gone out of focus in the hurly-burly of day-to-day developments and setbacks. Now she started to be enthused again.

George had assembled masses of specific information – all up to date, with many cross references between her sources. There had been much informed debate between the three of them (Ruth Fisher had also been present).

147

But then George had gone on to her queries. There were few places around the world where launching rockets and their satellites from airliners were in development. Practically everybody else – even the Scots in North Shetland – were using large, vertical rockets.

George sipped some of her wine before continuing.

'Everyone "knew" that this was environmentally more damaging and arguably more expensive. Pioneers like Newquay were needed, either to prove the alternative or to test it to destruction. Whatever the outcome, it was important for the world to know.'

George had obviously made a personal hit with both Spaceport leaders. The session had ended up with a commission for her to update and quantify their old business plan, in the light of new advances and their own experience.

A generous short-term contract had been agreed which would start in mid-April. But I could see fresh ideas were already jostling in her mind.

Our meal had been more lavish than usual this evening and now I could see why. It was great she had done so well, but not undeserved. We chatted for quite some time on how this might all develop.

Then, as our main meal plates were collected and we reached the dessert stage, she turned to me.

'I've done far too much of the talking, Peter. How have your inquiries been going?'

It was my chance. I told her, in much detail. Ending with the afternoon's breakthrough in the Molesworth cellar.

'So our hero, John Betjeman, spent the first half of the war in Dublin,' I concluded, 'fraternising with the Irish. Then, I don't know why, he was called home. There's nothing more that

I've found in any internet accounts, but now we know from the hotel records that he came down to stay in faraway Wadebridge – for the whole period between his time in Dublin and D-day. What on earth do we think he might have been doing?'

There was a pause. It was far from obvious. We each ate some of our Molesworth trifle and pondered.

'You've learned, Peter, that he'd been sent to Ireland by UK Security forces. So, either he'd failed so badly he'd been brought home in disgrace . . .'

'Or else he needed to be protected from someone he'd offended in Dublin. He was always reputed to be a bon-viveur – notorious, even. He might have said something unwise in the wrong company, perhaps at the end of a carousing evening.'

George ate more trifle and considered the idea. 'Mm. D'you remember, we found that poem he'd written about biking with Emily? He was obviously very fond of the land of Ireland. Do you think he might have been too sympathetic to the cause of Irish unification?'

I ate more of my dessert before answering. 'He was staunchly British, I believe. He'd tried to join up in 1939 but failed the medical. But never mind why he was brought back to the UK. The question for us is, whatever was he doing down here? I mean, what security interest might be at stake?'

There was silence and then George thought of where she'd been working. 'The nearest military establishment to Wadebridge, I'd say, is Newquay airport. That was heavily used during the war, I believe, by American forces.'

Then I recalled the period he'd been staying. 'Would that make sense of when the poet was down here? I'm thinking, his time here didn't last beyond D-day. But why on earth Wadebridge? It's ten miles from the airfield. How did that feature?'

George had picked up a smattering of local history in her time at Newquay. 'I understand that the airfield was used to transfer troops and planes over from the United States, ready for the Normandy landings. Might there be a security issue in keeping them all safe?'

I sighed. That wasn't very credible. Betjeman was hardly going to patrol the security fences on his own. 'But they weren't in Newquay for long enough, surely? The troops had to be got down to the South Devon coast. That's where the D-day invasion sailed from in June 1944.'

Then I remembered one of the displays in the museum.

'George, I wonder how they got there. It couldn't have been via trains from Wadebridge station, could it?'

'If that was what happened,' said George, 'it might be sensible to have a security presence in the town here. Though it's hard to see John Betjeman, a man who'd failed his medical, being much good at that.'

We cogitated for a few minutes. Coffees were ordered to round off our meals.

'What John was always best at, apart from genteel poetry, was social drinking. After all, that was his role in Dublin. D'you think they might have wanted him to talk to American troops as they passed through Wadebridge, to find their state of morale? That would be useful to high-ups in London, don't you think?'

'I suppose so,' George replied. 'Can't think of what else he could do here that made much sense. But where might that take us?'

Neither of us could imagine. It seemed that, for now, the Betjeman trail had gone cold.

CHAPTER 27

Betjeman in Wadebridge: Thurs April 6th

For now, Thursday was the last day I would be researching on my own. The next day was Good Friday, a public holiday; George would be off duty. I was looking forward to that, though I must admit I was starting to enjoy being an investigator.

The experience made me wonder whether I should have specialised in history rather than mathematics, though it was much too late for that now.

I had one or two avenues to revisit. The first was the John Betjeman Centre in the old railway station. Their poet expert, Sally, should be in today. Now I had some information to share with her.

When I got there, the residents were busy with dominoes and Ludo. I drank some coffee then asked for Sally. A cheerful-looking lady came out of the rear office to help me.

I explained I was researching John Betjeman and was interested in the Centre's artefact collection. We went through for a closer look and I asked about the more distinctive items. They'd come from all sorts of places, mostly from his friends in the years shortly after the poet's death. I made a few notes, though I didn't see how they would help me.

Then I told her about my research in the Molesworth Arms

151

cellar and how I'd found Betjeman's name amongst the wartime residents.

It wasn't as much of a surprise as I'd expected. Sally had already known from his friends that the poet had been here in the war years. But it was good to get confirmation.

'What I noticed,' I went on, 'was that he was only staying in the hotel on weekdays. What happened at weekends?'

But Sally wasn't beaten. 'He'd go back to his cottage in Trebetherick, I should think. Wouldn't you?'

'And how did he get there? There wouldn't be many buses.'

'Oh, that's easy,' she smiled. 'We had an armoured defence engine here; it ran down the line every night to Padstow. I'm sure someone as garrulous as Betjeman could wangle a ride in the cab – especially if it was only once a week. It'd bring him back on Monday morning too, I expect.'

'But he'd still need to get across the Camel,' I observed. 'Wouldn't that be a problem, especially in wartime?'

'Not to Betjeman,' she grinned. 'He could talk the back legs off a donkey – and make every line rhyme as he did so.'

My enthusiasm for this man was growing apace. I was assembling a portfolio of material that I was sure would appeal to my writers' circle.

On the way back from the Centre I dropped in on the museum. It still wasn't very busy.

'I was here on Monday,' I told them. 'I have two further questions where you might be able to help me.'

'Go on,' said the guide.

'You've a lot of material on trains in Wadebridge,' I began. 'Am I right in thinking these continued to operate during World War Two?'

'It was a reduced service, but yes – though not as far as

Padstow.'

'Right. And did these trains take US troops from Newquay Airport over to the South Devon Camps, ready for D-day?'

'That's a good question.' She signalled to her companion, and he came across to join us. I repeated my query.

'I believe they were,' he said. 'For the six months up to the Normandy landings, at any rate. Lots of troops came in via Newquay Airport, of course. They had to extend the runway to cope with the larger planes. Local residents reported the noise was almost incessant.'

I nodded. 'Thank you very much. That supports the idea I've been working on. And secondly, can you tell me anything about the armoured defence train that ran down to Padstow?'

'It ran every night, I think. From 1941 to the end of the war. With a Polish driver and fireman – brothers and both refugees. By 1945 the pair had settled in these parts, in a small cottage near Padstow. They'd be dead now; I don't know if their families are still there. That was a long time ago.'

I went back to the Molesworth Arms. I had one more idea that might clarify what Betjeman was doing in the war years.

'Laura,' I said, as I passed her on reception. There was no-one else around. 'I've been thinking about what we found in the cellar yesterday. What I'd really like to know is what kind of things Betjeman was doing here in the war years. He obviously wasn't writing poetry.'

'I'd like to know that too,' she responded.

'You and I are far too young to answer the question. But George mentioned to me in passing that your mum used to work here. Would she have been here in wartime?'

I held my breath; might I have offended her? But it seemed not.

'Hey, that's an idea. Mum and I don't often talk about life in the hotel. Things have changed so much, you see, and we don't always agree. But we'd be alright asking her about the war years – she'd be the expert. Leave it with me.'

There was nothing more I could do for now. It might not lead anywhere. But there was a chance that it might.

At dinner that evening I put forward my idea of us cycling to Padstow then crossing the Camel and walking on to St Enodoc.

'I can see two things wrong with it,' George said judiciously. 'First of all, cycling to Padstow and enjoying the place is a good day out on its own. St Enodoc as well would be too much.

'But secondly, there'd be no point in going there tomorrow. It's Good Friday. There's bound to be a service in the church at some point. If we do go, it needs to be on a day when it's empty and we can get into the building. We want to check, remember, whether that was the location of the church mouse poem. And also to take a few photographs.'

She could see I was looking glum and proposed an alternative. 'But we could do the walk from Rock on Saturday. Then go on to my cottage. That's where we'll be all next week, remember. My first week of proper holiday this year.'

CHAPTER 28

St Enodoc's Church: Sat April 8th

We moved out of the Molesworth Arms on Saturday, telling the Spaceport admin in case someone else needed Room 14. We didn't need to drive separately to Tintagel; George suggested I left my car here, I'd need it to get back to Polkerris in a week's time. 'The hotel carpark will be safe enough,' she affirmed.

It was a gorgeous spring morning, with a clear blue sky and fresh daffodils and celandines abounding on the verges. George had a trick to avoid parking fees at Rock: we parked for free, halfway up the approach road. Then, boots on, we shinned up a narrow footpath and onto the golf course.

I'm always wary of golf courses, particularly on Saturday mornings when the gung-ho gang are letting rip. But I saw they had a well-marked footpath, running alongside the fairways, with a view to the left over the Camel to the cliffs beyond. I could see George was in her element, as I would have been around Fowey.

Soon we had to cut inland, across a fairway and along a narrow path to a tiny church, almost hidden in a hollow. It had a surrounding wall and a solid lynch gate.

'I'll let you take the pictures,' she said. 'Betjeman's grave is close to the gate. The words are clear enough. Some might say it's rather large, compared with the other gravestones here.'

I took pictures from several angles, I wasn't sure what I'd

155

need. The best one looked past the grave down to the shoreline, though that missed his friends' tributes. I wondered if the poet himself would have found these slightly over the top, but I suppose we'll never know.

'Right. Let's have a look inside.' George led the way into a modest porch, which had plenty of notices and timetables – this was a thriving community. Then on into the church. There was no-one else here.

The interior was a beautiful soft stone. I'm sure Betjeman would have found it to his taste – if that's the right word. Maybe "rejoiced in its historic design" would be better. A fitting place for his funeral, anyway.

It was small, only twenty-five or so metres from the altar at the front to the rear wall. A dozen wooden pews, lovingly polished, were arranged on either side of the central aisle. Yesterday's hymn numbers were still on display. There were several gaps in the far wall, covered by velvet curtains, presumably with storage behind. Spare hymnbooks, maybe? And a door into a vestry near the front, from which the minister would emerge, wearing his or her robes of office.

I pulled out my now rather-battered collection of Betjeman poems from my kagoule and thumbed through for the "Church Mouse".

There was no certainty: the location had not been specified. It could have been written with this building in mind – one of this size, anyway. We sat on a pew at the back and studied his poem together for some time. I felt very much at peace.

Later we emerged and headed across the golf course, then over a second course, through a caravan park and down to Polzeath. I'd been to this famous beach a few times before, but it was good to see it in context.

George led us into the Galleon Café, looking out across the sand. On Easter Saturday plenty of people were here. 'I always come in here,' George said, 'they have a cunning deal. The first mug is the usual price, but refills cost a pound. Very clever marketing, actually. Especially for customers on this sort of beach.'

I suspected there was another story here. Maybe I'd extract it from her over supper. I reflected: much of George's time in Cornwall had been spent here after she'd lost her husband and was on her own. The course she'd chosen, independent consultancy, had meant she couldn't hide away, she'd had to relate to lots of people in all sorts of situations. I hoped, if we stayed together, I would learn to do the same.

After coffees, we decided that it was too early in the year to be going into the sea. We headed back to Rock on the path along the estuary, past Trebetherick and Daymer Bay and the side of Brea Hill, then over the estuary sands into Rock. It had been a good walk and I felt pleasantly exercised.

After a light lunch, we drove on to George's home in Treknow: Ivy Cottage – completely new territory for me. The second bedroom, which I'd been given, had a view down into Trebarwith Strand. I could see another beach here, this one less busy than Polzeath.

I sensed George standing behind me. 'You can only see the beach at low tide,' she said. 'At high tide there's no beach at all. But when it is there, it offers really good body boarding. Is that your bag, Peter?'

I turned around. 'There's less surf on the south coast, I'm afraid. But I'd be happy to learn if you'd teach me?'

It occurred to me that, for George, having a special friend here was almost as new to her as it was for me. This was her home rather than a place she came on holiday. We'd need to

157

work at it.

'Right,' I said. 'We need a plan. We've got a week, what'll we do with it?'

Gradually, mostly from her, we compiled a list. The beach on Trebarwith Strand and the walk along the coast to Tintagel. A trip to Bude and what she called the "Canal Walk".

For something different, there was a museum next to an old airfield beside Bodmin Moor. And if the weather still held, a longer trip to Bedruthan Steps, close to Newquay Airport. 'Perhaps we could do that at the end,' she suggested, 'on our way back to Wadebridge?'

'You lead and I'll follow,' I told her. 'There's no point in us going far this week, the roads will be too crowded. We don't need to jostle all the way to Land's End, for example. What will we do about food?'

'This is a holiday, we could eat out a little,' she mused. 'I'll book us Sunday lunch in the Boscastle Farm Shop – you'd like that. You'd see their cows from the window. We could amble up the coast afterwards – or stroll up the Valence valley.'

'If it's OK with you, I'd be happy to cook on Monday,' I offered. 'Chilli Con Carne or something; we can get two days meals out of that.'

George nodded. 'Right. In that case I'll do Sweet and Sour chicken for Tuesday and Thursday.'

'Then we can eat out again on Friday,' I asserted.

'Or maybe fish and chips from Camelford – the best in Cornwall. See how we feel.'

Reviewing the plan, I could see George wasn't one to splash out on her holidays. But that was alright with me: Annie had been much the same. I'd make sure we had some appetising puddings, though. Those never went amiss.

I won't go into details. Just to say that, looking back, it was the best week I'd had for years. Away from her consultancy, George was fun to be with – willing to take a joke, open to correction, not intense at all. I did my best to match. After all, I was off duty too.

No forfeits were required: we stayed off all work topics for the whole week.

The nearest we came was at Davidstow Museum, next to Bodmin Moor. We wouldn't have gone at all, except that it was raining and we didn't fancy getting soaked on Rough Tor.

The place had been built by an army fanatic after World War Two and comprised military bits and pieces from all over Cornwall. There were twenty odd buildings, mostly Nissen huts from the old airfield. It wasn't warm but it was at least dry.

For us, the most useful section was a hut devoted to Newquay Airfield. This told us how it had come about.

A small aerodrome had been built on the site in the 1930s and was taken over by the military in 1939. The Americans had arrived two years later; for many years, till the 1990s, it was a US Base. The runway had been substantially extended to point straight out to sea and take larger planes; it was now one of the longest in the UK. That was how the airfield had caught the attention of the Spaceport team.

I hoped they might have lists of the troops arriving in the war years that we could browse, but that level of detail had been lost (if it ever existed). It was clear, though, that it comprised a wide range of personnel of all ranks. Betjeman would have his work cut out to talk to them all. Would he focus on the higher ranks?

There was no mention of forced entry. American troops were welcome in those days. The biggest problem was making sure they all returned from local lindy-hops and barn dances. Rugged, handsome soldiers, bronzed from years in the mid-west sun, were popular with the local girls, even if they spoke a different form of English.

The only conversation of note came on Friday evening.

I'd been dispatched to collect fish and chips from Camelford. George stayed at home, making sure the oven was hot enough to reheat the meals on my return.

When I got back, she'd also found time for a lightning shower and complete change of clothing. She was at home now, no longer limited in her choice. Tonight she was dazzling in a bright red dress that I found almost irresistible.

She noticed me staring at her and smiled. 'Why don't you change too, Peter?'

I rushed upstairs. Another appearance for my best jacket. This had the makings of a special meal.

George had laid out her best cutlery and chilled a bottle of Sauvignon: high-class catering for a small cottage.

It would be folly to let the opportunity pass. 'George, you look stunning. Even better than you did in the Fisherman's Arms.'

She ate a piece of her fish and chortled. 'Peter, I haven't worn this dress for years. Not had the opportunity, actually. I'm glad it still fits me – also that you like it.'

Which was the start of a very personal conversation indeed. But it was not one for wider dissemination.

CHAPTER 29

Bedruthan Steps: Sat Apr 15th

Our previous night's conversation had been long and intimate. There was a lot of ground to cover, many presumptions to unpack on both sides.

But it couldn't all be done in one evening, even perched in front of a glowing wood burner, assisted by Sauvignon and slices of cheesecake. George was still wearing her red dress when we parted on the landing for our separate bedrooms.

Now, though, we had a sort of understanding. Some stages of life, like courtship, were too deep and precious to be hurried – but neither must they last a minute longer than necessary.

There was something different in the air as we sat in the kitchen the next morning: our relationship had moved on. The challenge now was to make the most of the last day of our holiday. We'd both be hard at work by next week.

The plan was to return to Wadebridge via the coast, past Padstow. We would drive on round and park at the National Trust café next to Bedruthan Steps. After a coffee we'd walk along the cliffs, get down to the beach if we could.

George was driving, I sat back to enjoy the views. I didn't know this part of Cornwall that well. The rugged cliffs were overlooking the vast Atlantic. Which today, fortunately, was calm.

We reached the Carnewas Café just after eleven. It was fairly busy, this was still the Easter holidays. George went to place our order and I saw a table in the corner, part-occupied by a couple in their forties.

'Mind if we join you?' I asked.

'Great, so long as you've no young kids,' the woman sniffed.

I blinked and she hastened to explain. 'I'm head librarian in Newquay. I prefer to avoid children completely on my day off. My name's Judith.'

Her companion saw a need to introduce himself too. 'And I'm Will. Part-time coastguard when I'm not coding in Truro. This is where I really belong.'

They were certainly friendly enough. 'My name's Peter,' I responded. 'I'm on holiday too, normally a maths teacher in Fowey. I'll be back at the chalkface by Monday.'

George was back now and completed the pattern. 'I'm George. Another mathematician. Currently on a project at Newquay Airport, now on holiday with Peter. Pleased to meet you both. Are you walking far?'

The two didn't immediately rush to respond. Odd, it wasn't a difficult question. Something was wrong. My teaching instinct was aroused.

'Is something the matter?' I asked, sounding as gentle as possible. 'George and I have just come for a day out. It's so peaceful round here, isn't it?'

I had never expected that the remark would have reduced the librarian to tears. But once she'd started it was hard to stop. There were a few paper napkins on the table but she'd soon exhausted them. George reached for more from the next table. She and I knew not to speak, as did her friend. We would learn more when she was ready.

The café continued to reverberate with life of all ages.

Fortunately, the couple were facing into the corner and no-one else seemed to notice anything amiss. Eventually Judith stopped crying, drew breath and sighed.

'It's not a peaceful place, Peter. Not all the time, anyway.'

I looked at her. 'Whatever d'you mean?'

She sniffed. 'I was here two weeks ago, with my Climbing Club. Our spring meeting. We were going to climb the Steps – you know, the stacks. I was with a pair of youngsters on the most northerly one, the Queen Bess Rock. From which we saw a body, in a crack on Diggory's Island, just a bit further along.'

Will sensed she was struggling and took over. 'Judith climbed over the Island to check. It was a young woman – horribly bloated. She contacted me as duty coastguard and I called out the Air Ambulance. She and I had to ease the body out of the crevice, then help winch it up into the helicopter.'

I didn't know at the time, but George had more experience of trauma than I did and reached for Judith's hand.

'Judith, you poor, poor woman. Horrible. What a dreadful experience. Right out of the blue. And you can't get over it?'

Will replied on her behalf. 'We'd never met before, but this brought us together. Judith wanted to come here again today, to see where it happened and try to steady her nerves.'

'Judith,' asked George, 'have you been able to share this with a close friend?'

'Just the police – for what it's worth. They had no idea who the victim was. No-one of her description had been reported missing. Mind, they don't know when she died. It was probably two or three months ago.'

There was silence for a few minutes. I'd no idea what to say. This was a bigger problem than I was used to. But George sensed there was something that could be done.

'Look, Peter and I came for a walk along the Bedruthan

Cliffs. Would it help if we walked along with you, so you could share the event with a sympathetic outsider? Peter and I would be happy to help if we could.'

Judith wasn't really up to making decisions on anything but Will was glad of any help. A few minutes later we were on our way.

I chatted and walked along with Will. Behind us, George walked beside Judith, listening hard. There was a good path that led us along, with the usual ups and downs. The local beach, and the half dozen Bedruthan Steps, were far below us.

'There are regular rock falls round here. That's blocked the usual route down,' explained Will, as we came to a "No Entry" notice. 'The climbers had to go further along two weeks ago.'

We continued walking along the cliff top until we found ourselves looking down a steep slope toward Diggory's Island.

'If you're not regular climbers, I'd advise you not to scramble down,' said Will. I remembered he was a coastguard and used to giving consistent advice. But even standing at the top we could see the island where the body had been found.

The women caught us up and we all stood looking down.

'It does look peaceful here,' admitted Judith. 'The police thought she'd probably died much earlier, further along the coast. But this was where her dead body was trapped – on the far side of the island. It's completely out of sight, unless you happened to have climbed up the Queen Bess Rock and looked across.'

She pointed out the rock, which was a bit further along. To me it looked like a smaller version of the Matterhorn. I wouldn't like to climb it.

'Peter and I have been staying near Tintagel for the past week. So we haven't picked up any local news from Newquay.

Has it made the headlines?'

Judith shook her head. 'Nothing at all, to be honest. The police don't want to scare everyone, especially not the tourists. Best if Newquay doesn't get a reputation. They don't want to say much – or for me to say much – until the victim's been identified. That could take some time. They're in no hurry; after all, she died several months ago. I can't see a few more weeks will make much difference.'

But she wasn't sobbing and her voice was level. It seemed that seeing the location again was calming Judith down.

We walked further along. I noticed a deserted beach below us, one that looked even harder to access. I wondered if George might be persuaded to go there one day for skinny dipping. But I wouldn't ask her till we were on our own.

By now it was after twelve. 'Why don't we go back for our cars, then have lunch together somewhere?' I suggested. No-one dissented, Judith looked pleased to be doing something different.

'You two know the area better than us,' I said. 'Is there a local pub you could recommend? Preferably out of town. I'd rather not go as far as Newquay.'

Half an hour later we were back at the Carnewas carpark. Will suggested the Trevarrian Inn, just past Mawgan Porth. 'It's quite near the airport, but there won't be many planes today.'

Neither George nor I had been there before. When we got to the inn, it had a good view down into Mawgan Porth; Bedruthan Steps were beyond the horizon. I went in first and saw they had toasted sandwiches: that would do fine. We'd be having a full meal in the Molesworth Arms this evening.

'My shout,' I said, once we'd got a table. 'Cider for all of us? And cheese toasties?' I stood in the queue at the bar.

I could see they had plenty of staff – most of them not on duty today. There was an ID display board behind the bar. Some very attractive ladies, presumably local. Not many jobs around here for them to try. I knew none of them, but then I was from Fowey.

I returned to our table ten minutes later with a large tray and we started to tuck in.

'I was asking Judith about identifying the body,' said George. 'The police had a computer reconstruction of what the bloated body might once have looked like. It seemed faintly familiar, she said, but she'd no idea where she might have seen it.'

'They've got a staff ID board behind the bar,' I told them, trying to be helpful.

'Hey, let me buy the next round,' said Judith.

'Let's get through this one first.'

But when, a little later, she did so, she came back animated. 'I can't be certain, but they had someone on their staff who looked exactly like my victim. I spoke to the manager. He remembered her, said she'd been hired to help cope with Christmas and New Year. Her name was Yvonne. It'd certainly be worth passing that on to the police.'

CHAPTER 30

A Shared Supper in Wadebridge: Sat April 15th

Judith's identification of the suspected victim at the Trevarrian Inn had been exciting for us all. It raised a number of questions, especially for George. But as we left our new friends in the inn, swapping contact details and agreeing to keep in touch in the future, she insisted that we parked these worries for the rest of the journey; we'd chew over them during supper in Wadebridge.

I didn't understand her logic but for the time being submitted to her deduction.

George had some questions of her own. 'What I'd like to know first, Peter, is how close is this inn to the airport? Is it walkable?' A glance at the map showed it was no more than a mile.

'Let's drive the route.' Whilst we were heading for the airport, George surprised me with a different question. 'Peter, d'you think you might be going over to Dublin one day, to complete your profile on John Betjeman?'

'Why ever would I want to do that?'

'Well, he was based there during the war. Returned home at short notice. It's probably the most exciting thing that ever happened to him. Wouldn't your writers' circle like to know more about it?'

I considered for a moment. 'It's way beyond what they'd

expect but that's no reason not to try. Trouble is, I'm incredibly busy with my sixth form from now on. I couldn't get away before the half-term break at the end of May. And I've no time to plan much beforehand.'

But George had anticipated the difficulty and already had a response. 'What about Aunt-in-law Nesta? You told me she lives in Dublin. Could you wangle an invitation to visit her?'

'I'll still do the Hall Walk and see Nesta's sister in Polruan, so that might help. But it'll cost me a fortune, won't it?'

George smiled. 'That's why I'm raising the topic now. They do regular flights to Dublin from Newquay, you know. At least twice a week. Why don't we go in right now and find out the days and fares? See if a visit could be fitted in over the half term holiday.'

I was learning that George had acquired a steely drive in her years as a business consultant. She'd actually do what I'd scarcely even contemplate. But if it was a fault, it was one I could live with – even hope to emulate.

Half an hour later we emerged from the airport with the latest flight plan for Dublin to hand. The flights were £37 each way. Easily affordable. I'd double-check holiday dates at school, then book it later in the week.

'I'd love to come with you,' said George as we headed back to her car. 'But I fear the next two months are going to be flat out for me on the Spaceport Business Plan. They need something that can be shown to government by the end of June. And I'm doing it mostly on my own.'

I was disappointed, of course, but this was the nature of a relationship between two busy people. We'd just have to make it work.

We got back to Wadebridge late in the afternoon. My car

was still safe in the carpark and I set about doing my packing. I'd be heading back to Fowey first thing tomorrow morning.

We'd reserved a table for six thirty. I felt sad. This might be our final meal together for several weeks. But it wouldn't be our last. I hoped that George wasn't going to tease me with banned words or forfeits. But it seemed that tonight she had other issues to ponder.

The stunning red dress was back in Ivy Cottage; tonight she was wearing the ice blue one again.

The waitress came and we ordered our meal – we chose the Chinese option, with a bottle of Merlot. Tonight we weren't in any hurry.

'Peter, weren't you bothered by what we learned at lunch time?'

I frowned. 'Not especially. Though I hope Judith wasn't simply confused.'

'That was alright for me; I was convinced she'd seen the victim on the display board. It was something else altogether.'

The wine arrived at that point. I filled our glasses and took a sip.

What on earth was George on about? I remembered what had happened straight after lunch. 'You mean, the victim was working close to the airport. How does that affect things?'

'Not just that. There's also the timing.'

I thought some more. What had we been told about dates? 'You mean, she could have died in January, around the time of the failed space launch? But we've no proof of that at all. Have we?'

'Well, she was there during the Christmas holidays or she'd have been missed. Probably working her socks off. And she'd disappeared soon afterwards – no worry for management, her

169

contract had expired. No call to the police. But that's almost exactly the time when the launch failed.'

'It's an odd coincidence, I agree. But . . .'

George was looking impatient now. 'Alright, Peter. Let me put it another way. On Jan 9th a rocket was launched from the Spaceport, which for some as-yet-unknown reason failed in flight. Almost to the day, a waitress disappeared from the Inn nearest the airport.

'No-one missed her. It was assumed she'd ended her contract. Her battered body was found wedged in Diggory's Island, just up the coast, three months later. Don't you think it's worth asking whether the two events – the launch and the disappearance – are connected?'

There was a pause. I drank some more of my wine but it didn't help.

'Won't the police have thought this through already?'

'Without Judith's identification, Peter, there's not enough to go on. I'm combining two items: location and timing. We haven't had either of those till today.'

It was high time I said something useful. 'But it all hinges on the exact date she disappeared. Two days before the rocket launched wouldn't matter at all. Whereas two days afterwards is devastating.'

George nodded. 'That's true.'

'So shouldn't the police be interviewing everyone on that identity board, asking when they last saw the victim. With so many witnesses, you'd hope something solid would emerge.'

Our starters – Peking Duck, hoisin sauce and pancakes – were brought at that moment and provided a useful breathing space.

'Let's assume for now that the dates do match. It would be a coincidence if they didn't.' We'd finished the starter and George was back on the case while we awaited the main course. 'All sorts of questions would follow.'

I didn't want to miss out and I'd been thinking too. 'For a start, can we find any link between the missing waitress and the airport? Was she ever seen there?'

'And also, where did she come from? Was there any reason to think she might be a security risk?'

'Did she have any key associates? Was she a special friend of anyone else at the Inn?'

'And where did she live? Mawgan Porth, maybe? Or down the coast in Newquay?'

'In fact,' I concluded, 'there's a huge amount of policework ahead, once they accept Judith's identification. Hey, I presume she will tell them.'

'We've got Will and Judith's numbers. I'll be around Newquay from now on. I'll give her a ring next week.'

At that point our main course was brought and we were distracted. We didn't return to the subject till the meal was over and we'd returned to Room 14.

Our thinking was far from over. George realised that she needed to tell her friend Maxine what we'd learned today.

'This is your friend. D'you want me out of the way?'

'Peter, I wouldn't dream of it. We're in this together. Maxine did the security assessment. Here, sit next to me.'

A few minutes later George had called Maxine on Zoom. A round faced, honey-blonde woman appeared on the screen.

'Sorry to disturb you on Saturday evening,' said George. 'By the way, this is my friend Peter. He's been staying with me but tomorrow he's off back to Fowey. He's a maths teacher.'

Maxine looked slightly puzzled, but she said nothing. George continued.

'Peter and I today learned something you ought to know about the Newquay Spaceport. It might affect your assessment of security.'

'I finished that three months ago,' protested Maxine. 'What's the problem?'

'We met a woman today, Judith, who'd found a drowned woman at Bedruthan Steps; she'd died some time ago. We later had lunch with Judith at the Trevarrian Inn.'

Maxine nodded. 'I know the place. Near the Airport. I went there with the Technical Director. Go on.'

'They've a staff ID display behind the bar and Judith saw it. And she recognised the drowned woman. She'd been a waitress at the Trevarrian.'

Maxine was keeping up. 'Hey, I might have met her.'

George didn't agree. 'I don't think so, Maxine. She disappeared around Jan 9th, you see, probably before you got there. No-one else is worrying about it, but we thought it was rather suspicious.'

'Thank you for letting me know, George – and Peter. Keep in touch, please. And let me know anything you learn about the dead woman. I could get the security trackers here to chase it.'

They said their farewells and Zoom was closed down.

'We've alerted her anyway,' said George. 'We can't do anything more at this stage. But I bet it'll go a lot further.'

I was less certain; but then, I hadn't been in as many dramas as George.

PART FOUR
THE JOYS OF SPRING
APRIL - MAY 2023

George & Peter's weekend away: Church Cove, Lizard

173

CHAPTER 31

Summer Term at Fimbarras Academy

I thought I knew what to expect, but going back to my home in Polkerris was still a shock. I'd had two weeks staying with a very special friend. Now I'd be on my own; and to be honest, I didn't much like it.

Teaching sixth form maths was still enjoyable. I had some great students and was motivated to help them do as well as they could, wherever they'd end up. My long-standing colleagues were in turn boisterous, hilarious, empathetic. My "old" world was still the same; but now I had glimpsed something wider. I couldn't combine both of these worlds for long.

For some reason I've now forgotten, I had a copy of the Wadebridge Gazette in my suitcase and I skimmed it as I ate my porridge. It was well-written, similar in style to the Fowey Exchange and, from my point of view, interesting to compare. Then I spotted something relevant to my torn-in-two situation. The much-respected head teacher at Wadebridge Academy had just announced she was to retire at the end of term; applications to succeed her were invited.

Idly, I wondered what kind of person they were looking for. I'd got a good maths degree, had taught at Fimbarras Academy successfully for many years, knew how to make a school work harmoniously. I'd updated the school timetable many times. I was Cornwall born and bred. All useful attributes for a job in

Wadebridge – but for a head teacher they'd surely want much more.

I didn't really have much back story. Why bother, when you lived in a beautiful place like Fowey? But that was no answer. It was true, I had a boat moored in Fowey harbour, but I didn't take it far beyond the estuary – never even sailed it as far as the Channel Islands. Perhaps that could be remedied – though not before the summer holidays.

Annie and I had holidayed in interesting places in our younger days, before she was taken ill. But that was years ago. All I really had these days that was extra-curricular was supporting George in her adventures (which I could hardly boast about, in case they were confidential); and researching John Betjeman.

The closing date for the application was the end of May. How big a splash could I make with my poetic research in the next six weeks? For it to be remotely significant I would certainly have to make that half-term trip to Dublin. I could start by contacting aunt Nesta – after a chat with my mother-in-law. That was one project to set in motion, alongside my regular teaching.

It was the next Sunday before school work and finer weather allowed me to undertake the Hall Walk again and I could drop in on Annie's mum, Angela.

I was hardly into her cottage before she was enquiring after my "new friend George". I told her about my recent time on the north coast, though many things (including the stunning red dress) remained private. Angela seemed delighted that the relationship was progressing.

Then I told her about my project for the writers' circle – the life and times of John Betjeman. 'I saw on the internet that he'd even spent the war years in Dublin.'

As I'd hoped, the bait was taken. 'Nesta's always taken an

interest in poetry,' said Angela. 'She's written plenty of poems herself – they have writers' circles just for poets over there. You must let her know what you're doing. I'm sure she'd love to see you when you've time.'

Which was how I got Nesta's contact details. My carefully worded email went out the same afternoon and her reply came back the following morning.

My dear Peter,

Thank you so much for writing to me. As my sister told you, I was, and still am, very interested in poetry. It's one of the things you can do as well as ever as you grow old (though I'm only in my seventies). Dublin has produced lots of poets, of course. Probably the best in recent times, Patrick Kavanagh, was a contemporary of John Betjeman. They became close friends in the 1930s – when Betjeman was "Biking with Emily", even before he was sent over here for some unconscionable reason during the British War. (That was before my time, of course). Kavanagh even wrote a poem to celebrate the birth of Betjeman's daughter, Candida. That was in a Dublin hospital in 1943.

Kavanagh, like me, was very supportive of Irish Independence but died in 1967. His wife, who has relatives, was even more active in the Movement. One of them sometimes attends our poets' circle, which meets in a pub in central Dublin once a fortnight. It's always a rowdy occasion, where much Guinness is consumed. Even I sometimes have the odd half.

I don't travel much these days but I always welcome visitors. And I do have a spare room. If you would like to come and see me in person, that would be wonderful. You mentioned the UK school holiday in late May. We have a holiday here too at that point; come for as many days as you want.

When you have more details, please let me know when you'll

be coming, I look forward to meeting you again.
Your loving aunt and friend,
Nesta

I checked on times from Newquay airport. There were flights to Dublin on Tuesdays and Thursday afternoons; and return flights on Wednesdays and Fridays.

That was tricky. If I was going as far as Dublin I needed some time there, not just three days. But when I checked at the school office, I learned that Friday was an "Inset Day" for Fimbarras Academy. No regular lessons, just administration.

Maybe, as a sixth form teacher whose classes were now almost over, I could make a special case for not being there at all? Or what about a diplomatic headache? Visiting an elderly, distant relative that I hadn't seen for years, on the only flight that made sense, was surely some sort of pastoral emergency?

I booked a short meeting with the head teacher for late on Monday afternoon. He wouldn't – couldn't – give me an official exeat. But he made it clear I had his blessing for leaving the Academy on Thursday lunchtime.

I booked the flights – out on Thursday, May 25th, back six days later, on May 31st. And sent a confirming email to Nesta.

Like George, I could be proactive. It was all going to happen!

Now I had to use any spare time, in the run-up to polishing my youngsters' A-level skills, to learn all I could about the poetry scene and the wartime context in Dublin.

CHAPTER 32

Phone call from Tintagel: Sat April 22nd

George and I had agreed when we parted that this was a busy term for us both. There'd be short WhatsApp messages between us, of course. But if we couldn't be together, we'd at least treat ourselves to one long phone call a week on Saturday mornings, to give each other encouragement.

Her call came as I'd almost finished frying the bacon – bad for my waistline but a longstanding Saturday treat after the rigours of the classroom. I transferred both rashers one-handedly from the frying pan to an already-heated plate and headed for the table as we greeted one another warmly.

'I'm running a bit late,' I confessed. 'Still eating my breakfast. You've probably been up for hours?'

She laughed. 'I haven't had mine yet. I'm out for my weekly run over to Tintagel, currently sitting on top of Barras Nose. It's a bright morning, the sky is blue and there's a fabulous view back over the Tintagel Castle headland. I wish you were here too.'

I told her about my latest teaching highlights and disasters. Then I moved onto the news about my half-term trip to Dublin. She sounded pleased at my initiative.

Then it was my turn to ask the questions. 'So how've things been for you?' I'd eaten my bacon by now, settled into an easy chair. This could take some time.

'My remit here is to update the Spaceport business plan. I'm on their books till the end of June – I've even got my own set of security keys. The Operations Director is friendly and has given me a desk in her annexe, but the rest of the top brass seem uninterested. It's not as easy a place to work as I'd hoped.'

'Even with the keys, you're still an outsider,' I counselled. 'Presumably they don't want you to rubbish their assumptions?'

'I don't know. Yes, the launch was a disaster; but that doesn't mean it was a bad idea or wouldn't work perfectly next time. But whatever the case, the company needs to know.

'If their hopes are over-optimistic or financially suicidal, they need to know that. What management do about it is up to them. I'm just trying to make sure their numbers are correct.'

It sounded a lot more interesting than my daily schedule. My contribution to the Fimbarras youngsters' educational journey would soon be over. I'd have a new tranche to teach in the autumn. Perhaps I really did need a new challenge? But I wouldn't mention thoughts of Wadebridge at this stage.

'So who've you seen this week?' I asked.

'I've been spending time in the Finance Department. The Director's a cold fish, I'm not drawn to him at all.'

She couldn't see me but I smiled. 'You mean he's an upstart accountant? Dresses like an undertaker?'

'Like a very wealthy undertaker – sombre tie and smart dark suit. Whereas I'm trying to look colourful, cheer the place up. We're quite a contrast.'

We had agreed these calls wouldn't last more than an hour. I had to move on. 'Apart from this clash on dress sense, are you making any headway? Are you getting the numbers you've asked for?'

'It's a drip rather than a full flood. Painful and slow. I have to be very patient.'

'He's probably afraid you'll find numerical errors.'

'I don't think so. All the numbers I've been given so far add up. The arithmetic's fine, the question is the assumptions behind them. Those aren't written down anywhere. Or at least, nowhere that I've yet found.'

'What sort of things are you after?'

There was a pause before George answered. Maybe talking off-the-record to me was helping to clarify her thinking?

'I want to start with the costs and benefits of what happened last time. You'd think that would already be known. I mean, the shareholders will want the figures, if no-one else. Is the place making a profit? Or would it have done, if the flight had gone to plan?'

A pause and then she continued. 'The balance sheet on a space station is unusual. For years and years there are costs of building: manpower and equipment, buying or leasing, rent on the airfield; but no benefits at all. The crux comes when Cosmic Girl flies off and the satellites are launched. The profit will come from the dues paid by the firms supplying the satellites. And I haven't yet set my eyes on those contracts.'

It sounded like they needed a good accountant as well as a top-class mathematician.

I glanced at the clock on the wall. Our time was almost up.

'Right, George, you've got plenty to keep you busy. I look forward to hearing the next episode. Before we close, though, have you heard anything about the bloated body from Bedruthan Steps?'

A hollow laugh came down the phone. 'I caught up with Judith on Friday. She was quite upset. Told me that the police were very relaxed, far too relaxed, about the whole thing.'

'How d'you mean?'

'Their view was that matching a face reconstructed by

computer to a mug shot taken four months ago, was never that definitive. Without new evidence, they're inclined to put it down to some sort of freak accident.'

I was astonished. 'But . . . but Judith told us the body she found was completely naked. How do they think that happened?'

'Judith told me that, given the suggested location, the police made enquiries around Mawgan Porth. And they found that the township had had a New Year's Day swim of their own. Local girls baring everything for a short time on the local beach. They'd even acquired a photograph. There was someone that might well have been the victim among them. So even if she'd been at the Trevarrian Inn over New Year, that gave a plausible explanation of how she'd drowned while completely naked.'

CHAPTER 33

A Surprise Visit to Polkerris: Sat Apr 29th

The following Saturday I was cooking my bacon slightly earlier, hoping that this time I could finish eating before the expected phone call, when I heard a ring at the door.

I felt slightly aggrieved. I didn't usually get visitors this early in the day. Was tempted to ignore it. But then the ring was repeated. I turned down the grill, hastened to the front door, unbolted it and looked to see who it was.

It was George.

We grinned at one another like a pair of meerkats, then I remembered my manners and ushered her inside. 'I'm still having my breakfast. Would you like some bacon?'

'After a welcoming hug, perhaps.'

For a few minutes we made up for our two weeks apart. Finally, reluctantly, I let her go and added two more rashers of bacon to the frying pan. This wouldn't be as lonely a breakfast as I'd been expecting.

I sought for some explanation. It couldn't just be a breakdown in her self-discipline, surely. 'Has your phone stopped working?'

She laughed. 'Not at all. But have you looked at next month's calendar?'

'What on earth d'you mean?' I reached over to the notice

board and turned the page over, then I saw it. Monday May 1st was a designated Bank Holiday – the one I sometimes forgot.

'The Spaceport's got government funding,' she explained, 'they expect us to recognise Bank Holidays. Ruth didn't tell me until Friday: there'll be no-one working in the Spaceport office until Tuesday. So, I can either work at Wadebridge alone – '

' – or you can come to Polkerris and share the time with me.' I blinked in sheer pleasure. 'That's amazing, George. Though coming without warning was risky. I might have thought the same. You're lucky I'm not currently knocking on your door at Ivy Cottage.'

For a few minutes we enjoyed imagining the problems that might have arisen. Surprises are not always successful.

Then another problem struck her and she looked apprehensive. 'Hey, Peter, I just assumed your Academy wouldn't work on Monday either? I hope that's the case.'

I smiled. 'As it happens, you're right. But having you here is a complete bonus. What should we do with it?'

A wild thought came into my mind, and I spoke it out loud before I'd processed it fully.

'George. How about us taking a room at the Fisherman's Arms?'

Whatever was I saying? And how would she respond?

And if the response was positive, if she did say yes, I realised there was no way I could possibly backtrack. I gulped.

There was something of a pause.

Then, 'Peter, let's think about this. I mean, my instinct and my emotions all shout "Yes please". I've brought that red dress you liked so much. Maybe I too was hoping, subconsciously, for something like this. Which would be unfair to deny you.'

Another pause, then she went on, 'It's been many, many years since I've felt like I do now. When I was first in love, I didn't know what I was letting myself in for. Now though, a tiny voice of caution tells me that we should wait – though not for very long.'

She drew breath. 'After all, Peter, we're not kids. We don't need a society celebration with masses of guests. Just our closest friends and family. Needn't take months to organise.'

For a moment she'd run out of words. She stopped talking, sobbed and threw herself into my arms.

After quite a while we disengaged and she spoke again. 'Peter, I do love you. I don't think I can live much longer without you. Even the last fortnight has seemed too long. We're both over fifty, life's too short to hang on and hang about. We're both aware of what we've gained and what we've lost from our first marriages. Let's not miss the boat this time.'

I don't know how this might have continued, or concluded, but suddenly I smelt something burning. It was the frying pan. Four sad-looking rashers of bacon, grotesquely frizzled and reduced mainly to carbon. It had gone right out of my mind that I was aiming for an early breakfast when that doorbell had gone.

Later in the day we set out for a walk down the coast at Mevagissey. Still in our dream world that we'd fallen into.

'Have you any friends that are ministers or anything?' asked George.

'No-one I'm close to,' I replied, 'how about you?'

'I've got one friend that could handle it. She lives on the Lizard: Joy Tregorran. She's the vicar of Church Cove, about fifty metres from the beach. It's a traditional church, which was a place in one of my adventures.'

I smiled. 'Sounds idyllic. I'd like to meet her.'

'Well. The wild thought I'd had, as I drove over to see you, was that you and I could drive over to the Lizard tomorrow and meet her – provided she's not on holiday or anything. D'you want me to give her a ring?'

'Fantastic idea,' I said. 'Be good to get away from Fowey. Make it feel more like a holiday weekend. Find somewhere we could stay tomorrow night, if you like. I'll leave the arrangements to you.'

We ate that evening in a busy pub in the middle of Mevagissey. Less posh than the Fisherman's Arms but still cosy. I'm afraid I can't remember what we ate. Though George was quite busy on her phone. She concluded, grinning, with the words, 'Sorted.'

As we drove over toward the Lizard next morning, we allowed ourselves to talk for a while about Newquay.

George had had more sessions in the Finance Department last week. After several long tussles she had narrowed down the nature of the contracts agreed with the satellite building firms.

'They certainly pay the Spaceport well for the expected journey into space,' she observed. 'It's the same rate for every satellite, with no success guaranteed; and all paid in advance.

'If you added up the levies for every satellite,' George said, 'that exceeds the short-term cost of the launch. So, in that sense, the launch in January *was* a financial success. That's probably what accounted for the bizarre publicity after it failed.'

'So the satellite makers bear the risk. How do they offset that?'

'They take out what they deem to be appropriate insurance.'

'And does the Spaceport know what they pay?' I asked.

'Afraid not. They'll know the cost of making their orbiter. They'll have to make a judgement on the chance of failure.'

I thought for a moment. 'Presumably not too high or it wouldn't be worth flying?'

'Well, we've some data on that. About five percent of satellite launches are known to have failed. Given the unusual launch method at Newquay, the insurers will want more than that. But their whole business is gambling with risk, so maybe not much more.'

It was all very complicated. And no single group knew the whole story.

We were through Helston and reached the Lizard about half past ten. We'd decided to attend the Sunday morning service at Church Cove that started half an hour later. I looked forward to seeing Joy in action, before George and I took her out somewhere for lunch.

I'd really no idea what to expect. Was she a similar age to George? Then I was greeted at the church door by a cheerfully attractive woman, little more than forty, with a sparkle in her eyes, who looked a lot fitter than I was. I learned later that she went for an hour's swim every day, whatever the season or weather. (Though she conceded, she did wear a wetsuit in winter.)

The congregation numbered around thirty and the service was fairly modern. No "thee" or "thou". Joy had brought on several couples in their twenties to take different parts of the service and it all flowed smoothly. The sermon was part of a series on modern meanings of Biblical standards, and Joy spoke well. Afterwards no-one was in any hurry to rush away.

When it was all over, Joy walked back to the car park and, directed us to a restaurant she and George had chosen for lunch.

We each ordered a Sunday roast, then the conversation flowed. George and Joy hadn't seen one another for some time and plenty of catching up was needed. I mostly sat and listened, admiring Joy's humour and clarity of thought – it turned out that she had once been a science teacher. That meant she and I could have a conversation while George listened.

Our meals were brought and then Joy turned to me. 'So, Peter, where did you and George meet? Answering that took some time but she listened hard and asked some sharp questions. I felt we were on the same wavelength, and I would like to know her better.

Perhaps, one day soon, I would.

CHAPTER 34

Findings from Finance: Sat May 6th

After the excitement of our face-to-face weekend away, next week's phone call from George was bound to be an anticlimax. But still worth having. We had to keep in touch.

This time I'd finished grilling the bacon and it hadn't burnt at all by the time the call came. We spent longer than before on personal details of how we felt and where things were going, before we moved on to swap our latest news.

This week I had something to share. 'George, I'm in a friendship group from my Bristol Uni days. Mostly mathematicians of our sort of age. We have a volunteer secretary who keeps in touch and circulates the latest details every spring. Keeps us in contact, anyway.'

'Good idea, Peter. We've all got our networks. The trick is to make sure they're working when we need them.'

I continued. 'This year, feeling more outgoing than usual, I read the circular more carefully. There was someone on the list with a newish job that I think you might be interested in.'

I paused, waiting for her reaction.

'Intriguing. It's not a budding politician?'

I laughed. 'They're not close friends of mine. No, this is someone who's also got a role in the space economy. She's called Joanna. She's strategy manager for SaxaVord – that's . . .'

'Hey, I know something about that,' interrupted George. 'I

spotted it on last month's internet trawl. It's in the Shetlands? On some remote island in the far north? The UK's alternative starting place to launch its own satellites. The back of beyond. But it's a long way behind Newquay – or at least that's what I was told at the Spaceport.'

I wasn't so sure. 'Mm. The plodding tortoise can sometimes overtake the rushing hare, especially if the hare falls over. I'm not sure how close the race is. But I thought you'd like to know. Would you like me to send on her details?'

George considered. 'Eventually. But the first stage, surely, is for you to renew contact. You don't need to mention Newquay. See how she's getting on and what she'll tell you. It'll depend on the informality of your group and how close you are. Mind, Shetland is probably as tight as Newquay. Well done, Peter,' she concluded. 'It's another piece of the overall jigsaw.'

It was now my turn to ask the questions. 'So what's been happening in Newquay this week?'

George took a moment to organise her thoughts. 'It was only a four-day week, remember. Shorter than usual. But I felt I had to go back to Colman Carter and ask him more questions.'

'That's the finance man with the top-grade suits and the minimal office? Not a loose memo in sight?'

I sensed George smile. 'That's the one. There was something not right about some of the contracts he'd funded, you see.'

'Not the arithmetic?'

'No, that was fine. But I drilled right down to the emails that had come in from the requesting departments. Especially the Technical Department, they'd spent by far the most. Primarily the rockets, of course; and also the hiring of Cosmic Girl.'

'Presumably Finance had approved them?'

'Well, I've talked a lot to Carter this week. And listened. You know, he's no technology man. Rather sad for someone in the space business. Knew less about the launch than I did.'

'So what floated his boat, then?'

'Oh, his thing was funding. Negotiating the many loans needed in an efficient manner; and making sure they were paid back on time.'

The description wasn't making much sense to me. 'But, George, that's what he's there for, isn't it?'

'It's a key task, certainly. He has to keep the shareholders and investors happy. Mostly in the City, where they know even less about space than he does. But he ought to be the longstop on other departments, making sure they're not overspending – especially the technical gang.'

I reflected for a moment. 'Intriguing. Can you tell me what you found, or is it all far too complicated?'

'I can give you some idea. The first thing that caught my attention was the wording on the emails about the rocket stages. There were either too many emails or else too many rockets. They might almost have been duplicate emails, but the descriptions varied minutely, just enough to keep them distinct. So, by careful wording they'd ordered both stages of rocket twice over.'

I was staggered, I couldn't believe it. 'Wow. That's a major overspend. You think that someone's on the fiddle?'

'Seems like it, but I'm not quite sure who. It all depends if the Technical Department took delivery of twice as many rockets as they actually needed; and if so, what on earth they intended to do with them.'

There was a meditative pause then she continued. 'And I found something similar happened on the satellites as well. More of those had been sent to the Spaceport than could actually fit into the second rocket.

George and I went round and round it all for some time. 'You mustn't say a word about this to anyone, Peter. It's top secret. Might all be my misunderstanding. Or it could be a matter for the police.'

Finally, she concluded, 'I've got a meeting booked with the Technical Director, Tom Willoughby, first thing on Monday morning. I mean, I can't hope to produce a business plan for the future if the Spaceport can't properly account for the past, can I?'

CHAPTER 35

George's story; Technical Insights: Mon May 8th

I'd collected all my evidence, reported George, including copies of the various dodgy emails, and went to see Tom Willoughby in his lair on Monday morning. It was about eleven o'clock.

There was no-one else present and I'd booked to be with him for a couple of hours.

Tom was at his desk. I took the chair opposite and opened my briefcase. Then I cut straight to the chase.

'Tom,' I began, 'I'm puzzled by this series of emails, which I found in the Finance Department last week.' I laid the emails out across his desk. He didn't reply immediately but a glance at his face told me that I was right to be confronting him.

'Any one of them on its own looks authentic,' I said. 'An order for one or other major piece of equipment. To a reputable supplier in the United States or France. With plenty of detail. No problem with financial approval, you might think. But if you look at them very carefully, they are not identical but there's a great deal of duplication. Laid out side by side like this it's obvious; but for a busy Finance Director, asked to sign each one off separately, several months apart, in between masses of other material on all sorts of other issues, it's not obvious at all.

'I'm sure Colman Carter's staff will have checked the fine print of the arithmetic. They're internally consistent. But I reckon the far bigger question – how many rockets were we buying in total – was missed altogether.

'Tom,' I said, looking him in the eye, 'Am I making a colossal misreading here? Or is there something else going on?'

I'd presented my evidence and had said enough. I stopped talking and waited for a response.

It took some time. Tom was obviously battling with conflicting motives. Was he going to wave the white flag and offer me full disclosure; or was he trying to fabricate an even thicker layer of obscurity? How obscure would it need to be?

I glanced around the office. Was the substance of his defence already prepared, waiting to be pulled out from a drawer of the nearest filing cabinet?

The silence continued. It was dreadful, Tom looked so woe begone. I was almost sorry for him.

How much did he trust me, I wondered. For that matter, why should he? I was a "here today, gone tomorrow" business consultant, I'd be off the Spaceport site for ever by July. Would he try to buy my silence? Was he even now contemplating where the funds would come from? And how much would be needed?

I was an independent consultant and valued that independence. There was no big organisation behind me. I wasn't going to be muzzled or to owe loyalty to anyone. I prepared myself to resist whatever bribery or sweetener might be about to come my way.

And continued to await his response.

'This'll go better if we're not sitting across a desk.' He nodded to the easy chairs beside the window, and we moved over to them.

'Your friend Maxine who was here in January told me quite

a lot about you,' he began. 'Told me you were at college to-gether, wrestling with higher mathematics, and by the time you both graduated she knew you very well indeed. I'd asked her opinion, you see, in the few days before she was to leave, and I'd heard you'd be coming after her.

'I must say, she painted a glowing picture. Said you were an uncompromising woman, dedicated to uncovering the truth. Loyal to whoever you were working for, but not to the extent of hiding their corruption: no interest in finding an easy way out. She had a lot of respect for you, George, and I got on well with her. I believe the picture she painted was accurate.'

He paused for a moment. It sounded like he wasn't going to bribe me, anyway. Or at least not directly.

'If this ever came to court,' he said, 'I'd find ways to obscure it. But in essence, George, you are correct. Over the last six months we did order, and take delivery of, second items of all the main pieces of equipment that we'd need for a space flight.

'Not to sell on for private profit, mind. The items are still on site.'

I was relieved that Tom was coming clean, but I wanted to understand every detail. 'So where d'you keep them?'

For the first time I saw the ghost of a smile. 'They're locked away in the Delivery Unit, behind where we are now. It's the place no-one ever visits unaccompanied.'

'How d'you mean?'

'It's the most secure building on site. We've declared the place "space-pure", you see. It has to be kept clear of contamination. We don't want to put our earthly bugs out into space. They won't want measles on Mars, or jaundice on Jupiter.'

'Ah. You mean, like a Scene of Crime location?' Given what I'd been thinking, that was a barbed comment.

'Far tighter,' he replied. 'No-one goes in there without

194

putting on a full protective suit, from head to toe. None of the top management team – Suzanne or Ruth, or even Colman – have ever been inside. And I hope and pray they never will.'

'I want to hear a lot more,' I declared. 'But is there any chance we could talk over mugs of coffee?'

Five minutes later the conversation resumed. There was less tension now. Though I needed much more explanation.

'Tom, when did you start this double-booking regime? And why ever was it needed?'

He sipped his coffee and sighed. 'It all started with the big bust-up over where we'd buy the second rocket – the one to carry the satellites. I'd made endless enquiries and made my decision. But Colman Carter, who knew nothing about procurement, for space or anywhere else, wouldn't let us buy it from the United States – some nonsense about "diversification of supply". He'd even got Suzanne Kennedy behind him.

'I fought and fought but they were both adamant. My whole remit was providing engineering expertise on what we needed. The choice of kit was my baby. But none of that counted when up against the Chair's favourite bean counter.

'I considered resigning. But I'd been here almost from the start. My family were settled in St Merryn. If I went at that point, and for some reason the launch failed, I'd be the obvious scapegoat. An angry gesture wasn't the answer.

'Then we had some mix-up over a minor item, wanted by two different teams, and I realised too late that we'd ordered it twice over – and the mistake had not been spotted. There was a gap in the financial procedures. And I thought, if I had to buy one French rocket, why not buy two? The orders went in a couple of months apart. And, a little to my surprise, we got away with it.

'Of course, if I had been spotted, I'd have been in big trouble. Though I did have a defence ready. The French rocket had a more modest track record than the American one I'd wanted, so I needed something in reserve. And two French rockets were still cheaper than the one I'd really wanted.

'I wouldn't be in as much trouble as Colman. As Finance Director it was his responsibility to check for mistakes like that. He'd signed it off – twice over. And "keep costs under control" was his primary remit. He wouldn't keep his job.'

The inner workings of a high-tech company. I started to see where this was going. 'So Tom, then you tried again. Ordered another stage one rocket? The big one. Being shot of Colman had become a secondary objective?'

'Looking back,' he said, 'it was almost funny. But Colman still didn't spot that we'd double ordered and signed them both off. And now we had both key items for a launch, twice over. We made jolly sure, though, that they were never on display together.'

'But, Tom, isn't that fraud?'

He considered. 'If I'd sold the second one on for my own profit, it certainly would have been. But if it had been spotted by Colman, I'd have said I was looking ahead. If the first launch was successful there would doubtless have been others.'

There were a few moments silence while I mused on his answer and pondered my next area of uncertainty.

'Tom, wherever does this go next?'

'I need to stress, George, that what I'm planning now is not for wider dissemination. Not to Ruth of Suzanne or anybody. It's a secret within my own management team. I wouldn't be telling you, except that you've uncovered the key details. I'll first need to sketch out the background.'

He had certainly got some spark. 'Go on then.'

'My team was dumbfounded when our launch failed. We just couldn't understand it. We double checked all our calculations and got the same answers. We could find nothing wrong.

'Then your friend Maxine was sent to check independently for external interference. The Russians or whoever. She looked hard and asked lots of questions but in the end her report gave the Spaceport an all-clear.

'I'd even sent Reuben to French Guyana. He'd come back very impressed with their rocket-launching team. He'd told them our tale and they were baffled too.

'But, for whatever reason, the launch had failed.

'My team and I still believe there must have been some sort of sabotage. I couldn't prove that, of course. The only thing I could think of was, what if we'd made the flight without any publicity? If the outside forces, however they were alerted, didn't know a flight was coming, then they couldn't possibly activate a plan to destroy it.'

I had to intervene here. 'But Tom, I understand that the decision to go was only made on Monday lunchtime – less than twelve hours before the flight. That's not long enough to activate any plan, is it?'

'That's true. But everyone here, the whole population of Newquay for that matter, knew for days that a space flight was imminent. Time to make plenty of preparations. Someone must have slipped the final details out to them just after lunch. The only way to test that, in my view, is to carry out a second launch in the strictest secrecy.

'And, using my backup rockets, I'm sure that's now possible.'

CHAPTER 36

George's Hopes and Dreams: Mon May 8th

Tom and I had got ourselves coffee refills. Then we went back to our easy chairs.

'As you can see, Tom,' I said, 'I've taken no notes. My memory is good but not that good. I've got the main thread but I might need to come back for details. But you can't leave your account here, can you? I promise I won't tell anyone else on site, but if it's possible, can you tell me what's going to happen next?'

There was a pause as Tom collected his thoughts.

'One way or another we've got all the equipment we'll need to fly again. And since we've done it before, we know they'll fit together. There's plenty of rocket fuel left in the big tank from January. But there are two things we are missing.'

'Mm. You've not said anything yet about Cosmic Girl,'

He smiled. 'Well done, George. That's one gap. But that's not impossible.'

'How's that?' I challenged him.

'Well. I talked to the captain the morning after Cosmic Girl returned to Newquay Airport, following the flight on Jan 9th. The whole crew were gobsmacked over the rocket's failure, took it as a professional slight. It would be a lasting blot on their careers – especially the captain. All of 'em were keen to do anything they could to put things right. So emotionally, at least, they're up for trying again. And to do so under the condition of total secrecy. They understood my anxiety.'

'That's all very well, Tom, but how will you get hold of the Cosmic Girl plane again?'

'There are documents in the Finance Department that you're yet to get hold of, George. One of them is the contract between Newquay Spaceport and the commercial airline that supplied Cosmic Girl. I was very careful how it was drafted.'

This was a very elaborate scheme indeed. I confess that my respect for him was growing. 'In what way?'

'The time on the contract doesn't just cover the week around Jan 9th. That would be silly: bad weather or a technical glitch might have prevented a flight happening for ages. So it's a call-off contract over seven months, starting in December and going up to the end of June.

'All it needs is a call from me and Cosmic Girl will be back to try again. With exactly the same crew. But they know the ropes. This time they won't need to spend a month practising take offs. They can just arrive on the day of the flight.'

We were racing over a lot of ground. Tom brewed and poured us more coffee, then I stirred again.

'Tom, you said there are two things you're still missing. One's Cosmic Girl. But what's the other?'

'Can't you guess, George?'

I racked my brain. What had he not mentioned this morning that was part of the overall scheme? Then it hit me. 'The satellites?'

He smiled again. 'Right again, George. We had plenty more satellites than the nine that fitted snugly into the second stage rocket. We've still got eight; but there's room for one more. We need a full load to replicate the flight of Jan 9th. To be frank, that's what's holding us up. In all other respects, I'd say, we're ready to launch.'

'Before we get onto that,' I said, 'can you explain the finances behind the satellites? I'm bothered by the funding paid by the reserve eight, you see. Has the Spaceport already claimed that? And, if so, isn't that fraud?'

'I wondered when you'd get to that, George? But that's OK. When each satellite arrives, the sender pays launch fees into an independent trust – an escrow bond. Which we can't access until the thing's launched. If they want to take their satellite back, they'll get the fee back too. But all of 'em want a launch. They're no use to anyone resting on planet earth.'

There was a longer pause. Imperceptibly, I felt the focus of the meeting switching. Up to now I'd been a supplicant, talking to an expert, trying to make sense of a legal anomaly.

Now we had reached a problem for Tom which overlapped with something I was already planning to work on, as part of a new business plan.

'Tom, can you tell me how the firms that were chosen as satellite builders for Jan 9th were shortlisted? Was this a task for Technical? Or did someone else in the Spaceport outfit do it?'

He saw the line of my questioning and grunted. 'When we reached the point of needing customers, everyone was invited to suggest names. That led to quite a large list. Some of my team went through that and eliminated quite a few for various reasons. This was a UK project and we wanted firms based in the UK. Preferably in southern England or South Wales. Ones that would aid our longer-term publicity. With satellites intending to undertake some interesting projects.

'Marketing contacted firms on this shorter list, telling them about Newquay to see if a deal could be struck. How big was their satellite; how much would they pay to put it into orbit; how soon would they be ready to launch; and so on. The viable list reduced to just seventeen.'

'Of which nine variations went on the first flight and failed to launch?' I suggested. 'Hey, could we ask them if they've a reserve satellite, for us to try again?'

Tom considered the idea. 'Well, we could. But there's no guarantee the invitation would be kept quiet. Some firms are upset at the moment, looking for alternative ways of launching their next satellite. We need another new firm who is keen to make up our full load. And it's not clear where we'll find them.'

We were pretty well talked out by this point. Tom suggested we drove to the Trevarrian Inn for a bite of lunch. 'It's where I always go when I need to clear my head,' he said. I was happy to join him.

'This is a long way round,' I commented, as we drove along bumpy, narrow roads for about four miles before we reached the Inn. 'It's only a mile or so direct from the main Airport.' A question occurred to me. 'Hey, is there any way across from the Airport, straight into the Spaceport?'

'Nothing official,' replied Tom. 'There's a high boundary fence with barbed wire along the top that surrounds the Spaceport. It used to be a military base, remember.'

'But if you knew a back way?'

'Oh well,' he replied. 'There's a tiny gap in the fence that's been there for years. But you'd need to know where to look. And to make sure no planes were taking off or landing – it'd be a shame to be mown down on the way across. It'd be easier to find if you were going into the Airport. Why, d'you fancy walking back or something?'

'I'll explain when we get to the inn.'

Tom ordered halves of cider and toastie sandwiches, then we found a table outside with a view along the coast. No-one was nearby, we could talk freely. Though our morning's conversation would not be referred to directly.

'It's your comment on catching the wind of the launch,' I said. 'There's something I learned a few weeks ago that might be relevant.'

I told him about the bloated body found just up the coast by the Newquay librarian in early April. And our subsequent conversation in this inn.

'The thing is, Tom, the librarian, Judith, thought the woman looked like a waitress on the ID display hanging behind the bar. "Staff serving over New Year". It's gone now. But the police reckoned the woman had died around Jan 9th. It seemed an odd coincidence.'

Our toasties arrived at that moment, so he didn't have to comment. By the time we'd finished eating the moment had gone. Or maybe there was nothing he could say, on the smattering of ideas I'd fed him.

We moved on to talking about his children up the road in St Merryn. I had to admit that my only daughter had grown up years ago and was now living in New Zealand. Fortunately, he didn't ask about her father. There was a maze of topics there that I wasn't keen to get in to. But the conversation helped our relationship to solidify.

Once we were back on site, I had to think harder about finding a firm that might want to put a satellite on board the next Newquay launch. That would require a fresh burst of energy.

CHAPTER 37

Peter renews an old friendship: May 17th – 20th

The following Wednesday I came back to a previous link with an old friend from Uni, Joanna. We'd been having an email exchange for a while, then she rang me from the Shetlands.

I recognised her distinctive voice at once. I'd almost forgotten, she'd had a soft Scottish accent. Not unpronounceable Glaswegian, it was as clear as crystal. Living among Scots, in the far north island of Unst, had made it even stronger.

I'd known Joanna at Bristol; she was another mathematician. She'd also been into Scottish independence, so it was no surprise that after university she'd headed north and her career had happened entirely north of the border. Too far for us to keep in face-to-face contact, I hadn't seen her for years.

It was good to talk. We chatted for ages, catching up and sharing bits of our lives. I told her about Annie and then about my new friend George. Joanna was still proudly single, though I suspected there'd been a few entanglements along the way. Joanna and I had both gone into teaching early on, but she had bailed out of a position she'd held in Aberdeen. Then she told me about her new work, in the rocket launch base at SaxaVord.

'I'm their strategy planner. Quite exciting. I suspect there wasn't much competition for the job, actually. It's miles and miles even from mainland Scotland – I suspect we're closer to the Arctic Circle.'

'But you'll be enjoying the long days,' I reminded her. 'None of the 'dark by ten' nonsense that I have to put up with in Cornwall. And the days will get longer still over the next month.'

Her laugh tinkled down the phone. 'Don't get me wrong, Peter, I'm not complaining. When the weather's kind, as it is at the moment, it's absolutely fabulous up here. I'm even thinking of buying a boat, to moor in the local harbour. No tourists on Unst, you see. It's as quiet as anything. Or at least, it is till we start launching our rockets.'

She'd reached a key topic. 'Will that be soon?'

'Not for a couple of years, I reckon. You've got a rival outfit down there at Newquay, I gather?'

I nodded then realised she couldn't see me. 'We do. My special friend George is working there at the moment. She's doing some sort of planning job as well.'

'There aren't many of us. It'd be good to meet her. We could exchange notes.'

'But surely that's impossible? Don't you have tight security up there, Joanna?'

She laughed. 'It's called the sea. Plus our remoteness. We might need more, I suppose, when we're in business, but right now we've no secrets to steal. Ones that I know of, anyway.'

I probed a little further. 'I don't suppose you ever get sent on conferences down in England?'

'Thank goodness we don't. The flight cost would knock a huge hole in my budget, apart from everything else. I wouldn't fancy coming to London, anyway.'

'Fowey's nothing that,' I protested. 'But Newquay's spaceport is more advanced; they may have more cash. If George were to fly up to you, would you have time to meet her?'

'I'd be glad of the company, Peter. I could show her round one or two of the islands. Hey, you could come too if you liked.'

'I'd love to, Joanna. I've never been north of Carlisle. But I'm in top gear, teaching A levels at the moment. I couldn't get away before July.'

'I'll still be here then, Peter. It'd be great to meet up.'

The next evening, Thursday, would be the last meeting of my writers' circle before I flew to Dublin. I wondered whether to share my hopes. Then decided it would be best to keep everything a surprise until I'd got back. After all, I might learn nothing at all about John Betjeman, then I'd have nothing to report but disappointment.

It was clear, though, from the chat over mid-evening coffees, that several others were into poet projects of their own. We'd have plenty to share when we all reported back in June.

When George and I talked again on Saturday morning, I told her at once about my conversation with Joanna. 'She said she'd be happy to meet you. But you'd need to go up to her. That's a long way. Is it worth it, d'you think?'

George considered. 'Until a week ago I wouldn't have thought so. But we and SaxaVord do have something in common that I'm now very interested in.'

'What's that?'

'Potential customers, willing to pay for flights into orbit. For a realistic business plan I need to get a grip on it. Basically it determines whether it's all worth doing.'

'Joanna told me she was SaxaVord's strategy planner. So she'll have thought about it too, I should think.'

'I hope so. The problem is, Peter, that using any of these methods – whether launching by a rocket straight from planet earth, or via a 747 jet – only makes business sense if there are plenty of firms wanting to use them at a commercial rate.

Obviously there are one or two – they had nine satellites in the Cosmic Girl launch. But is that the tip of a large iceberg, or just the majority of a tiny fringe?'

I had one more idea of what might be gleaned from a visit to the Shetlands.

'The other thing you could talk to Joanna about, George, is how SaxaVord assesses the difference in costs between launching directly with a big rocket, like they plan to do, versus using a jet plane, as they've already tried at Newquay. She might have got numbers she'd be willing to share. Or at least to intimate.'

We chatted around Spaceport challenges for some time.

Then George observed, 'Halfway through next week, Peter, you'll be flying to Dublin; have you got everything you'll need?'

'I believe so. I've had several email chats with Aunt Nesta and sketched out what I need to know. Got a return ticket with Aer Lingus. I'll drive straight over from Fowey after my last class and park at the airport. If I'd more time I'd park further away and use a taxi, but it's going to be tight, anyway. It'll be a big adventure; I'm looking forward to it.'

'Well, bon voyage, Peter,' she said 'And you'll be back in a week's time? I look forward to hearing how it's gone.'

PART FIVE

DUBLIN AND BEYOND

MAY 2023

The O'Connell Bridge, Dublin

207

CHAPTER 38

Arrival in Dublin: Thurs May 25th

Thursday, my last day of term, had been a mad rush.

I left Fimbarras Academy with my case already packed and drove across Cornwall to Newquay airport. I was there by one o'clock, collected my boarding pass, handed over my luggage (a rucksack), then sat in the foyer to enjoy my packed lunch.

The Aer Lingus flight was called at half past two and the plane set off just after three. An hour and a half later we were landing at Dublin Airport. Much larger than Newquay and thriving with custom: Ireland looked a prosperous country.

A fifteen-minute coach journey down the M50 took me into Dublin.

The coach stopped at the city bus station. Nesta was due to meet me here; the first challenge was mutual recognition. We hadn't met for a quarter of a century and must have looked very different from the occasion of my wedding to her niece Annie.

I'd told Nesta I would be travelling light: a rucksack and no suitcase. But so was everyone else. It was a beautiful spring afternoon, I'd no need for a coat.

But Nesta knew which bus I'd be travelling in on and greeted me a moment later.

'Peter! It is Peter, isn't it?'

'Nesta.' I shook her hand. 'It's good to see you again.'

I saw a tall, grey-haired woman in her seventies, looking very alert. She had a serious face, but now she'd found me it was creased with a cheeky smile.

I had a sudden flashback to my late wife Annie, she'd been tall as well. And felt an unexpected wave of affection. 'Gosh, Nesta, you remind me of Annie.'

She gave me a small hug. 'I still think of her too, Peter. My only niece. Though she's been gone a long time now. Come on, my friend, we need to make the most of today.'

She spoke with a gentle, Irish accent. Something her sister Angela had lost over her long years in Cornwall. One Annie had never had at all. I had come to a very different country.

Another bus took us to her home. 'Service 63,' she told me. 'Remember that, Peter: 63. You might be down here on your own by Saturday.'

It was a smarter bus than any we had in Fowey. Powered by Liquid Petroleum Gas, I think. And quite full. We took a double seat upstairs. Nesta gave me a commentary on key features as we passed through the centre of Dublin.

'That's the O'Connell Bridge. The most distinguished bridge across the Liffey – said to be wider than it's long. The Liffey is the lifeblood of Dublin. Many a gory tale starts here.'

I tried to imagine the seven-arch bridge in Looe being as wide as it was long. The mind boggled. And I'd never heard the River Fowey described in such a lyrical manner. Nesta was more poetic than I'd expected. That might be helpful. She'd at least have some interest in John Betjeman.

She pointed out a glistening set of stone buildings, laid out on a well-tended lawn. 'That's our oldest University, Trinity College. It was started by your first Queen Elizabeth. It's produced hundreds of famous graduates.' She listed many. It was obviously a great source of pride.

The old lady lived several miles out from the centre. We

passed plenty of green space on the way. Her home was a neat house in the middle of a long terrace.

'Right, Peter,' she said, once we were in and I'd been shown my room, 'I'll bet you've not eaten much today. Would you fancy some Gaelic stew?'

I didn't ask what was in it but it tasted delicious and there was plenty. I guessed we wouldn't be going out this evening.

After we'd finished the meal I helped her wash up. Afterwards she turned to me with a determined look on her face.

'Right, Peter. It's lovely to have you here and I hope you'll be happy enough to come again. But perhaps you could explain what you're hoping to discover in our few days together?'

She led me through into her comfortably furnished lounge and we sat facing one another.

'It started with my writers' circle,' I began. 'D'you have anything like this in Dublin?'

'Oh, we certainly do. Lot and lots. Ours often meet in a pub. And are more geared to poetry than stories. We are very proud of our poetic legacy, you see.'

I'd been looking up Irish poets on the flight over and mentioned a few that I'd memorised. 'There was Oscar Wilde, of course. Though he was perhaps more of a playwright. And died quite young.'

'Chucking him into Reading Gaol for several years didn't do much for his health.' I saw Nesta was well able to hold her own.

I continued. 'Then, last century, you had Patrick Kavanagh. An exact contemporary of John Betjeman. Both born at the start of the last century. But Kavanagh died in his sixties.'

'Probably the effect of too much Guinness,' she declared. 'It's handicapped quite a few of our poets.' Then my words sank in. 'Ah yes. It was Betjeman that you had uncertainties over, wasn't it?'

I felt grateful. Nesta had latched on to my problem without me having to labour over it.

'That's right. It all stemmed from our writers' circle, you see.' I explained about our spring project and how I'd chosen Betjeman on the advice of someone I'd met on a local walk.

'I knew almost nothing about him. Except that his poems were said to rhyme. I read a few and started to enjoy them. But the most intriguing thing, from my point of view, was that Betjeman was clearly in love with Ireland; and he was also based here in World War Two.'

Nesta stirred. 'That's a British way of putting it, Peter, if I might say so. We tried to stay out of that war, here in Ireland. And didn't have much time for people sent here from England. Not even proper poets like Betjeman.'

We seemed to have reached the core of my problem very quickly.

'I'm glad you've said that, Nesta. It's good for me to hear a different view. Because, for my writers' circle project, I've been trying to follow Betjeman's early life on the internet.'

I paused to draw breath. 'He was sent here in 1942 but was called back to the UK the following year. So not a long visit. And what I'd love to know is, what caused him to be called back so quickly?'

CHAPTER 39

A first taste of Dublin: Fri May 26th

Nesta retired for the night early, giving me the chance to study the paraphernalia in my guestroom – posters and the occasional sepia photograph. I was surprised to find a Nationalist tendency - if that's the right word. Nesta's family had been far more Republican that I'd ever dreamed of. I had come to a different country.

My Annie hadn't talked about that sort of thing – not to me, anyway. Maybe her mother had been re-tuned by the calm of Fowey? Her dad had been a fiery Cornishman, I recalled; maybe that brand of politics was enough for both of them?

It was a useful warning for me to take nothing for granted.

'I'm hoping, Peter, that you could put aside one day of your visit to take a simple tour of Dublin. That would give your aunt Nesta a great deal of pleasure.'

I took another mouthful of muesli before I replied. 'I'd really enjoy that, Nesta. How will we go about it?'

'They have bus tours here that last two or three hours, with extensive commentary. You'll just have to look and listen. That's probably the fastest way of bringing you up to speed. I'm guessing you won't know much Irish history?'

I confessed my ignorance.

212

'Have you heard of the Irish Potato Famines?'

'Dimly. The 1850s, wasn't it? Palmerston? Quite a long time ago.'

She sighed. 'You're a typical colonialist, Peter. In the dash for Empire, the British mucked up countries all over the world. From Africa to India, not forgetting poor old Ireland. You were always the landowners; we were the peasants. Just about survivable until the potato blight arrived. It took years for news of that to make an impact on London. By then it was far too late. Half our population had emigrated.'

I could see that, even at her age, Nesta was capable of a major rant. But then she controlled herself, took a grip and gave me a broad smile.

'I won't hold you responsible for all of that, Peter. Times change and we must change with them. Not blame the next generation. Now, what d'you want on your toast, marmalade or lemon curd?'

The tour started at eleven o'clock from the centre of Dublin. It was another fine day and we took seats on the open top deck. The commentator was seated behind us and had plenty to say. I don't recall all of it, just a few of the many highlights.

The most northerly point we reached was Croke Park, the rugby stadium. I'd seen that on television during the Six Nations Championship; it was good to see it in real life.

Nesta had obviously done the tour before and nodded appreciatively as we went along. I decided I'd save up my questions for her until it had finished.

By then it was almost two o'clock and we found a bar serving a light lunch. We picked avocado salads. I also ordered a white wine for Nesta and a Guinness for myself – I hoped to look local, anyway.

'He was very full of Joe Biden's visit, wasn't he?'

'It was a big event, Peter, and just last month. Showed Ireland had a recognised place in the world. I was just thankful that Sleepy Joe didn't pass away while he was over here – he's about my age, I reckon.'

This was something we could agree on. 'Trouble is, Biden's eighty going on ninety, while Trump's hardly younger but going on seventy.'

Nesta nodded her agreement. Then, 'Biden's not the first President that's been here, you know – not by a long way.'

'There's more of them from Ireland, then?'

'Half of all American presidents claim Irish ancestry. Twenty-three out of forty-six. It's the effect of the Potato Famines, you see.'

'Even Barack Obama,' I joked.

'Him too. Goodness knows how. But there's a massive Irish vote in the United States, you see.'

I delved into my salad and then asked, 'Who's the first president to visit here that you can remember, Nesta?'

I was expecting the question would keep her quiet for a few minutes while I ate more of my salad, but she came back immediately.

'John Fitzgerald Kennedy. He came in the summer of 1963. Just a few months before he was assassinated. I was twenty years old at the time and he captured my heart – I was smitten. He made a great speech in our parliament about the Irish dream – I'll never forget it.'

She basked in the memory as we finished our salads. I did some mental arithmetic and recognised a date match.

'So, Nesta, you must have been born in 1943. That's the same time as – '

'– John Betjeman was in Dublin.' She smiled. 'Actually,

there's a personal reason I know that. It was the same year his daughter was born – the same hospital and the same month. Candida, her name was. Pretty name, not very common.'

That was a shock. Why didn't I know that already?

'Did your family ever meet him, then?'

'Briefly. There wasn't much post-natal care in those days. And he was English, my parents were staunchly Irish. Not too much in common. He left soon afterwards, anyway.'

Which brought me back to my reason for being here.

'So what's our plan for the rest of the day?'

'We could stroll around the centre for the afternoon. Gently, mind – pretend I'm Joe Biden. Can't move too fast.

'Then we could have an early evening meal in the Ginger Man. That's one of the pubs I was thinking of with a poetic circle. They meet every Friday evening. There's someone comes there whom I'd like you to meet.'

We pottered around Trinity College for most of the afternoon. Most buildings were white stone. As smart a campus as I had ever seen. And it had been started in the sixteenth century by the first Queen Elizabeth. It was hard to get my head round this: was Ireland a colony in those days or just part of the British Isles? I expect Nesta would say it always felt like a colony.

In the early evening we went to the Ginger Man. There was a massive sign outside advertising Beamish Stout; I assumed that was their alternative to Guinness. The food inside was fine for a casual evening meal.

It was busy but not overcrowded. We found ourselves a table in the corner and had a break before ordering any food. Nesta sat where she could watch for the newcomer she was hoping to meet.

215

I'd gone to place our order – fish and chips were fine for Friday – when I noticed Nesta waving to a newcomer, who came to join her. When I got back to the table they were in animated conversation.

'Peter, do meet Siobhan,' she said.

I seized another chair before shaking her hand. Age-wise, I would put her in her sixties. Her hair was a hazel blonde heading for grey, neatly arranged in a bob.

'Siobhan is a professional poet,' said Nesta.

She frowned. 'In the sense that I don't do much else, I suppose that's true. In the sense that I can live on the proceeds, it's not true at all.'

'And do you write poetry, Peter?' she continued.

'Afraid not,' I replied. 'I'm a maths teacher from Cornwall.'

She gave a sigh of regret. 'I wish I could do maths, Peter. Or live in Cornwall. It's a beautiful place, isn't it?'

I felt relieved. At least she wasn't going to make me write a limerick. Not yet, anyway.

'So you're just here for a few days holiday?'

I explained about my writers' circle and the poetic project I'd started on. Her eyes lit up when I mentioned Betjeman.

'Ah. He was a great poet. And also paid his way. My grand-father was a close friend of his.'

So this was why Nesta had bought me here. 'What was your relative's name?' I asked.

'Kavanagh. Patrick Kavanagh. They were more or less blood brothers in the thirties and forties. Betjeman's daughter was born in Dublin, you know. Patrick wrote a poem celebrating her birth. If you're trying for a rounded biography, it would be worth including.'

'Thanks for the counsel,' I said. 'I'll certainly get hold of it.' I saw she was still listening, so I continued. 'There is one bit of

Betjeman's story that I'm rather hazy on. He came over to Dublin in 1942 but left just a year later. I've spent ages browsing the internet, in between my teaching, but no-one seems able or willing to give a reason.'

Siobhan considered for a moment. 'Of course, none of us were here then. But I do know someone who might be able to help you, Peter. If you came to my house tomorrow – hey, why not come for lunch? Nesta knows where I live – I could arrange for you to meet him.'

'That would be wonderful, Siobhan. Thank you very much indeed.'

CHAPTER 40

Solving one problem raises another: Sat May 27th

I'd wondered if Nesta would want to accompany me to lunch with Siobhan, but she declined.

'These days I've got to look after myself, Peter. I'm nearly eighty. If I have a busy day like we did yesterday, I need a quiet day afterwards, otherwise I'm wiped out for ages. Siobhan lives not far from here. You can easily walk over there by noon.'

I nodded my acquiescence.

'I'll leave it to her to explain who'll be joining you,' Nesta continued. 'In fact, it's probably best that I'm not there. I wouldn't want to interrupt any disclosure, or to learn things I shouldn't. Just listen hard and pick up all you can. Mind, it'll be best if they see you're not taking notes.'

This was a strange world. A long way from teaching. 'OK. But I may need some guidance when I come back.'

Nesta gave me the address for my phone and I arrived at Siobhan's just before noon.

It was an old house, quite large, with a well-tended garden. I was welcomed by Siobhan herself and invited into the sitting room.

'I asked her but Nesta wouldn't tell me much about you,' I explained. 'Said you'd prefer to tell me yourself.'

'Fine. Shall we start with coffee?'

A few minutes later it was time to begin. 'Peter, how much d'you know about the Irish Republican movement?'

'Hardly anything,' I confessed. 'The BBC covers politics in Ulster but goodness knows how well they're covering Southern Ireland – as they choose to call it. I'm willing to learn.' I looked at her hopefully.

Siobhan took a deep breath. 'There's a vast amount written about the history of Ireland, from all sides. I'm a poet so I can't do it justice, or even explain the emotions aroused. But let me tell you a little about my own family's story in the last century.

'I won't bore you with the tangled relationships that preceded me.' She laughed. 'Our family tree looks like a thicket. The person that I'd like to tell you about – my great grandmother – was Kathleen Barry Moloney. To me her life illustrates the struggles Ireland has endured over the last century.'

'Please, Siobhan, tell me more.' So she did.

'Kathy came from a big family of Irish republicans. Her brother Barry was charged with murdering three British soldiers during the 1916 uprising and was executed. His death turned Moloney into a full-time activist. Later she toured the United States, speaking to large crowds, fundraising for the republican cause. She was jailed and at one point went on hunger strike.'

It sounded grim. 'How are you related to her?'

'Kathy had several children. One of them, also called Kathleen, married Patrick Kavanagh in 1968, just before his death.

Siobhan glance at her watch. 'There isn't time right now to unpack this, Peter. My other guest is due shortly. But the message I want to tell you is: the republican cause has been going for a long time and is deeply felt by many citizens. Much of that overlaps with Irish poets. My grandfather Patrick Kavanagh, to take one example, was a well-recognised poet who was also a staunch republican. It's no coincidence, I'd say, that his best poem was "The Long Hunger"'.

Siobhan would doubtless have said plenty more but at that moment the doorbell rang.

'Ah, that'll be Archie. If anyone can tell you about Betjeman's mishap, it'll be him.'

Archie's arrival signalled the early stages of lunch. The two of us sat round a polished oak table at one end of the kitchen while Siobhan was unloading a very hot meal from the aga. It was what I'd have called shepherd's pie, though doubtless it had a different name in Dublin. There were also plenty of trimmings.

I'd gone past a corner shop on my way and bought a bottle of their best Merlot as a gesture of goodwill. Archie wrestled with the cork and poured us all generous portions. I started to regret not having bought a second one. But there was no problem, Siobhan had a second bottle of her own.

'Archie, Peter is a visitor to Dublin,' she said. 'From Newquay, in Cornwall. I met him yesterday in the Ginger Man. He told me he's been set a problem you might be able to help us with.'

Archie had a much stronger accent than Nesta but I heard him clearly, maybe my ear was becoming attuned. 'What's your problem, young man? I'll help if I can. As long as it's not mathematics.'

He bellowed at his own joke. I decided I wouldn't tell him I was a maths teacher. Discretion was sometimes the better part of valour.

'I'm trying to build up a picture of an English poet by the name of John Betjeman.' I saw a grimace flit across his face and then vanish: Archie had heard of him, at any rate.

'I know the name, right enough, Peter. He was lurking here

in Dublin for half the European war. My dad had dealings with him.'

It took me a second to recognise Archie's name for World War Two. I recalled that Ireland had remained neutral in that conflict.

'I've been told that he arrived here in 1942 and disappeared a year later. Have you any idea why he left so quickly?'

Archie sighed. 'Pour me another glass of that Merlot, Peter, and I'll do my best to remember. It was a long time ago. But my dad did tell me something. After the news of his death, I think.'

I hastened to comply. Generously refilled his glass and gave the remainder to Siobhan and me.

She saw the first bottle was finished and fetched out a second.

Archie refuelled and then began. 'We never really trusted the British. I mean, a posh-speaking Englishman arrives here in wartime, based at the British Embassy, without any obvious job at all. All he seemed to do was to drink with the locals.

'He could hold his drink, though. My dad gave him that. But who was paying for it? It certainly wasn't the Irish.'

There was a pause, but I'd long ago learned the value of silence and said nothing. After a minute he resumed.

'We – I mean, my dad's gang – started to collect together information: where had Betjeman gone, who was he talking to? Several of his drinking partners were in dad's outfit. A regular one was a poet called Patrick Kavanagh – have you heard of him?'

'Siobhan was telling me about him just before you came.'

Archie glanced at his hostess quizzically before continuing.

'We've learned, over decades, to be suspicious of the English, and to take action to protect ourselves where necessary. Sometimes, Peter, it's a choice between being brutal or being butchered. If that's the case, we don't want the latter.

'Time went on and the list of Betjeman's contacts grew and grew. In the end it went from suspicion to certainty. This man was spying on us. So it was decided, action would be taken.'

He looked at me, awaiting comment, but I remained silent.

'We knew where he worked, you see. And the time he went home in the evenings. That was the easiest place to find him.' He paused, choosing his words carefully. 'Our top hitman was selected. We showed him the photographs. Then he crouched in the top flat, facing the embassy. And waited.'

Archie paused for the tension in the kitchen to rise. Then he let it fall again.

'For the whole of that week Betjeman did not appear. The hitman was withdrawn – he was needed elsewhere.

'In the meantime, my dad decided to deal with Betjeman directly.'

This was almost unbearable now. It took all my composure to remain silent.

'My aunt – then in her twenties - was told to dress alluringly and wait outside the embassy. This time Betjeman did emerge and she sidled up to him, took him by the arm. Led him through darkened streets to our home. Blindfolded him. Then Dad met him in the cellar.

'What happened next?' I poured myself some more wine.

'Dad never elaborated. Betjeman told him some sort of story about being a poet and meeting other poets like Kavanagh. Recited one of his poems and persuaded him he was innocent. They were convinced and simply let him go.'

'That was the end?' I asked. It sounded almost too simple.

'The British transferred him out of the country within the week. He was never seen here again. So he got away with it – that's what my dad thought, anyway. Now does that give you the answer you want, Peter?'

Lunch continued in a boisterous manner. Plenty more delights came out of that oven. I'd got the answer to my question, one which I would never have guessed. We got through the second Merlot and then onto a third. Archie was in his element, which seemed to be alcohol. I was glad I wasn't driving anywhere; and that Nesta wasn't with us.

Later, when he was seriously inebriated, Siobhan and I were told more stories of life in Dublin from a Republican viewpoint. A few were outlandish, others were brutally horrific.

It was on my way home, much later in the afternoon, that I asked myself the thousand-dollar question. Were John Betjeman's loyalties as much on the side of the British as Archie's dad had first believed? Or did he have an instinctive support for the Republicans and their cause?

Could he have been a bosom friend of Patrick Kavanagh, for years and years, unless that was truly the case?

So was Betjeman to be exalted – or to be condemned?

CHAPTER 41

An Arctic Intrusion: Sun May 28th

Nesta and I had a quiet breakfast, not too early. Then she announced she always went to Mass on Sunday mornings. Would I like to accompany her or would I prefer to remain in her home? I must have looked a little weary as I opted for time on my own.

When she'd gone, I made myself more coffee and settled in the lounge. Then switched on my phone. To my surprise there was an email from George, sent late on Saturday evening.

Peter,

I have news of an adventure of my own. And a request for your assistance.

I'm currently on the Shetlands with your old friend Joanna! I'll tell you more when we meet, but here are the highlights.

I've seen SaxaVord from the outside. A huge launch pad, more unsightly than Newquay. But there are few to complain. Not many live on Unst, apart from those employed on the site. Those who do are grateful that at least there's now a shop; they don't have to take two ferries to Lerwick to collect their provisions.

Your friend Joanna is lovely - she adores the peace. The development team is small, but there's a way to go before blast-off. No doubt it will expand. They might even need a maths teacher one day!

She was willing to share information on an off-the-record basis. We talked a lot as we walked around her bay.

Why had they gone for a rocket base here: was that the most cost-effective method? She'd been asked the same question by the Scottish government, who are backing this whole project.

On her calculations, if you happened to have a two-mile runway to hand, pointing out to sea, launching satellites from a plane would be about five percent cheaper. But if you had first to build or extend the runway, it would take longer and be far more expensive. So both sites in the UK, here and Newquay, have logic behind their different launch methods.

When we got back to her croft I moved onto satellites. How much would it cost for a satellite firm, say in Glasgow, to get their satellite to SaxaVord? What would it add to their costs?

'These days they're small,' she said. 'Low Earth Orbit ones, the most common, weigh 5-10 kilograms. Someone could drive up to Aberdeen and bring it with them on the plane. Wouldn't cost much at all – once you've got the satellite.'

'No big security checks before it goes on a plane?'

'There will be at a big airport. But everyone knows Lerwick is special. People bring all sorts of things over here. They don't worry that much about legislation from Edinburgh.'

Over lunch I moved onto the satellite "market". It was easy to assume, in these days of climate change and telecom growth, that it must be huge. But from a business point of view it had to be, to support future space flights.

Joanna had thought about this. She was paid to think

further ahead. She'd done university surveys, not just in Scotland but across the UK.

It was quite tricky. Most of her sample had been research departments. They could all see lots of potential, but their horizon was often no further than their next grant: would they be here at all? Which in turn depended on government. There were plenty of things a government might want to know, in Scotland or England – but no-one had unlimited funds.

'So which demand is bigger? Satellite launch sites, seeking customers to use them? Or satellite builders, seeking someone to launch them into space?'

There was no easy answer.

After lunch I was taken for a road trip round the island. I saw a nature reserve, several tiny harbours and, to my surprise, a Viking boat, resting high on the shoreline.

The boat prompted a new question. 'Joanna, you've talked about your search for customers. But has anyone contacted you?'

'No-one from Scotland. That's our prime source.'

'But from anywhere else?'

'There was one outfit in Dublin that sounded keen,' she replied. 'A firm operating from an industrial unit linked to Trinity College. They called themselves "Bridging the Gulf". Trouble is, they'd built their satellite and were almost ready to go. We won't be ready for another year. In any case, they're not part of the United Kingdom.'

'I thought the Scottish Nationalists wanted to rejoin the European Union? Dublin's our nearest neighbour; it's hardly the Balkans. Anyway, what was it intending to do?'

'Something to do with Gulf Stream temperatures. Hence

the name. D'you know much about that, George?'

So here's my question, Peter. Any chance you can contact "Bridging the Gulf" while you're in Dublin? Even visit them. Check they look authentic. They're well ahead of Joanna. But they might be exactly what Newquay is looking for.

CHAPTER 42

Further contact with Republicans: Mon May 29th

Nesta had returned from Mass encouraged. A friend she'd met there had invited her to Sunday afternoon tea. Somewhat regretfully I opted to miss the occasion.

I had plenty to think about from my encounter on Saturday with Archie and his tale of Betjeman's near elimination. And my subsequent disquiet about whose side he was really on.

I read plenty more about him on the internet without being fully convinced either way. Betjeman obviously was very fond of Ireland, had spent much of his time here in the 1930s. How much time he'd spent with Emily, after their poetic bike ride was over, was not recorded. And after the war he'd wanted to set up home in Ireland but his wife wouldn't agree.

It still wasn't completely clear why he had been brought back to Britain. Was British security fearful, after what had happened, that he might still be shot – and therefore had to be removed from the scene? Or did the British deduce, from the fact that he hadn't been executed, that the republicans had found him to be on their side – and therefore had to be brought home, to avoid him doing further damage?

Further browsing had shown me that, after John had returned, he'd been sent to security's admiralty headquarters in Bath. Maybe they had not been sure either?

Sending him to Wadebridge, to keep track of the morale of United States troops arriving at Newquay Airport, sounded a good move. And where he couldn't do much harm. There'd be no Irish Republicans lurking in Wadebridge to divert him.

I went round and round without reaching a conclusion. How could I disperse the fog?

In the end, I decided it would be worth taking the chance on another conversation with Archie. We'd swapped phone numbers at the end of our wine-soaked afternoon. It was now mid-afternoon on the day after. He was probably drinking wine again somewhere, but it was worth a try.

The phone rang and rang. I was about to give up when it was answered. There was a muffled croak, the man didn't sound well at all.

'Archie,' I said. 'Hi. It's Peter here. I'm still bothered about Betjeman: whose side was he was really on? I'd love to get it clear in my mind before I leave Dublin on Wednesday. Is there any chance we could meet – or if you're not up to it, maybe there's someone else I could talk to?'

Which was how I was given another name, a man called Dennis. And some really complicated instructions on how I could find him on Monday morning.

Next day I caught the 63 back into the middle of Dublin. That was easy. Then I had to travel five stops on the 87. Followed by a ride to the terminus on the 137. I hoped I was travelling in the right direction – these buses ran both ways, of course. I had to wait ages for the next one, when it came I was to get off after seven stops. And wait to be collected.

I had no idea where I was but I was grateful to see a seat by the bus stop. It was very quiet indeed. Suddenly, without warning, a hood was dropped over my head. 'Give me your hand,' said an Irish voice, 'I'll guide you the rest of the way.'

Which was how we reached Dennis's house – at least, I assume it was him. He didn't ever say. It was a little scary. I was guided down into a cellar. Still with the hood on, I wasn't going to remove it before I was told to.

'That was how we brought John Betjeman to meet the Chief during the war,' Dennis said. 'Archie said you were asking about it, I thought it would be good to give you the experience. Right, take the mask off now, Peter. I don't mind you seeing me – but please don't try to take my photograph.'

I pulled it off and waited for my eyes to adjust; but the room was almost dark. There was a dim light on the stairs. Dennis was silhouetted on the chair opposite me.

'With John, one of my predecessors strapped him to the chair, but I won't bother with that for you. I assume you're not carrying a recorder?'

'Certainly not.' I wasn't that foolhardy.

'So what's your problem, Peter?'

I took a deep breath. 'In the considered view of the Republican movement, looking back, was John Betjeman a loyal Brit, an undercover Republican or just a man facing both ways?'

In the gloom I thought that Dennis had almost smiled.

'That's a very good question, Peter. It was one we asked ourselves many times, without ever being completely certain.'

I didn't speak, waited for him to continue.

'When the Chief let him go, we were pretty convinced that John was primarily a poet, not politically astute at all. Then he disappeared a week later. We knew that wasn't us, it had to be British Intelligence. Whatever their byzantine reasoning, he was out of our hair. On the whole my predecessors pegged him as a loyal Brit.'

That was an answer but not a fully convincing one. 'Was

there anything that made you doubt?' I asked.

'D'you know what they did with him back in Britain?'

'As it happens, I believe I do.' Someone, at least, was interested in my research.

'He was sent first to a security headquarter in Bath. Then posted to a little town in Cornwall called Wadebridge. He was there for seven months.'

Dennis stiffened. This must be new information – not surprising, really, it had taken me a while to find it. 'Have you any idea what he was doing all that time?'

'I can only guess,' I replied. 'Wadebridge was the railway station used to move American troops from Newquay Airport across to the South Devon sands, ready for D-day. I think John was probably mingling with the troops, keeping an eye on their morale. Social drinking seemed to be his main skill.'

'That's one thing we can agree on, anyway,' laughed Dennis. 'But I've one piece of information that might fit alongside that.'

I was silent, waiting for him to tell me.

'We heard, years later, from Irish sources in America, that Betjeman had been given a parcel of some sort that he had promised to transfer to our movement in Dublin. But it never arrived. Put that alongside what you've just said. It's almost certain, I'd say, that John must have been given that by an American soldier he talked to, drank with, on their way to invade Europe.'

'What on earth was in it?' I had to ask.

'We never knew. And we never will. It might have been something that as a loyal Brit, he deemed it wise to destroy before it reached us.'

'John was never that organised,' I affirmed. 'I'd say it's more likely that he mislaid it before it went anywhere.'

'But in that case, Peter, you can see why our doubts about him continue. Whose side was he on? Will we ever know?'

CHAPTER 43

Bridging the Gulf: Tues May 30th

Tuesday was my last full day in Dublin. I'd contacted "Bridging the Gulf" on Monday and been welcomed for a visit this morning. In the evening I would take Nesta out for a farewell meal.

The firm operated in a small industrial unit not far from Trinity College and I found it without difficulty.

The receptionist greeted me warmly and I was taken to the Director's office. A willowy, sensible-looking woman of around forty. She spoke with a gentle Irish lilt.

'Hi, I'm Marie,' she said, rising to give me a warm handshake. 'And you must be Peter Jakes from Newquay Spaceport?'

Not completely accurate but I didn't correct her. George had asked me to make this visit on her behalf. Today I was her ambassador.

'Their business planner, George Gilbert, heard I was here, you see, and asked me to call in and meet you. She said you were building a small space satellite?'

'Would you like to see it?' No legendary Irish small talk here. She was an astute business woman, keen to show me her wares.

I was led through a door at the back of Marie's office into what looked like a television detective's open-plan work space.

Large computers on many desks, maps and diagrams plastered on every wall. In the far corner, protected from floor to ceiling by clear glass, was a box-shaped metallic object. A dozen staff, mostly below the age of forty and all in white coats, were conversing freely, animatedly, as they wandered between monitors.

Marie saw me staring at the activity, gobsmacked, and smiled. 'We're ready to go, Peter. The theoretical work was done in the University Space Department; the components came from all over the place.

'We brought it all together three months ago and finished construction last week. That's the satellite in the far corner - we have to keep it dust free. And of course, make sure we've a way of transporting it safely to the launch site, once we have one.'

I'd come at very short notice; this scene couldn't possibly have been staged for my benefit. No tight security but there was a hum of purpose. They were all working together. I couldn't believe anyone was after a destructive cargo here.

I recalled George's most recent email. The reason Dublin hadn't been picked up before, she'd guessed, was that it was outside the UK. Was there anything I could discover that might offset this?

'So what's this satellite intended to do?' I asked. 'In everyday English, please.'

She grinned. 'I'll let Ronan explain. Use my office if you like.'

I followed Ronan back to her office, which I now noticed had a map of the North Atlantic, southwest of Ireland and Cornwall, on one wall. I seated myself to face it and waited.

'You've heard of the Gulf Stream?' he began.

I'd done some reading following George's email. 'It's the flow of warm water from the Caribbean. It comes right across the Atlantic, warms Northwest Europe by several degrees, compared with the temperature in Newfoundland. Vital to the tourist industry in Cornwall, and I guess, Ireland. As well as heating northwest Scotland.'

'Well done. That's the standard view, anyway. What's less well known is the effect that global warming may have on it.'

'Which is . . . ?'

'As you probably know, the Arctic icecap is melting year by year. In turn, that reduces the pull on the Gulf Stream. That's a serious long-term threat to our well-being.'

'But only one of many,' I retorted.

Ronan smiled. 'As long as it's only a best guess from learned geographers, no-one will give it much attention. But what if there were detailed measurements, day after day? And you could see the rate at which it was slowing down?'

'Is that possible?' I asked. 'Aren't there so many factors that affect it, which will confuse the long-term trend?'

'That's certainly true, close to shore. But with a satellite in the correct orbit, able to measure ocean surface temperatures at a location many times a day, new research would be possible. Stronger projections would soon emerge.'

I started to join up the dots. 'So that's what your satellite is designed to do? That's as long as you can get it into orbit.'

He nodded. 'There's only one launch pad now open to Europe: French Guyana, on the equator. All its satellites are equatorial. What Dublin needs is a low earth orbit that passes over the Poles. Which I believe the Newquay launch should do.'

Enthused, he advanced his ideas, making much use of the map. We debated constructively. At some point Marie rejoined us. When eventually there came a pause, she raised a different issue.

'Peter, you can see the opportunities here. Especially for Ireland and Cornwall. Quantify the scale of the problem, start a wider debate, experiment with fresh responses. Our team has been in touch with fellow academics in Falmouth. They're as keen as we are to get the thing into orbit.

She gave me a smile. 'I've got a proposal for you. I'd love to get our satellite over to the Spaceport in Newquay. I want to make sure we're in the queue this time, not just a reserve. And then I remembered, you mentioned, you're flying back there tomorrow.

'Now, we've completed the travel paperwork and our satellite is ready to go. We can get it packaged up this afternoon, ready to travel tomorrow morning. How would you feel about taking it back with you on the plane?'

CHAPTER 44

Spaceport Surprise: Wed May 31st

My last morning in Dublin – for now, anyway. The previous evening I'd taken Nesta out for a farewell dinner, a splendid meal which we'd eaten with mixed emotions. Today I'd managed to persuade her she needn't accompany me into Dublin to see me onto the airport bus.

The truth was, I wasn't sure she would entirely approve of what I was going to do with Bridging the Gulf on the way.

It wasn't that my conscience was troubled. It had been the firm's suggestion, and it would be their risk. I assumed they had insurance on the satellite which started at the unit door and ended with it orbiting in space. After all, I'd be taking it direct to Newquay Spaceport.

I'd emailed George on Tuesday to check for her approval and she'd replied enthusiastically. Told me to get it addressed to her, she should be around on Wednesday morning.

I was slightly more worried about trouble with airport security, at one end or the other. But the satellite had been carefully wrapped, with plenty of bubble-wrap, inside a strong, well-sealed cardboard box. It fitted low down inside my rucksack; a good job I hadn't bought much in Dublin to take home. This was undoubtedly the most memorable souvenir I would ever carry.

What might possibly offend Nesta, with her Republican

sympathies, was the close links which Bridging the Gulf were forging with their Cornish counterparts. But that was her generation's issue and not mine. I left the firm, with my special parcel, on the best of terms.

Thanks to the paperwork, no questions were raised at either end of the flight. I used the time while in the air to record as much as I could remember about all that I had found out. This was going to make a spectacular finale to my writers' circle presentation.

Newquay was a small, friendly airport. I'd not used it before but I would certainly do so again. My car was waiting in the car-park, I laid the precious rucksack carefully inside the boot and headed round to the Spaceport. I'd never been there before, this was going to be a memorable experience on its own account.

George had said she hoped to meet me at the entrance, but if she wasn't there, to say I had a parcel for the Delivery Unit. Now, for the first time, I ran into proper security.

It was two men in uniform at the gate. They'd had no warning of my arrival. No notification of my car registration. They wanted to see my proof of identity and to know exactly what I was bringing.

I presumed this was a sequel to events in January. Maybe things had been tightened up after the failure of Cosmic Girl, and the extended visit from British security?

I had the embarrassment of having to open the boot and un-pack my rucksack in front of the guards. The item I was bringing was hidden beneath my spare clothes, which didn't look good.

'It's a delicate object. A satellite. I hid it here to keep it safe,' I muttered, to a frankly unbelieving gaze. Eventually I got to the satellite parcel and handed it over.

Fortunately Bridging the Gulf was a professional outfit.

There was a heap of information about them on the package, as well as the name of George Gilbert, the intended recipient.

The firm's information was credible; but George was also an unknown.

I racked my brain for a name that would be recognised. Then I remembered Willoughby.

'I understand the final recipient is to be Tom Willoughby, the Technical Director,' I told them. 'Ms Gilbert is working directly with him.'

I watched, heart thumping, as a series of calls were made from inside the guard kiosk. Eventually a less hostile-looking guard reappeared.

'That's alright, sir. Mr Willoughby will arrange for someone to meet you at the Delivery Unit. You'll find it over there.' And with a final wave I was on my way.

The Delivery Unit wasn't the easiest place to find. It was tucked away behind a unit entitled "Technical Department". I parked right outside the front door and rang the doorbell; would anyone greet me?

A moment later someone appeared. This was getting like Dr Who. It was a human, I suppose, but covered by a white space suit, including a helmet with a darkened visor. I couldn't even make out whether the occupant was male or female.

'You have brought the satellite?' It was a gruff voice, maybe artificially distorted. 'Follow me.'

I nodded, picked up the precious package and followed them into the building, There was a small reception desk, then a second door.

'You want to leave it here?'

'Is there any chance I could see the rocket for myself?' I was never normally that presumptuous, but I wanted to tell Bridging the Gulf all that I could.

'You will have to put a suit on. We must minimise dust.'

Fair enough. I followed them through the second door and into a changing room. Several suits were hanging at the far end and there were a dozen lockers standing against the wall.

Not much privacy here. I peeled off my outer clothes and stacked them in the nearest locker. Then climbed into the space suit. If only my students could see me now, I thought with a grin.

'Ready?' I was asked.

I tried to nod but the helmet wouldn't let me. 'OK'. My voice sounded husky. That couldn't be nerves, could it?

My welcomer turned and headed for the door into the main unit.

I was in the core of Newquay Spaceport and gazed around me, awestruck.

To my right was a pair of huge, folding metal doors, currently closed. That was where the big stuff must come in or out.

Opposite the doors, lying on its side in a massive metal rack, was a huge, silver rocket, some twenty metres long. This must be the driver for stage one.

And on the third wall, also on its side, was a second rocket, much smaller. This must be stage two, which would presumably hold the satellites.

Behind me, beside the door I'd just come in, was a series of smaller racks. These contained all sorts of items, including boxes of different sizes.

'Your satellite goes in there.' My guide pointed to a space beside the other boxes. I turned and added mine to the collection. Delivered!

But now I was here I wasn't going to walk out right away. I might never come inside a space gallery again, not a real one, anyway. I wanted to soak in everything I could.

I walked over to the stage one rocket. It was massive – almost the length of the Delivery Unit. I wondered if the unit had been built with it in mind.

Then I moved across to the second rocket. That was where the Bridging the Gulf satellite would reside – until it was propelled into orbit.

'Where do the satellites go?'

My guide stepped forward and pointed. I saw the faint outline of an opening, a metre wide and two metres long. With a catch sunk into the rocket at the top end.

I couldn't resist it. Boys and their toys. The largest Lego kit you could ever imagine. Before my guide had realised my intention, or begun to stop me, I leaned over and heaved on the catch.

And it worked. I heard something click inside the rocket. Then slowly, ever so slowly, the doorway slid sideways, to reveal the space underneath.

I didn't know what to expect. But it certainly wasn't this. For there was another body in a space suit, lying along the cavity.

I gasped, then turned to ask the guide what on earth was going on. But much to my surprise, they had vanished.

The comatose space suit being and I had been left on our own.

CHAPTER 45

An Unexpected Reunion: Wed May 31ˢᵗ

I didn't know if Space Suit One had gone for help but my instinct, if I could, was to help the person lying inside the rocket. It was possible they were still alive.

I looked harder at them this time. Yes, I did sense a flicker behind the visor. Then - this was certainly not my imagination - an arm began to twitch.

I held onto it gently and pulled.

There was a groan and then more movement. The whole body was now starting to shift itself out of the hold. I put my arm behind, to give an extra shove. Then, slowly, they twisted, until they were sitting facing outwards, both legs dangling outside the rocket.

But not for long. They had further plans in mind.

I held both hands in mine and helped the casualty to slide out until they were standing on the ground. Then I took a left arm as they wobbled, not too steadily, towards the exit door.

We reached the locker room. There was no-one else in here now and my companion slumped, exhausted, onto a bench. It was time for me to change.

Getting out of my own Space Suit took a while. Then I was standing there in my boxers, reaching into the locker for my clothes. My companion stared at me as I did so.

Once dressed it was time to help them. I knew better what to do now. Off came the helmet and at last I saw who it was.

It was my special friend George.

Whatever the outcome of our unfinished forfeit games over dinner, this was no time for modesty. I helped to remove her space suit and a few minutes later George stood there, shivering in her underwear.

'Which locker did you put your clothes in?'

She pointed to one near me and I opened it. There was nothing inside. Quickly I checked through the rest, but they were empty too. What on earth should we do now?

'My car's right outside the door,' I declared.

She looked extremely doubtful. Arriving at the Molesworth Arms, dressed as flimsily she was now, was bound to arouse comment – and could we even past the guards on the gate?

Suddenly, I had a brainwave. 'Wait there.'

I slipped out of the Delivery Unit and over to my car. All my spare clothes were lying in the boot. Not that many, and they wouldn't fit her properly, but they would give her some decency. Enough for us to drive away, anyway.

I seized everything I had and headed back to the locker room.

I managed to drive past the guards without comment. Slumped in the passenger seat, my largest jumper down to her thighs, George was hardly visible. She was obviously in a bad way. I wondered how long she'd been locked inside that rocket.

I drove on, hoping she would volunteer more once she was ready. In the meantime, she brooded in silence. This wasn't the kind of journey I had been expecting.

We were almost at Wadebridge before she spoke. 'Peter, I don't think it's a good idea for us to stay the night at the

Molesworth Arms. A lot of staff at the Spaceport will know that's where I've been staying. It might be best to keep away till things start to get sorted.'

'I'm in your hands, George. I'm a teacher on holiday till next Monday. Where d'you suggest, then?'

'Well, let's first go back to Ivy Cottage. That'll give me the chance to pick up some replacement clothes – ones that fit me. But it's probably unwise to stay there either. Anyone who was after me could find out my address from my Spaceport application form.'

I considered. 'So should I take you to Polkerris, then?'

For the first time today, I saw George smile. 'I'd love that, Peter. But it would take me away from the issues now facing us.'

'In that case, where should we head for?'

There was another pause. 'I was wondering what my friend Maxine was doing this week. She did the security survey at Newquay back in January. Gave the place a clean bill of health. But I don't think that can really be true, can it?'

'Does she have any children?' I'd never met this woman, was starting from a low base.

'A three-year-old. Rosanna. But she's probably not in nursery this week. All educational establishments in Bude will be closed until Monday.'

'Might the family be away – on holiday or something?'

'Unlikely. Her husband's a key Bude policeman. He probably needs to be on duty in half term week.'

'But would she have room for us for a day or two?'

'I bet she would. Maxine and I go back a very long way. It wouldn't be that hard to share a room, would it?'

We drove onto Treknow. George had a shower and a complete refit while I made a pot of tea. Then, mug in hand, she rang

Maxine.

I tried not to listen but I got the drift. Maxine indeed had a guest room, which she'd be happy for George and me to use for a few days. She was at home over half term, pottering about with her daughter. But that was no problem. Rosanna could easily spend a day or two with a nursery friend, if her mother had to come away; she'd regard it as a treat. It sounded like Maxine was eager to get back into the Spaceport problem.

We set off again. George was more talkative now. But she said it would be better not to say much about where I'd found her and how that had come about until Maxine could hear it too. Likewise, she discouraged me from saying much about my time in Dublin. 'I'm desperate to hear it, Peter, but Maxine needs to hear it as well.'

So we filled up the journey from Treknow to Bude with George telling me about her earlier adventures there with Maxine. That made for an entertaining car ride. They'd had some hairy moments.

Maxine was very welcoming when we reached their home and showed us her guest room, which she obviously expected George and I to share. I wasn't going to turn her down.

We unpacked and settled ourselves in while Maxine finished giving Rosanna her tea. A little later her husband returned from work at the local police station and took the little girl for a bath and then bed.

'I've got Chilli con Carne for supper,' Maxine told us. 'It was meant to be a two-day meal for my Peter and I, but it'll do just as well feeding the four of us today.' This was a sociable woman, I was starting to like her.

It turned out that Wednesday was Peter's chess club evening, so we'd have the whole evening to exchange our various pieces of the jigsaw and try and pull some of it together.

We had a lively meal together, the home couple were astute in unpacking my background, including my life with Annie. They were obviously both used to gentle interrogation in their working lives. The husband asked nothing at all about why George and I had landed on their doorstep. I later learned the two kept a nominal Chinese wall between their working environments.

Once Peter was out and Rosanna was asleep, our data swap could begin. From this, I hoped, a plan would emerge.

CHAPTER 46

Adult Story Time: Wed May 31st

George was the immediate cause of our having to take refuge in
Maxine's home, so Maxine made sure she began our exchange.

'I flew back to Cornwall on Monday afternoon,' she began.
'I'd love to have stayed longer in Shetland but I've a tight deadline: I have to finish the business plan by the end of June.'

'What on earth were you doing on the Shetlands, George?'

'I'd been to see Peter's friend Joanna. She works on the Saxa-
Vord Vertical Launch base. She's given me lots of useful material. Costs on different ways of putting a satellite into space. And
including the "Bridging the Gulf" firm in Dublin that I asked
Peter to visit next day.

'So I was back in the Spaceport office by Tuesday morning,
talking to Tom Willoughby. He has a cunning scheme to launch
a second rocket, you see. It's hush hush.'

Astonished, Maxine interrupted again. 'What?'

George summarised Tom's plan for another launch, this
time not giving anyone advanced warning. That took some time.

'I told Tom about the Dublin satellite firm,' she said. 'I'd
need his backing before that went any further, but it was a way
to complete the satellite load he needed for the launch. He was
enthusiastic, said he hated the notion of UK-only limits anyway.

'I reassured him that I had a colleague visiting the site in
Dublin to check all was well. The idea that Peter could bring
their satellite back to Newquay in his rucksack had not yet

emerged.'

Maxine was looking gobsmacked. 'George, you did all this under the guise of being their business planner? A good job you hadn't been hired as a detective, eh. What happened next?'

'Of course, I couldn't share anything directly with anyone about this possible new supplier from Dublin. But I had to make sure the made-in-UK limit wasn't binding for some reason that Tom had missed. That was a legitimate part of any business plan. I needed to get a handle on the size of the satellite market that Newquay might attract in the future.'

'I guess so.' Maxine didn't sound remotely convinced. But I recalled she had given the whole place the security all-clear, back in January.

George continued her account. 'That question took me to various other Spaceport staff during the day.'

I feared we were losing the plot. 'Somehow or other, George, you must have alerted someone,' I asserted. 'Was there anything you said to anyone which might have done that?'

George considered for a moment, trying to recall the nuances of two-day-old conversations.

'Well, somewhere, I floated the idea that the dead girl found in Bedruthan Steps, who'd once worked at the Trevarrian Inn, might have leaked the timing of the first launch. But no-one was interested.'

For Maxine this was another bundle of new information. Jointly unpacking our investigations was taking some time.

'So what happened this morning, George?' I was impatient now. My friend had nearly been killed. We needed the details.

'Next morning – this morning – I'd emailed you in Dublin to say we had approval from Willoughby to do a deal with Bridging the Gulf. Then I had a massive panic.

'I'd never actually been inside the Delivery Unit. Was the

Dublin satellite going to fit inside the rocket, once we got it to Newquay? Was it even the right shape? You both know me, I had an insatiable urge to check for myself.

'I knew the unit would be locked. I couldn't tell them why, but I needed someone to let me in. I asked Tom Willoughby, he said he'd "make arrangements". Told me to present myself at the unit door at eleven.'

'What happened next?' I was really impatient by this stage.

She paused to recall. 'I was met by someone wearing a white spacesuit, including a helmet. They explained the unit interior was a dust-free environment. I couldn't see who it was.

'They got me to change into one of these suits and took me into the rocket chamber. I saw the second rocket, the one that would hold the satellites, and asked to see exactly how they would be carried into space. My companion stepped forward and opened a cover on the side.

'"Hey, it's big enough to take a human," I said. The most stupid remark I made in my whole life. "Sure is," they replied. And scrambled in to show me. There was plenty of room.

'"Can I have a go too?" I asked. They got out. A moment later I'd climbed inside the rocket and was lying along its length. Not squashed at all. In fact I felt almost comfortable. And then – the moment will live me forever – I noticed that the lid had silently started to come down on top of me.

'For a minute I assumed this was simply a further part of the demonstration which I'd asked for. But the lid was soundproof. "I've seen enough now," I shouted, but I couldn't make out any response. Nothing at all. By now it was pitch black. I was trapped – completely trapped – inside a space rocket.'

There was a moment of silence. Maxine and I tried to imagine her predicament. It was truly horrible.

'How long were you in there, before Peter rescued you?'

'It must have been three hours, I reckon. Long enough. I'd started to imagine what might happen, if Tom went ahead with his rocket launch with me still inside the rocket. At some point I'd be ejected into the vacuum of deep space, I'd just explode. It'd be a horrible death. Nothing left for a funeral.'

'But even if that didn't happen, you could still suffocate inside the rocket,' said Maxine. 'Was the chamber airtight?'

'It must have been. It was fairly large, enough air for an hour or two. It was a good job Peter came when he did, though.'

I explained my side of the rescue and why I already had a car parked outside the door, with spare clothes in the boot.

There were mutual congratulations all round. George had had a narrow escape.

Then George moved us on to the key questions. 'But why would anyone want to kill me? And who was in that spacesuit?"

We all paused to consider. I had the first thought.

'It's probably safe to assume it was the same character both times. The person who let me in wasn't as tall as me, and the voice was distorted. I couldn't even tell if it was a man or a woman.'

There was silence for a moment.

'It must be someone who was expecting to meet you both,' said Maxine thoughtfully. 'It could be Tom Willoughby himself, or someone close to him. He wouldn't want an outsider in there, would he? Could it be someone in his management team?'

George considered for a moment. 'I couldn't rule anyone out. Trouble is, the Spaceport's a tight community these days. There are lots of friendships across the company. And they do talk to one another.'

'I don't know any names at all,' I said. 'I used Tom Willoughby to get past the security gate but I've no idea what he looks like, or who the guards talked to on the phone. It would need a police investigation to trace it any further.' I looked to George for a response.

'The trouble is, Peter, we don't want that at this stage. Not before Tom's fired his secret rocket. I'd go to the police, but I'd want approval from the top: either Ruth Fisher or Suzanne Kennedy. I can't imagine either would be very keen. After all, I'm still alive and well. So where's the evidence?'

'Let's leave that for the moment,' said Maxine. 'I'd also like to hear Peter's tale.'

I was pleased to tell it. 'I've been studying John Betjeman in wartime. He was sent to Dublin in 1942 to build better links with the Irish, who, you'll remember, were neutral in World War Two. But he came back home in 1943. I wanted to know why.

'And now I can tell you. He found himself on a Republican hit list, would have been killed if he wasn't away from the office at the time. He was taken to meet a Republican chief but persuaded him that he was simply a poet. Off the hit list; but threatened enough for the British to bring him home.

'But there's more. I met a senior Republican myself on Monday. Apparently, Betjeman was given a package while he was based in Wadebridge, to get to the Republicans in Dublin. But they never received it. They still feel they were shortchanged – even today.'

'Where on earth would he get the package?' asked Maxine.

'We know he stayed at the Molesworth Arms for the months leading up to D-day. I've seen the hotel's records. We believe his role was to mingle with US troops as they came from the airport at Newquay into Wadebridge, to catch a train to South Devon, ready for the D-day landings. Betjeman was to keep track of their real state of morale. Useful data for British D-day planners.'

'Well done, Peter, and very interesting,' said George, 'but do we need to worry about this at the moment? Has it the remotest connection to today's problems at Newquay Spaceport?'

'Probably not,' I admitted. 'But there is a real question about Betjeman's loyalties, to Britain and to Ireland. You can read most of what happened to him in several ways.' I went through my ideas.

'It's an interesting question, anyway,' conceded Maxine. 'Have you any ideas, Peter, on where this research might go next?'

I took a deep breath. 'It all depends on what happened to that package. Betjeman was a good choice, had close Republican contacts in Dublin. It might simply have got lost on the way, but I doubt that. He'd been entrusted to deliver it, wouldn't just stick it in the post. Yet it was never received. It's probably still somewhere in Cornwall.'

'But Peter, why wouldn't he send it? It wouldn't be a plan, say, for the Republicans to break into Newquay – US security was always better than that.'

'But he would at least have looked at it, read any message. Maybe felt conflicted. Conflicted enough to hide it away, anyway. If we could find it, and read it for ourselves, it might clear up the uncertainty.'

'Maybe.' But I felt Maxine was just humouring me now. 'So what's your next move, Peter?'

'Well, if Betjeman had been given something precious, that he wasn't willing to send but daren't destroy, and he'd hidden it somewhere round Wadebridge, he might have left a clue in one of his Cornish poems. They're idiosyncratic enough. So my next move, ladies, is to browse them carefully, see what I can find.'

PART SIX

CONCLUDING ACTIONS

JUNE 2023

St Enodoc's Church. Final resting place of Sir John Betjeman

CHAPTER 47

Back to Wadebridge: Thurs June 1st

After our stories finished, there had been a long debate on what to do next.

George didn't want to go back to the Spaceport on her own. But there was a tight deadline facing her: she couldn't afford to stay away for long. And who or what was she keeping away from?

Maxine saw that her clean bill of health for Newquay's security back in January needed revisiting. She'd only just heard about the unexplained death of the Trevarrian Inn waitress, working a stone's throw from the airport. That body had not been discovered when she'd completed her review. But now it had. Was anyone pushing the case any further?

In the end Maxine and I persuaded George that she could go as far as the Molesworth Arms for a day or two and work on her business plan there. Now she was on her guard, in an established hotel, she'd be secure enough.

I would stay there too for the rest of the week. That should make it safer. And allow me to ask one or two more questions in Wadebridge.

Maxine declared she would take her own car to visit the Trevarrian Inn and follow up where necessary. But she would return to Bude at night to be with her daughter Rosanna.

And so we left Bude. My goal in Wadebridge, once we'd reached the Molesworth Arms, was to pursue the question of John Betjeman's loyalties. Was there any other witness to his time in Wadebridge? It was a very long time ago.

The only lead I'd had no time to pursue had been his weekly journey to Trebetherick. I headed back for the Wadebridge Museum, where I'd seen the photograph of the armoured engine. Had they any more information on the name of the driver or fireman?

Of course they hadn't. But they told me the source of the photograph. It had appeared in the Wadebridge Gazette.

Half an hour later I was in the Gazette's office. I explained my quest. 'Our older newspapers aren't on the computer,' they said, 'but we do have a hard copy of every edition we produced. Would you like to look through them?'

'Not that much' would be the honest answer. But I was, after all, looking for a distinctive black and white photograph – a lot easier than seeking a particular name. They took my contact details. Then I was shown down to the basement and seated at a table, with a massive file of old newspapers from the 1940s in front of me.

It didn't take long, though I had to make sure I wasn't sucked into reading the newspapers as they covered the war years. The photograph of the armoured engine appeared on the front page in September 1943.

And glory be, the name of the engine driver was also given. Stefan Sadnicki. A refugee from Poland. He'd arrived in 1939 but hadn't been able to enlist in the British army for medical reasons. He'd driven steam trains in Poland before the war and was happy to do the same here. Especially if it would help the war effort.

The article didn't give an address, of course. Primitive

safeguarding applied, even in those days. But he must have stayed somewhere close by. My only chance was if he had stayed on after the war. And also had a family.

I'd never have found him if he was called Smith. But Sadnicki was an unusual name and the Gazette had its own database of Wadebridge residents with news value. This was computerised; you could search it in lots of ways.

Half an hour later I had drawn a complete blank.

'Bad luck,' said the Gazette man who'd been assisting me. 'So he can't be here. The only thing I can suggest is that you contact our sister paper in Padstow. I'm sure they have a similar database.'

I decided the best way to get to Padstow was along the Camel cycle trail. I could hire a bike. Avoiding parking charges would make it cheaper than a car and the exercise would do me good. I'd actually be travelling the way Betjeman had gone home every weekend.

The Padstow Post was as helpful as the Gazette. They did have a database of their own, listing residents of interest. They could let me peruse it. And there was a Sadnicki among them. In a small cottage, close to the old railway line. I'd already cycled past it.

Ten minutes later I was knocking at the door. It was opened by a harassed looking woman of around thirty. A wide-eyed toddler was staring at me in the hall behind her.

'Good morning,' I said. 'I wonder if you can help me.'

'Maybe,' she said, 'but I'm not buying nothing.'

I smiled. 'I'm not selling anything. But this is the Sadnicki household?'

The fact that I knew the name caught her interest. 'It is. I hope you're not after the man that drove the armoured train in the war? I'm afraid he's long gone.'

Was this going to be a wasted journey? 'Is there anyone here that might remember anything from those days?'

She pondered. 'Well, there's always Grandpa Michal, I suppose. Would you like to come in?'

Which was how I came to meet someone who had actually met John Betjeman at work in the war.

Michal was sitting out in the back garden, basking in the sun. 'There's someone here that would like to talk to you,' said the granddaughter. Then she slid away.

'Glad to talk to anyone,' he said. Then my heart sank. I perceived that the man was blind.

I stepped forward and shook his hand. 'My name is Peter, sir. I'm a teacher from Fowey. I'm doing a project on John Betjeman.'

'That's the poet? He's dead isn't he?'

'I'm afraid so. But I heard from the museum in Wadebridge that he was there in wartime. And he used to come on the armoured train to Padstow at weekends.'

Michal's face lit up. 'So that's who it was. John Betjeman, eh. Well I never.'

'You must have been very young then,' I suggested, trying to do the arithmetic on his age without causing him offence.

'I was twelve, Peter. Could see in them days, of course. I used to travel with dad on the train to Wadebridge, it was really exciting. We never caught any Germans though. I'd have enjoyed that.'

I wasn't so sure but I didn't like to argue. 'So you remember someone travelling in the cab with you?'

'Every Friday evening, he came. Regular as clockwork, armed with a document wallet. Never told us his full name. "Call me John," was all he said.

'That's great. I'm doing a project on him,' I said. 'It's wonderful to meet someone who actually met him. Can you remember anything about him?'

There was a pause. I wondered if Michal was going to sleep but it turned out he was just thinking.

'It's odd, you know, Peter, I can remember the old days much better than recent ones. Is that unusual, d'you think?'

'I think it's perfectly normal, Michal. So what can you remember about your passenger?'

'We never knew what to expect. He could be as gloomy as anything. Other times he would chatter like a garrulous parrot. . . There's only one thing that stands out. It was the time John told us he'd something precious inside that wallet. "It's very special," he said. But he'd promised someone he'd met that day that he would hand it on.'

'Course, I wasn't going to let him get away with that. I was a twelve-year-old lad, wanted to know everything. But this time he was very tightfisted, wouldn't tell me anything.'

'Mm. Perhaps he hadn't been told much about it himself?'

'Maybe. It was just something he'd been given at work.'

There was a longer pause. I realised Michal had reached the end of his reflections. He was starting to go to sleep.

'That's really helpful, Michal. Thank you very much indeed.'

CHAPTER 48

Deconstructing a Waitress: Thurs June 1ˢᵗ

Maxine had been more concerned than she'd let on to George that a dead body had been discovered at Bedruthan Steps, whom, it seemed, had worked at the Trevarrian Inn. That was where Tom Willoughby had taken her for lunch back in January – far too close to the Spaceport for comfort. Was there anything else known that might augment her inquiry?

It was worth arranging for Rosanna to play with her friend from nursery while she drove down to check for herself.

She reached the inn at half past ten. It was already open serving coffee; Maxine was glad to buy a drink herself while she collected her thoughts. Then she approached the landlady behind the bar. The inn was still very quiet.

'Hello,' she began. 'I work with British security. You might be able to help me.' She displayed her security card.

'I'll do my best, dear. What's the problem?'

'I'm interested in one of the waitresses that was employed here over the Christmas holidays. I'm afraid I haven't got the name. But I'm told you had pictures of your staff.'

The woman pondered for a moment. 'We did at one point. A display of all our staff, including the short-term hires. But it's out of date now so we took it down.' She sighed. 'Mind, I like to hang onto them. If you don't mind waiting a few moments,

I'll go and have a look.'

A short while later she reappeared, holding a photo-populated display board. 'This is everyone that worked here over Christmas. Who were you interested in?'

This was the question which Maxine could not answer. 'Could I borrow it for a short while?'

'Keep it for a week if you want, dear. But I'd like it back sometime.'

Maxine carried the board back to her car and tried to remember what George had told her about their source. She'd been called Judith. Then it came to her; she was a Newquay librarian.

Half an hour later Maxine had parked in the centre of Newquay and headed for the library, display board under her arm.

'Is there a librarian here called Judith?'

The woman nodded. 'In that office over there.'

A moment later she was introducing herself to a serious-looking woman with a big pile of books on her desk.

'My name is Maxine Travers. I'm with British security. I wonder if you could help me.'

'I'll do my best. Hey, is that the display board from the Trevarrian Inn?'

'It is. And I wonder if – '

'I could tell you who the woman I found in Bedruthan Bay was? Sure.' She glanced at the board. 'It's that one there. Yvonne Magorran. Hey, does this mean the authorities are finally doing something?'

Maxine blinked. 'I'm very sorry, Judith. I wasn't given the whole story. Would you mind telling it to me?'

She found it a very interesting story indeed. Judith was a

librarian, used to refining fringe details. But there was nothing to refine here. The find had made a major impact on her life. Maxine was amazed when the story came to an abrupt halt.

'Judith, you'd even identified the dead woman for them. Why did the police give up?'

Judith sighed. 'They said the most suspicious circumstance was that the woman was completely naked. I'd raised the notion of the New Year's Day skinny swim, but they'd checked; she wasn't on the one in Newquay. Then, somehow or other, after I'd shifted their focus further north, they heard there'd been a similar event – much smaller, of course – in Mawgan Porth. With a bit of trouble, asking around the village, they found someone who had been there and taken a photograph.

'Yvonne was on that photo. So if she'd got into trouble during the New Year swim, gone out too far, caught by a rip tide and not managed to get back, that would explain why she was naked when I found her on the Steps three months later. "Case closed," they said. "Just an unfortunate accident."'

There was a pause as Maxine considered. Then she raised a different question.

'You know, I wouldn't mind seeing that Mawgan Porth photograph. You don't happen to know who they got it from?'

Judith grinned. 'Oddly enough, I do. Not from the police, mind. The woman herself uses the Newquay Library. She came in here the next day, indignant about her privacy being abused. Wanted advice on whether she could sue. I'm afraid I told her it wasn't worth the bother. But I did get her details.'

Ten minutes later, energised, Maxine was on her way to Mawgan Porth. A diplomatic challenge lay ahead. But that was the kind of thing she was paid for.

She found the house without difficulty. Facing the beach,

next to a shop selling umpteen games and beach toys.

She rang the bell and heard someone coming to the door.

'Mrs Trewinter?' she began. 'My name is Maxine Travers. I'm from British Security. Could I come in for a few moments, please? It's about your New Year's Day photograph.'

Mrs Trewinter didn't know whether to be annoyed at yet another official visit or pleased that something was happening. It would be easier to talk to another woman about this kind of thing, anyway.

'Come in, m'dear. Would you like some coffee?'

Maxine declined the coffee and moved on to the photograph. 'I did a New Year Day skinny dip myself once,' she confessed. 'When I was much younger, twenty years ago. Down at Kynance Cove. All I really remember is that it was incredibly cold. I lost all feeling in my legs, could hardly walk back for my towel. I never had any urge to do it again.'

'Well I never,' said Mrs Trewinter. 'What British Security will do to keep us safe, eh.' A short pause, then 'I did it myself once – never again for me either. But I was very pleased to see the young ladies stripping off and lining up. A tradition maintained, I thought.

'They didn't want to be photographed – most of 'em just wanted to get into the water, swim a few strokes and then out again – but I'm a bit of a legend here and I got them to line up for me. Though to make it happen I let them hang on to their towels. Would you like to see the picture?'

'If you wouldn't mind.'

The lady disappeared and came back a moment later, an A4-sized print in her hand. It had been taken with her back to the sea, with Mawgan Porth behind the swimmers. Some fifteen women, of all shapes and sizes, wearing nothing but a towel, were grinning at the camera. Maxine recognised Yvonne

261

towards the back.

Then, unexpectedly, she recognised another face on the photograph. It couldn't be – but it was. It might be just a coincidence, but still . . .

Fifteen minutes later Maxine had persuaded Mrs Trewinter to forward a copy of the original image, which was still on her phone, in exchange for a promise to keep her informed of developments. 'That's as far as I can, of course.'

'Of course, m'dear. I guess that's the nature of British Security. But I'll look forward to the identity parade.'

Soon Maxine was on her way back to the Trevarrian Inn. The same landlady was on duty, though now she was a lot busier. Maxine thought she might get her attention more quickly if she bought herself lunch. It proved a successful gambit.

Finally, she could address the landlady. 'The person I'm interested in from your display board is called Yvonne Magorran. This is her picture; what can you tell me about her? And you can have your board back.' She could afford to be generous: Judith had helped her take an enlarged copy of Yvonne from the board, in the library.

'Well. She came on the staff here the week before Christmas. Served drinks behind the bar and at the tables, till just after New Year. She was a good worker, great social skills, could talk to anyone. Given the short interval she was here I didn't bother taking up references; and she didn't ask for one when she left. I'm sorry, I can't say much more.'

'Were there any unusual incidents while she was here?'

'Not that I can recall, Maxine. She kept a very low profile.' Then something came to her. 'One thing I do recall: she was very reluctant for me to take her photograph for the display board. I had to tell her it was a condition of employment before she'd let me take it. Slightly odd: most young women love being photographed. I never worked out why.'

By mid-afternoon Maxine was back in Bude, visiting the GCHQ Cleave Listening Station where she normally worked. Two reasons brought her there in a week that she had taken off to be with her daughter.

Firstly, she wanted to access the UK's security database, to see if anything was known about Yvonne Magorran. She hoped the picture she'd acquired from the library might aid the search.

While that was being done, she had a short meeting with the station boss.

'Something has come up which may mean I need to revise the report I produced in January, on the Newquay Spaceport. Have I your permission to take a couple of days out to look into it?'

Her boss asked a few questions and then nodded.

'I trust your instincts, Maxine. If there is a problem I want to know. And if there is something odd going on, it's better that we find it out ourselves before it makes it to the Sun. We don't want to get the blame for it all having gone wrong.'

It was the outcome Maxine had hoped for. Now it was back to the database team.

'We couldn't find anything in the UK, Maxine,' said their manager. 'Even using the photo, in case she was using a false name.

'But you'd sounded highly suspicious. So we tried the databases of neighbouring countries. And found her name in the wanted list for Ireland. She's a second-generation member of the Detached Irish Republican Army. Usually based in Dublin. I rang my opposite number over there. He admitted that they haven't seen or heard of her for months.'

'Ah, I can account for that,' said Maxine. 'The Yvonne that I'm on about was drowned in Cornwall at the start of this year. It seems to have been an accident, that's the police view anyway. But she was working close to Newquay airport.

'I'm afraid your finding makes me very suspicious indeed. Was the failed space launch back in January really just an unfortunate accident?'

CHAPTER 49

Peter's search for the lost missive: Fri June 2nd

In Cornwall, first light in June happens around five am. At that point, residents of Newquay who were awake, even those in a light asleep, were disturbed by a sustained, monster roar. It lasted almost five minutes. No-one could make any sense of it – until much later.

But when staff arrived at the Spaceport later that morning, they were amazed to see Cosmic Girl, the 747 jumbo jet last seen in January, once more standing outside the Technical Unit.

For almost everyone it was a complete surprise. And no-one knew what it might portend.

Wadebridge, fifteen miles away, remained in blissful silence.

In the Molesworth Arms I was awake and unable to sleep. I'd been woken by the sharp light of a clear dawn: the sky was a brightening blue, the chirruping of birds outside were the only sound I could hear.

Peter, I told myself, this is too beautiful a morning to waste in bed. There was something I could do – my last fling in trying to make sense of John Betjeman. I could look for clues, on the possible hiding place of the mysterious package, within his Cornish poems.

I got dressed, then seized the book of Cornish verse that

George had given me in Fowey and started to read. If Betjeman had hidden a clue in his verse, it must surely have described a hiding place around here. And it must have been written after 1943.

I knew from the engine driver's son, Michael, that the poet had taken a precious package with him to Trebetherick, presumably to open in his own home. At that point he must have decided, for some reason or other, that he couldn't send it anywhere. But if the missive was that subversive, he wouldn't want to leave it lying around. It must have been hidden pretty well straight away.

The most obvious place would have been somewhere in his own home. But that had been sold on his death, forty years ago. It was inconceivable that a small parcel would still be hidden in there.

I opened the book and skimmed through the Betjeman poems thought to have been written in, or about, Cornwall. There were dozens and I enjoyed reading them. But most could not be pinned down to an exact place. And the few with a name in the title – like the one on Port Isaac – were still too general to pinpoint a particular location.

The whole notion was ridiculous.

Then I thought a bit more about St Enodoc, the tiny church close to his home. He would worship there regularly when he was in Cornwall. Spend his time during long sermons gazing about him. Maybe that would lead him to spot a special hiding place.

Which brought me back to one gentle poem that might give a clue: the Diary of a Church Mouse. It was written to be broadcast on the BBC in the 1950s but must surely have drawn on his memories of St Enodoc.

I found the poem and read it again. I found it rather amusing.

The author (a mouse) had certainly wanted to remain hidden. He talked about a place where "the vicar never looked", where he was "nibbling through old service books".

I wondered if that might be a personal clue to somewhere that Betjeman himself had used to hide his parcel during the war.

By now it was just after seven. I remembered that I'd been to St Enodoc's Church before with George, across the golf course. I glanced at my watch. If I went straight away, I could be back for a late breakfast.

This time I wanted the fastest way to St Enodoc. I drove almost as far as Trebetherick, then down a narrow lane towards the sea. I found a parking area, gambled that no-one would check it before nine and strode over to the church. It hadn't struck me until I was nearly there that it might well be locked this early in the day. I cursed my impatience.

But it was alright. There was an early morning communion service already happening, close to completion. The congregation was small, just into double figures, but seemed tranquil. I sat quietly at the back and read through the Diary of a Church Mouse in its original setting. It made a lot more sense.

I don't suppose the place had changed much over the years. No doubt being on some sort of listed building scheme would stop it being altered very quickly.

Once the service was over the congregation moved away quickly but the minister stayed to tidy up. Would he be able to help me?

I stepped forward and caught his attention. 'Hi. My name's Peter Jakes. I'm afraid I wasn't here for the service,' I explained. 'I'm trying to follow up John Betjeman.'

'You're still welcome, Peter. My name's Graham – Graham

Hindle. You've presumably seen his gravestone outside?'

'Oh yes. But he may have hidden something in here. I've been looking for clues in the Diary of a Church Mouse.'

Graham roared with laughter. 'Another one on the trail. But I doubt you'll find anything. I've looked pretty hard myself.'

He led me to the alcove where "the vicar never looks", behind one of the baize curtains. There were plenty of hymn books in there but they didn't look mouse-bitten at all. I resisted the temptation to sift through them one by one. These books were in regular use, it wasn't a good place to hide anything.

'What makes you think there might be something?' he asked.

So I gave Graham a condensed account. He was very interested in my tale of the blind man who'd met Betjeman on the armoured engine.

'Well done for finding him. The trouble is, Peter, that lots of people have scoured this church, armed with that poem.'

'Well, have you any other suggestions then?'

'Betjeman was before my time, of course. And yours. But if he'd wanted to hide something, don't you think he might have hidden it inside one of his personal possessions?'

'You're thinking of the grave? Wouldn't it be a huge task to exhume it?'

He grinned. 'Almost impossible, I'd say. I was thinking of the possessions they still have in the Betjeman Centre, over in Wadebridge. Are any of his poems related to them?'

Forty minutes later I was back in Wadebridge. For there was one object that I'd seen in the Centre that would fit the bill. It had a charming poem written about it: "Archibald".

I couldn't honestly say that it looked to be a poem written to keep a secret. It was Betjeman's love-poem to his teddy bear, over his lifetime. That was at least "half a century" when the poem was written, so it must have been written in the 1950s.

But the bear was clearly a constant in his life. It lasted beyond the "freckled faces he had kissed". Just the sort of place, then, he might have hidden a precious remnant.

There was one line about a "drooping, pear-shaped head" which even suggested where to look. But I'd need to be very persuasive in that Centre, if I was to be allowed to tear the bear apart.

Before that, though, I needed breakfast. I parked behind the Molesworth Arms and headed for the restaurant. I found George was still eating.

'Where on earth have you been?' she demanded. 'You could at least have texted me.'

Perfectly true, and I offered her a grovelling apology. I began to explain as I started on my bacon.

'You mean,' she said, 'that you've talked to the vicar at St Enodoc and discounted the building altogether. Go on, then, what's your latest idea?'

I unpacked the notion that it might be hidden in the dowdy teddy bear I'd seen in the Betjeman Centre. The idea grew more plausible as I gave it air. Even George seemed less critical.

'The next problem is, will I be allowed to tear it apart?'

'You know the answer to that,' she replied crisply. 'So how will you get round it?'

I paused, eating more of my breakfast. Then it came to me. 'One of the staff specialises in the Centre's contents. I need to get her enthused, persuade her to gently open up the bear.'

I recalled that the Betjeman specialist, Sally, worked on Fridays. I made sure I had the poetry anthology in my backpack, then headed for the Centre.

'Can I talk to Sally?' I pleaded.

A moment later we were standing outside the possession cabinet. The bedraggled teddy bear was still on his shelf.

'I've been doing a lot of research on Betjeman', I said. 'Including his time in Dublin. I know why he came home in a hurry. But also how he let down the Irish Republican hierarchy. And yesterday I met an eyewitness to his train journeys to Padstow.'

Sally looked at me in amazement. 'I need to hear this, Peter. All of it.'

'I will tell you, I promise. But there's something even odder that I believe happened. I reckon there's something really important that Betjeman had hidden inside that teddy bear.'

Sally was excited now. 'Let's have a look, shall we?' She unlocked the cabinet and took out the bear. 'Come on, Archibald, you need some attention.'

Now he was in front of us I had a moment's doubt. If there was an envelope inside him, it would be very squashed by now. Was that really a good way to safeguard something special?

But Sally was a trained curator and could see the problem. Now she focused on the bear's head. 'You know, there's some stitching on his head that's not the original. It's coarser, the sort of thing Betjeman might have done himself. Why don't we take a look inside?'

She brought a pair of nail scissors out of her handbag. Then, very delicately, she started snipping the stitches on the bear's head. A moment later its crown came away in her hands.

She peered into the head. 'Peter, there really is something down there.'

I shared her excitement. Sally produced a small pair of pliers and reached inside. Slowly she drew out a brown envelope that had been turned into a long roll.

She looked up. 'Shall we see what John Betjeman was hiding?'

'I'll tell you my prediction, Sally. I believe it was a letter given to him by one of the United States soldiers as they passed through Wadebridge from Newquay. If I'm right, it was intended for senior Irish Republicans in Dublin. But I've no idea what it told them.'

She looked at me. 'Shall we see?' I nodded.

Sally unfurled the envelope. Inside was a handwritten letter:

To the leaders of the republican forces in Ireland
February 1944

Dear brothers at arms,

Greetings from your brothers and sisters across America. We follow your struggles against your colonial neighbours with admiration and interest. Once our present battles are over in mainland Europe, I guarantee that we will find practical ways of giving you support in the future.

Please let us know. Is your biggest shortage financial, military gear or diplomatic? What specific needs can you identify for us to work on?

For ever yours,
John F K

CHAPTER 50

The net starts to close: Fri June 2nd

'By the way, d'you have plans for this afternoon?' Maxine Travers asked her husband over breakfast. The two were alone; Rosanna had just been dispatched to wash jam off her face.

'Haven't got any,' he replied. 'It's supposed to be my afternoon off but . . .' He looked at her closely. 'Have you got something in mind?'

'Well. It's this Spaceport business. I found out yesterday afternoon that a waitress who was found on the beach, drowned last January, was a known terrorist from Dublin.'

He frowned. 'Wonder how she got into the country then. But what's that got to do with the space flight?'

'I'm not sure yet. She worked at an inn near to the runway. More or less beneath the flight path. Might she have shot at it somehow? There were no bullet holes or anything on the plane afterwards. I looked.'

Her husband mused. 'If the woman had access to power from the inn, I suppose she might have used some sort of laser gun. If she could get hold of one, that is. And she'd need to be an incredibly good shot. A jet plane takes off at hundreds of miles an hour. It would flash past you. You'd need to be completely ready – and right under the flight path.'

'You wouldn't be better waiting in a boat, just offshore?'

'That might work, provided you had gear like the British army are developing, the Dragonfire. With its matching support and tracking equipment. They'll use it to finish off drones. But that's asking rather a lot of a waitress from Dublin.'

He halted for a minute. Then, 'But you said she'd drowned? So she can't be the person you're after now. She must have had an accomplice.'

'Quite,' said Maxine. 'That's why I might need support this afternoon. Anyway, I'll let you know.'

Inspector Travers knew it was extremely rare for his wife to ask for this kind of help. He would make sure he was in the Newquay locality by lunch time.

Maxine didn't know yet how the case would end. She had some idea on the assailant; but not much on method and nothing at all on motive. Her policeman husband would need all three. It was going to be a busy day.

She dropped Rosanna once more with the family of her nursery playmate. Then she drove on towards the coast, close to Newquay airport. What time did the Trevarrian Inn open? Would the friendly landlady still be on duty?

When she got there, an hour later, she saw from the empty carpark that she was their first customer. The landlady was still there, preparing to serve behind the bar. She saw that Maxine was very purposeful, recalled that she had security connections and resolved not to stand in her way.

'Could I have a look round the back of your kitchens?' It was an unusual request but not one the landlady was minded to refuse. She knew Maxine was not here as a food inspector.

'Find your own way, m'dear. I'll keep minding the bar.'

Less of a problem for herself, thought Maxine, than there might be for an official police operation. The sisterhood had its moments.

What she was after was a spare power socket, close to a rear-facing door, not in regular use. Possibly in some sort of outhouse.

It didn't take long to find one. The inn had a few outbuildings to hold gardening gear, including a no-nonsense powered hedge strimmer. It wasn't plugged in, as it hadn't yet been needed this year. But, looking further along the wall, Maxine could see where it could be connected. There was a power socket behind a spare fridge that stood close to the door. That would be perfect.

Maxine didn't touch anything. There probably wouldn't be any DNA or fingerprints from five months ago, but Scene of Crime officers needed to be given the chance. Instead, she peered outside the door.

She had studied the large-scale map carefully. It showed a footpath from Trevarrian that ran half a mile across the headland, right under the flight path, ending in the village of Tregurrian. To her relief she could see the start of the path from the outhouse doorway. It ran between the fields, with overgrowing hedges and nettles on either side.

There probably wasn't anything to see but Maxine was a thorough analyst and walked over to have a look.

And there it was. A heavy-duty electricity cable, almost buried in the lane verge. You wouldn't see it unless you were looking very carefully. There'd have been less undergrowth, of course, in the depths of winter. And no wild flowers.

Maxine walked steadily along beside it. There was a connection after a hundred metres onto a second cable, which came to an end beside a closed field gate. Maxine glanced at the map on her phone. Yes, that would be directly beneath the flight path.

She didn't know precisely what kit had been plugged in there on January 9th. But she'd certainly found the bare bones of a way to disrupt a massive jet with a space rocket fastened underneath.

It was time now to head for the Spaceport.

Maxine mentally kicked herself as she drove along. Why on earth hadn't she looked for that cable five months ago, as part of her security checkup? She could only blame the remit she'd been given. With the Russian invasion of Ukraine making the headlines, the worry was on long-distance intervention. She'd looked hard at both ends of the flight – the Technical Unit in Newquay and the final tracking in Goonhilly – but paid no attention to anything in between. It had taken a drowned body, and its eventual connection to the Trevarrian Inn, to bring it into focus.

What she should have done before, she realised, was to ask for the Spaceport staff records and examine them carefully. That was what she must now do.

But when she got past security and onto the site, she had a shock. The gigantic Cosmic Girl was standing once more outside the Technical Unit, staff fussing around it. Something was going on here that she didn't understand.

And if there was to be a second space flight – and it looked pretty imminent – she needed to solve the case before it took off again. There was no time to lose.

The jet hadn't been shot down over Trevarrian last time, but there was no guarantee that it wouldn't happen on the next.

As a precaution, Maxine rang her husband before leaving the car. 'I've just reached the Spaceport site, darling. I've found hard evidence of a planned major crime at the Trevarrian Inn.'

The inspector didn't waste time asking for details. 'Use your phone to turn your tracker facility on, dear. It'll tell me exactly

275

where you are. I'll be with you as soon as I can.'

Maxine hadn't been on the site since January. She still had a security remit, her boss at Cleave Camp had renewed it yesterday, but she also needed high-level authorisation within the site before she would be allowed to see company staff records.

First she headed for the office of Suzanne Kennedy, the Company Chair. The quest was futile. She was told the senior executive wasn't there. 'She's gone to meet the crew of Cosmic Girl,' her PA told her. Maxine had worries about that, but this wasn't the moment to pursue them.

So she moved on to Ruth Fisher, the Operations Director. Ruth was in her office, trying to hold everything together. The shock arrival of Cosmic Girl, visible from her office window, had unsettled her. She was expecting Tom Willoughby shortly; had demanded a full account of what was going on. She didn't like not being the one in control.

When Maxine appeared in her office and told her she was reopening her security inquiry, Ruth wasn't in the mood to ask questions. But she was happy enough for her to see the Head of Personnel; 'Helen Smithers will show you the staff records, they're fairly comprehensive. No problem.'

A few minutes later Maxine was with Helen, introducing herself. She hadn't had much to do with her during her visit in January. But Helen still remembered her sudden entrance, on the morning after the failed flight. She was a Cornish girl too.

'We keep our core records on cards,' she explained. 'All the backup documents are on the computer. There are only a hundred staff here, we're not a vast outfit; and I know them all.'

Maxine was given a spare desk in the Personnel Office and settled to the task. There was plenty of information on each card. She wasn't interested right now in educational backgrounds or technical qualifications. She was after the remotest hint of any link with Ireland.

All that equipment at the Trevarrian still needed someone to tell the operator that the flight was imminent. You could wait in the lane for an hour, but not for a fortnight. So who might the Trevarrian waitress have a natural connection with? There needed to be some link, surely, between the waitress and staff at the Spaceport.

But an hour later she had drawn a complete blank. What on earth would she say to Peter Travers when he joined her? Where was the evidence that she'd promised to show him?

CHAPTER 51

Posse to the rescue: Fri June 2nd

I'd been given a photocopy of the letter hidden in John Betjeman's teddy. Sally and I had agreed its existence had to be kept secret for the time being. I watched her roll the master copy back inside the bear and resew his crown. 'There you are, Archibald. No harm done at all.'   •

After that I headed back to share the discovery with George.

But I'd hardly started to do so when we were joined by the other Peter, Inspector Peter Travers.

'Morning folks. I'm on my way to Newquay Spaceport,' he told us. 'Maxine and I have turned her tracker on. I know she's somewhere on the site, but I don't know the place at all. Would you mind coming with me?'

He was obviously addressing George, but I wasn't going to miss out. The last time I'd been there I'd saved her life. If Maxine needed some sort of rescue, I was up for the fight.

'We'll go in my car,' he said. 'I need you two to fill in as much as you can about a motive for the space flight that failed, while we travel there.'

Fortunately, Peter was in a large police car and there was plenty of room for all of us. I'd never been in a police car before, that was quite exciting, especially the way he drove it. I sat in the front and George was in the rear.

'So what possible motive is there for anyone to try to sabotage the January space flight?' the inspector began.

'I believe I may have the beginnings of an answer to that,' I replied. 'I was just starting to tell George. Would you like me to continue?'

So to both my companions' amazement, and missing out the abortive visit to St Enodoc, I told them about the letter Sally and I had found in John Betjeman's teddy bear.

'John had the bear as a child,' I explained, 'and wrote a poem about it in his fifties. For him it would be an obvious place to hide something precious. Like this letter.'

'I feel as though I've turned on a crime story halfway through,' observed Peter, as we hurtled along the A39.

'I've just got back from Dublin,' I responded. 'I met someone high up in the IRA. They still regard Betjeman as treacherous because this letter, which they'd been promised, never reached them. We can't be sure why. But the fact that Betjeman had hidden it so well suggests he found it too embarrassing to send them. And it also confirms his British loyalty.'

'That'll do as a catch up. Can you now read us the letter, please?'

I took it out of my pocket and cleared my throat. Then read the missive in its entirety.

'Wow,' said George from the back seat. 'I can see why Betjeman might have been embarrassed to send it. It's very pro-republican, isn't it? If it was traced back to him, say by his British security colleagues, he could well have spent the rest of the war in jail.'

We all considered that for a few moments.

But our driver was benefitting from only knowing a fraction of the whole story and had a different angle.

'But Betjeman's embarrassment wouldn't cause a rocket to

be sabotaged today. Not just on its own, anyway. Shouldn't we turn our attention to the person who sent it?'

'Someone called John,' I said dismissively. 'Hardly an uncommon name, then or now.'

George had a wiser thought. 'But his intended audience must have been able to work it out from the letter. Otherwise the rest is just empty promises. Who's the most famous JFK?'

'John Fitzgerald Kennedy,' I declared. 'He certainly fought in World War Two. He might well have been one of the soldiers travelling through Newquay airport that Betjeman conversed with at Wadebridge.'

Peter joined in now. 'Kennedy wasn't President in those days, of course. He was a young man in his twenties, with no special status. Mind, he came from a very powerful American family.'

I remembered what Nesta had told me on my own visit to Ireland. 'He visited Ireland when he was President. He was pro-Irish, proud of his Irish ancestry. He came to Dublin in 1963, three months before he was assassinated, made a rousing speech that the Irish found very supportive and still talk about today. I'm sure he could have written that letter.'

There was another pause for thought.

'Very interesting, but we still haven't answered my question,' said Peter. 'Why might that lead to an Irish assault on a Newquay rocket?'

'I can think of a sort of reason,' said a voice from the back seat. 'The Kennedy family is still active in American politics. They might find a letter from the 1940s a long way from their views today. Ireland has moved on a great distance.

'If the Irish had received it, felt let down that it hadn't led anywhere and threatened to publish it, it could have real impact. Suppose the Kennedy clan feared that and wanted to pre-empt the publicity. What action do we think they might take?'

The question would have to wait. We had now reached the Spaceport and Peter needed George to ease us past security. Fortunately, George had her own security documents with her and spoke up for her passengers.

Peter parked the car in the visitor section and consulted his phone. Where had his wife got to?

He fiddled with it for a moment and then swore. 'The bloody thing's broken. It's got Maxine inside the Spaceport, but she's shown as located in the middle of the runway. Something has gone dreadfully wrong.'

CHAPTER 52

The Absent Attendant: Fri June 2nd

'Are you certain you've got every member of staff here?'

Helen pursed her lips. She didn't like being cross-examined. 'Of course we have, Maxine. That's the crux of my job.'

'And that includes everyone who was here in January?'

'Well, we had to lay quite a few off, after the launch failed. We've still got their records, but they're in a separate archive.'

Maxine sighed. So her card review hadn't been watertight after all. On the other hand, George had been assaulted only this week. The villain must still be on the Spaceport books.

Then she glimpsed Cosmic Girl through Helen's window and the next question came unbidden. 'What about the crew of Cosmic Girl? I don't remember coming across them in your records.'

'They're not on the staff, Maxine. Professional aircrew, hired by the airline. If you want to check on them, why don't you go over and ask them yourself?'

Maxine realised she had annoyed Helen by questioning her accuracy. But as she left, she wondered if anyone else was also missing from her records.

Maxine remembered the place where she'd talked to the crew in January and made her way over there again. They were in the special aircrew annexe. Fair enough. You couldn't expect them to be sitting at the controls for hours, waiting to fly.

'Good morning, gentlemen – and lady. My name is Maxine Travers, I'm trying to ensure there'll be no problems with this flight. Can you help me on a few questions, please?'

The Captain and Chief Pilot, Greg, was welcoming. 'Great to see you, Maxine. This is all a bit sudden, I'm afraid. We were shifting sacks of grain round Malawi till yesterday morning. So what are your questions?'

'It's a matter of completeness. I'm trying to check the nationality of everyone that was working here at the time of the launch in January. No big deal, it's something I should have checked last time.'

'No problem with that, Maxine. Security's nothing like as cut-throat here as all they do in the States. We're very lucky, as an aircrew, to dodge most of it. Well, I'm American through and through. Born and bred in Kansas.

The co-pilot spoke up next. 'I'm Harry and I come from Denver.'

Then came the radio operator, Wally. 'I'm from Canada, Maxine.'

Lastly, Cynthia the navigator. 'And I'm from New York State.'

Maxine carefully wrote the names down. None were from the British Isles, anyway. And there was no obvious link with Ireland.

Then she said, 'Thank you very much, guys. And what about the flight attendants? I seem to recall there were a couple that you'd arrived with, that weren't around on the day I came. Someone joked that they were out shopping in Newquay?'

Greg responded. 'The flight attendants aren't part of the core team, Maxine. They're often hired for one trip at a time –

obviously they're highly trained, but they move around freely. They lap up the freedom that gives them.'

'Right. Can you remember the names of the two that came with you last time?'

'Gee,' said Greg. 'That's a tough one. We've been flying all over the world for the last five months, often with different attendants on each flight. I can't remember who came with us in December. We only took one of them home with us, anyway.'

It was a strange remark. Suddenly, for Maxine, bells started to ring. 'I'd really like to find the name of that attendant who disappeared. It might turn out to be important.'

Their latest flight attendant, who'd been sitting in the corner, spoke up. 'Hi, Maxine. My name's Jackson. I know it's not an official record, but we attendants do keep a list of those who've flown on each airplane. It's a notebook in the drawer next to the sink, in the rear steward section.'

Maxine paused. Right now she couldn't think of anything else that she needed to say. 'I think you've answered all my questions, guys. Thank you very much. If I go over to Cosmic Girl right away, will I be able to get on board?'

'I've got all the keys you'd ever need to start the engine and fly it away,' said Greg. 'So no-one can steal the plane. But I left the passenger door unlocked. Given the short notice, we didn't know what gadgets the staff here might want to put on board.'

'Great,' said Maxine. 'I think I'll go and look for that missing name now.'

'That's what the other lady said,' observed Harry. 'But she wasn't a polite lady like you, Maxine. She didn't introduce herself to us at all. Maybe you'll catch up with her inside the plane?'

CHAPTER 53

Confrontation: Fri June 2nd

Maxine thought it was pretty odd to leave the passenger door to a jumbo jet unfastened. But it was standing within a tightly controlled, secure site. Maybe the crew preferred to be left undisturbed, ahead of the forthcoming flight. This secret launch, at such short notice, was creating a welter of problems.

She wondered, as she mounted the aircraft passenger stairs, who the "other lady" might be. Though she had a nasty suspicion and, once she was inside the gloom of the plane, her suspicion was confirmed.

It was the forceful Chair of Newquay Spaceport. This was a confrontation that would need to be handled well.

'Good morning, Suzanne,' she began. 'What brings you here?'

The woman started, looking guilty, disturbed at her presence. Perhaps uncertain who her questioner was. It was five months since they'd met, there were no lights on within the plane and that from the porthole windows was limited.

'It's Maxine, isn't it? The woman who gave us such a glowing report. Have you come to revise it, dear?' Her voice sounded bitter, almost mocking. Maxine recalled their first encounter. She was a hard woman, not used to taking prisoners.

'I might need to,' Maxine replied. 'I found strong evidence this morning, behind the Trevarrian Inn, of how it had really

285

been done.'

Then she remembered how her policeman husband spoke approvingly of silence as a means of extracting information; and said no more.

Suzanne was weighing what had been said; and what it really meant.

'You found the wire, did you? All the way from the outhouse to the field. Or maybe you didn't find it at all. The landlord came across it and contacted the police. Who, completely flummoxed, contacted security. Who in turn sent for you. The far end of a very long line. The small pot at the end of a long rainbow.'

Suzanne drew breath. 'And now, I suppose, you'll want me to tell you what it all means. Well, I'm not falling for that, Maxine. You'll need a lot more evidence than a length of cable before you pin anything on me.'

The Chair was looking defiant now. Though slightly uncertain. She didn't know the full extent of the evidence that Maxine was talking about. What she had to gloss over and what she needed to explain.

Maxine remained silent, let the suspect tie herself in knots. And once again the quietness did its work.

'You asked me what I was doing here, Maxine. Come straight from my office, have you – sent on here by my Privacy Allergic PA? Huh. You've not got the first clue on what I'm looking for.'

Still Maxine said nothing. Silence was harder than it looked. She had answers to the questions, but this was not the time to share them. Suzanne continued, her temper rising.

She scornfully projected the newspaper headline. '"Chair of Newquay Spaceport found in the aircraft taking next rocket into space" – how suspicious is that? You think I can't explain it? Who else did you expect to be in here?'

She chuntered on, edging forward as she did so. 'Wait till you report that miserly factoid back to your bosses – or even the police, if they can ever be found. You think they'll come for me, do you? And charge me with what, exactly? And above all, what's my motive for doing so?'

She and Maxine were facing one another now, barely two feet apart. And Suzanne was very angry indeed. She'd almost got as far as destroying a key piece of evidence when she'd been disturbed. Policemen usually came in pairs but she sensed, now, that Maxine was acting alone. Perceived that, at this moment, no-one else knew exactly what she'd discovered.

Maxine had occasionally come across violence. She recalled her first encounter with George in Bude. At that point she had just been kidnapped from her shower and spent the night in a coal bunker. She'd also found the occasional dead body over the years. But she was not used to defending herself from direct attack. And the blow came out of the blue.

The analyst fell to the floor, dazed. And then Suzanne fell on top of her, held her down with her knees. Then reached for a syringe from her handbag. This would be someone else who wouldn't live to tell the tale.

Back in the Spaceport carpark, George had overcome Peter's moment of panic. She, too, had been shocked to see a jumbo jet on the runway, parked outside the Technical Unit. But she also saw that the blob on the Google map which marked Maxine's location was on exactly the same spot.

'Peter, Peter, Maxine's inside the plane.'

There were two Peters and both responded to her call. All three dashed towards Cosmic Girl, the policeman in the lead. What on earth was his wife doing in a jumbo jet?

The posse raced up the stairs and faced the passenger door.

But they quickly saw it wasn't locked. A second later the trio was inside, eyes blinking as they got used to the gloom.

And then they saw the deadly scene. Maxine was lying comatose on the floor. Another woman was on top of her, holding her down. With some sort of needle in her hand.

Inspector Peter dived forward and knocked the assailant off his wife. The syringe fell from her hand.

Peter Jakes jumped forward to make sure the villain stayed down. But were they too late? Had she already completed a lethal injection?

CHAPTER 54

Restoring the Calm: Fri June 2nd

An hour later some sort of calm had been restored.

Inspector Travers had slipped handcuffs on Suzanne Kennedy, marched her down the aircraft stairs and set off with her in the back seat, aiming for Bude Police Station. The syringe, now placed in an evidence bag, would be sent on to Forensics. It certainly had Suzanne's fingerprints on it. Hopefully they would also find something compromising about whatever she was trying to inject.

He wasn't going to risk Suzanne being interviewed by a policeman from Newquay who knew nothing of what had gone on. He was a direct witness to the assault on Maxine. Though, for the purpose of the courtroom, it might be safer to rely on the testimonies of George and Peter.

There was a separate case of the potential murder of the waitress. He couldn't start on that until he had time with Maxine and she had briefed him. And shown him the additional evidence.

As soon as Suzanne had been restrained, George had raced to tend to her friend Maxine. It turned out that Suzanne's jab had missed its target; the posse had arrived just in time. The analyst had been dazed but, it seemed, there was no lasting damage.

Peter Jakes was all for taking her to Newquay for a checkup but she steadfastly refused. 'I've got more work to do here,' she declared.

George and Peter decided they needed to take the afternoon off. Peter would be back teaching next week, and George hadn't planned to be in the Spaceport today anyway.

They'd had a police car lift to get here, but George's car was still in the Spaceport carpark from Wednesday morning. Maxine promised she would phone them later; maybe all three could have a meal together and catch up on each other's news?

'I suggest a stroll round Stepper Point,' said George. 'It's North Cornwall's answer to the Gribbin. Towns like Padstow or Wadebridge will be heaving today. It'd be good for us to talk.'

George knew a place to park for free near Crugmeer and they set out towards the coast. It was a beautiful afternoon. The sea was calm, an azure blue, as they walked along the coast path and round Butter Cove to the headland.

It was a relief to be at peace after the morning's hectic search for Betjeman's lost letter, the chase to the Spaceport and finally the fight within the plane.

Ten minutes later they came to the Lookout at Stepper Point.

'Let's go in and say hello to the volunteers,' said George. 'My Uncle Bill, who left me the money for Ivy Cottage, used to work here. This is where my first adventure really started.'

Later they came round the headland, above the Camel Estuary. St Enodoc's church, surrounded by the golf course, was on the other side. The sandbank that formed the Doom Bar was below.

'Are you thirsty? There's a special teashop along here,' said George. 'Just off the main path, the start of Hawker's Cove.'

Peter was impressed. There was much to enjoy on the north coast. Later, after tea and scones, the pair continued along the path beside the Camel until they could scramble down to the beach and sunbathe for an hour. Sadly, the swimming gear had been left at home.

Afterwards they went on till they found an inlet, then turned inland, back to the road and hence to George's car.

At that point Maxine phoned George. 'I'm fully recovered,' she began. 'I've learned a lot more. But it'd be easier to share everything face to face. Would you two be happy to have supper with me at the Trevarrian Inn – say half past six?'

They both agreed. There was just time to stop for a glimpse of Bedruthan Steps and Diggory's Island on the way round.

Maxine was waiting for them when they reached the inn and had reserved a table outside. It was a warm, sunny evening. Peter got white wine for the ladies and a pint of Doom Bar for himself. At last he understood the bitter's name. They also ordered light meals. It didn't matter if the food took a while to come; there was plenty to talk about.

'So what have you learned, Maxine?'

'I was here early this morning. And found out how the flight was disrupted.'

The proposition sounded ridiculous. 'What?'

'There's a cable running out the back down a lane. It'd give you power to operate a laser gun from right under the flight path. I'll show it to you after we've eaten.'

Maxine took a sip of her wine. Then continued. 'I met Judith in Newquay library. We identified the waitress that she had found drowned: she was called Yvonne Magorran. So now I had a name and a photograph. It turned out, from our records at GCHQ, that she was in an offshoot of the Irish Republican Army in Dublin.

'Now the attack on Cosmic Girl started to make sense as a terrorist assault which failed.'

Peter blinked. 'Wow. Maxine, you've achieved more in two days than George and I did in two weeks.'

But Maxine hadn't finished. 'There was one more thing. Yvonne was on the Mawgan Porth New Year skinny-dip, which is why the police decided her death was most likely just an accident. But I found a picture of the girls before they took the plunge. There was one other face I recognised: it was Suzanne Kennedy. That suggested Suzanne and Yvonne knew each other, at least a week before the launch. Which might be a crucial finding.'

Maxine stopped to sip her wine before continuing again.

'And I've found Yvonne's link to the Spaceport project. This afternoon I went back to the Cosmic Girl. I found her name listed as a stewardess on Cosmic Girl. So she was right on the inside. Incidentally, that's why she was never reported missing: Cosmic Girl flew off without her, months before anyone started asking questions.'

'How on earth did you find that out?' I asked.

'The stewards keep their own record of who's been on the plane. That notebook was inside the Cosmic Girl kitchen, with Yvonne's name included. That was what Suzanne was after as well, of course. And why she became so wild when I found her searching.'

At that point our meals were brought. After we'd started eating Maxine asked, 'So what have you two discovered since yesterday evening?'

Peter explained how he'd found the letter which John Betjeman had hidden, eighty years ago. 'It was signed "John F K". We think that could be John Kennedy. It's polarised towards the Republican cause. It might cause embarrassment to the Kennedy family, even today – if it was ever published.'

George took over. 'We imagined it might link in some way

to the attack on the space rocket. It seems unexpected enough; and could tie in with your findings about Yvonne. But we can't work out why.'

They ate in silence for a few minutes. 'There are still some facts we're missing,' said Maxine. 'I spent this morning on Personnel staff records. I could find no-one with strong Irish connections. But after my Cosmic Girl encounter with Suzanne – from which I'm very grateful that you rescued me – I went back to check. Yvonne, like the rest of the aircrew, was never on the records. But, it turned out, Suzanne isn't on the records either. So we don't know anything about her background; or how it might tie in with Yvonne – or with the JFK letter.'

George frowned. 'But your Peter's got Suzanne in jail, hasn't he? Isn't that one of the questions he can ask her?'

They had finished their meals by now. Suddenly they heard a distance roar. 'Whatever's that?' asked Peter.

Maxine knew but she wasn't yet saying. 'Guys, we need to move.' She led them behind the inn and out onto a narrow lane; then pointed out the cable hidden in the hedgerow.

'This cable starts within an inn outhouse and runs along here.' They paced along the lane for a couple of hundred yards until they'd reached a gate. 'And it stopped here. Let's just wait.' She took out her phone.

The noise got louder. It was definitely coming from the airport. Then Peter Jakes got it. 'Maxine, are we here to witness another Cosmic Girl space launch?'

She grinned. 'I promised Tom Willoughby I would not tell anyone. But you two have guessed it for yourselves. You might need your cameras shortly.'

It was clear now what was happening. The noise from the airport reached a higher pitch and sounded like it was moving towards them. They got out their cameras and pointed towards the sky over the airfield.

Then it was there. A huge jumbo jet, moving directly overhead, with a large rocket nestling underneath. Three seconds later it was past them and out over the sea.

Once it was passed, Maxine concluded. 'I'm heading back to Bude now. I need to spend more time with my Peter. By tomorrow morning we should know whether or not the flight has succeeded. But we can still congratulate ourselves: between us we've done everything we can to get those satellites into orbit.'

CHAPTER 55

Peter's case concludes: Sun June 4th

When we'd finished at the Trevarrian Inn, George had invited me back to Ivy Cottage in Treknow. 'You don't need to go home till Sunday, do you? Let's have a last weekend together.'

So we were together as we listened to the news on Saturday morning. But there was no mention of Newquay Spaceport. George decided that she would risk ringing Ruth Fisher, to find out what had happened. Was it a masterful success or a dismal failure; feast or famine? We had to know.

Ruth was still in her Spaceport office but didn't mind being pestered, she was on a high. 'George, thanks for ringing. It was a great success. Cosmic Girl came back just after midnight: as far as the crew were concerned, everything had gone perfectly. At much the same time, Goonhilly told us that they'd tracked both rockets and pinpointed when satellites were placed into orbit.

'It's all we could wish for. We've informed the satellite providers, now we're waiting for them to start processing their signals.'

George wrinkled her nose. 'So why isn't it on the news?'

'Well, Tom Willoughby had kept it so secret that it was hard for us to boast about it afterwards. The good news will creep out slowly as the satellite firms go public. I can live without the media right away. Maybe that's the best way for us to handle the publicity?'

'Sounds good to me, Ruth. I'll be in on Monday morning. Still aiming for that business plan by the end of the month. Have a good weekend.'

And George and I had a good weekend as well. We didn't mention rockets at all. Not until Sunday lunchtime, anyway.

Maxine and George had agreed late on Saturday afternoon that it would be good for the four of us to meet for Sunday lunch.

Sunday was the birthday of Rosanna's friend from nursery, and she had been invited to her party. We could book an outside table at the Farm Shop at St Endellion without any worries on her score. Share our findings and ideas.

I realised it would be my last chance to contribute before I was back in Fowey.

We ordered drinks and a magnificent Sunday roast and the catch-up began. First, Peter Travers brought us up to date. His team had worked all Saturday collecting evidence, mostly from around the Trevarrian Inn.

'It's looking good so far,' he began. 'SOCO found DNA on the cable, that's still being processed. But I also talked to the landlord's wife, showed her some pictures. She picked out Suzanne. Confirmed that she used the inn regularly over Christmas and her favourite waitress was Yvonne. Also told me that Yvonne was around the week before the launch – so can't have drowned in the Mawgan Porth New Year dip, as the local police had supposed.

'And I've learned something of Suzanne's background. Her mother, now dead, was British; her dad, still alive, is American. He's a distant limb of the Kennedy clan. Through him she'd heard something of the contentious letter to Ireland. I think she now realises that's a damaging admission, but I've got it on tape.

'But the whole thing's bizarre. Suzanne is the Chair of Newquay Spaceport. Whatever is her part in an assault on Cosmic Girl? I mean, if Suzanne had been found dead – say, in the lane under the flight path or even at Bedruthan Steps – and terrorist Yvonne had vanished, that would make some sort of sense. But what we're left with makes no sense at all.'

In the silence that followed I butted in. 'Before we go on with that, Peter, please can George and I have five minutes on the letter hidden by John Betjeman?'

George started. 'On reflection, the letter itself wasn't that explosive. But imagine the fears it might have aroused. John would return from war and tell his family about it. They could fear the reputational damage if it ever got published.'

I took over. 'Whereas, Republicans would get a hint of it from the Irish mafia in America and would be aggrieved: the support promised had never come. So from both sides the fear from the letter was worse than the potential reality. And that may be why it had so much impact today.'

Another pause, then Peter Travers took back the reins. 'What we need is a plausible link between the two women. I need something to work with when I re-interview her tomorrow.' He raised his cider glass. 'Ideas, please.'

Maxine began. 'Thanks to Peter Jake's research, we've got the actual letter behind the ongoing rumours. He's met Republicans who still resent its non-arrival. Both Republicans and Kennedys must have ideas on what it's about, and the scope for reputational damage.'

She mused before continuing. 'I can think of two ways the two women might come together.

'In Scenario One, Suzanne comes here for the job, completely ignorant, naive. But the Republicans see her name, confirm her links to the Kennedy clan and send Yvonne to make mischief. She puts a lot of pressure on Suzanne and, naturally, she resists.'

'She's not the sort of woman to mess with,' said George. 'That's sometimes a useful skill but it can be fatal. You can imagine the two women, once they had met, reaching loggerheads; and the stakes quickly rising.'

Peter Travers observed, 'Irish Security data shows Yvonne was a seasoned terrorist. She must be the one who obtained the laser gun and laid down the cables to provide the power.'

'Even so, you couldn't hang about in that lane for nights on end,' I noted, 'not in January, anyway. The assault, whatever form it took, would depend on knowing the exact launch time. Maybe Suzanne was the source for that?'

'So how would that work?' asked George.

Maxine considered. 'Well, on this scenario, Yvonne would bully her into providing it. They'd heard of the legendary JFK letter. Yvonne threatened to publish it unless Suzanne complied. Suzanne checked with her dad, daren't risk it being a false threat and decided to give in. Maybe the "Molesworth Arms Three" also came from that threat?

'So she ended up a very unwilling partner to a seasoned terrorist. And over the next weeks the disharmony grew.'

Peter broke in here. 'Until the moment of the launch. That evening, Yvonne forced Suzanne over to the inn and then out into the lane. Perhaps she wanted to give the Chair the humiliation of seeing the assault in person?

'It was when Yvonne started lasering Cosmic Girl that Suzanne realised the full extent of what she'd got herself into. And at that point took the law into her own hands. Probably just as Yvonne was aiming high, with both hands on the laser gun. Suzanne saw a small chance for redemption; and she took it.'

It was a dramatic statement. The arrival of our lunches provided a useful break.

For a few minutes the roast beef and roast vegetables took all our energies. Portions were generous and we had appetites to match. But though the talk had paused, our brains kept working. Soon we were debating again.

I spoke first. 'OK. Let's call that Scenario One. "Suzanne the Innocent". But does it really hang together? Would an innocent woman really have the guile to take out an experience terrorist?'

'For that matter,' added Maxine, 'would a missing letter from eighty years ago make Republicans blow up a space rocket today? It was a cosmic calamity, but not spectacular terrorism. So what's the alternative?'

There was a pause and then George started us off. 'Let's call Scenario Two "Suzanne the Eliminator".

'Both sides – Republicans and Kennedys – had some idea of the back story: Irish-bloodhound John had made rash promises to the other side, which had never been delivered.

'But on this scenario Suzanne wasn't innocent. She'd been carefully chosen by the Kennedy clan as a ruthless eliminator of the Irish threat. It was the Kennedys that got Yvonne installed as stewardess on Cosmic Girl, and Suzanne that got her a short-term job as waitress, in the only pub on the flight path.'

Maxine saw where she was going and took over. 'So on this scenario, there were two hostile women in the dark lane with the laser gun, on that fateful night when Cosmic Girl flew overhead. Yvonne was the only one with the skills to obtain, and fire, the laser gun. But Suzanne always intended to finish Yvonne off afterwards. In this scenario, that wasn't a last-minute accident, it was the crux of a deliberate plan.'

There was a significant pause. We ate more of our meals, then I followed on.

'Suzanne had been at the Spaceport for several months. She knew about rip tides and the dangers of being dragged out to sea. At some point she could have seen a track down to the coast, further up at Bedruthan Steps; maybe even driven down it beforehand.'

Peter had been listening hard to us all. Now he joined in.

'In either scenario, Suzanne wouldn't want Yvonne's body recognised or identified – or linked to Cosmic Girl. She didn't know if the flight had been successful. Even if she was innocent it was still vital to keep the two apart.'

He paused, mind whirring. 'So . . . Suzanne got Yvonne's body, her laser gun and any other kit, into her own car. She must have parked right by the lane entrance, so no-one saw her. Then she drove up the coast, off-road on the track above Bedruthan Steps, and stripped every stitch of clothing off her. After that, she dragged Yvonne's body down the rough track to the beach and pulled it into the sea.'

We'd got ourselves two distinct scenarios. Enough to be going on with, though with plenty of holes and no overwhelming evidence. Now it was time to order some desserts.

Once we started talking again it was George that began. 'Your interview will need a lot of care, Peter: we don't know which scenario applies. Or if there's something else, caused by factors we don't yet know. We've got ideas and a few killer facts but not all that much. Can you even prove that Suzanne was in the lane? She's a clever, determined woman. Is there any way she can concoct an alibi for the launch evening?'

The inspector smiled. 'While I was over in Trevarrian yesterday, I called in on Ruth Fisher – for some reason she was still in her office. I asked her who watched the first flight take-off. She couldn't recall every name. But she was certain that Suzanne was not among them. It had been a source of friction between them. The Chair didn't appear until Tuesday morning and then she was in a filthy temper.'

'Right. So you know where she wasn't. But can you prove she was at the Trevarrian Inn?'

Peter frowned. 'She is the Company Chair. Ruth told me she had a smart, silver BMW. Not many like that around here. It's a long time ago but it'd be worth checking if anyone saw it on that special launch night. And if so, where it was parked. I'll get my sergeant onto that tomorrow. At this moment Suzanne doesn't know that we've got anything on her at all.'

Our desserts were brought and we started eating.

This was my last chance to discuss this topic for some time. 'There is one thing I don't understand,' I said. 'Yvonne had all the equipment she needed to assault Cosmic Girl. But we also know the plane didn't explode. Was the assault the cause of the final rocket failure; or was that just a dreadful coincidence?'

'I've thought about that,' replied the policeman. 'And I've talked on the phone to military experts. They suggest it's just possible the laser gun was being aimed at the rocket being carried under the wing. And damaged a connection between the two stages. Enough to break the firing link between them. So it did sabotage the first flight – but not with the epic explosion that Yvonne had doubtless hoped for.'

I offered my final comment. 'Every cloud has a silver lining. If the fuel tanks on the plane had been hit, and it had exploded, it would have been curtains for many more than just poor Yvonne. Everyone in Trevarrian might have been a victim. We should all be very thankful.'

And everyone agreed.

CHAPTER 56

Confession: Mon June 19th

In Wadebridge, two weeks later, Inspector Peter Travers was working to a tight schedule. Suzanne Kennedy had been charged with deliberate assault on Maxine Travers. The syringe had been found by Forensics to contain a lethal toxin, botulinum. There were several reliable witnesses to the crime, including the inspector himself, and Suzanne had offered no explanation or defence. She was currently on remand in Launceston, awaiting trial.

But Travers also wanted to clear up the death of Yvonne Magorran, which he believed had also been the work of Suzanne Kennedy.

His team had slowly assembled the evidence. Her distinctive car had been spotted outside the Trevarrian Inn on the evening of the first launch. The landlord's wife had seen her in there in the early evening, then she'd disappeared. But the landlord was a car enthusiast, had remembered that the car was still there till late in the evening, though it had gone by next morning.

Furthermore, traces of her DNA had been found on the cable plug at the field gate.

But the date when it had been left was unknown. The case would be weak without a clear motive that linked Suzanne to the dead woman.

The dead woman's link to Republican terrorism was already known. Peter Jakes had given him an account of the way today's Republicans thought of the missing letter; and, miraculously, found the letter itself. Betjeman's last bequest. The first challenge was to nail down the link between Suzanne and the Kennedy family.

There are many studies of the families of major politicians, old and new, in the United States. Peter had an old friend in the FBI, James, who advised him where to look; and took a personal interest in his request.

'For reasons I can't say at this stage, James, I'm interested in any connection between the Kennedy clan and a woman called Suzanne Kennedy. I'll send you her details if it would help.'

A week had gone by. Then James had returned the call.

'A branch of the Kennedy family in Massachusetts had a relative called Suzanne, who was helping them set up a new business. She'd been there for several years but left last July. I can show them her photo if you like, Peter – make sure it's the same woman.'

Two days later James confirmed it was the same Suzanne; and passed on her full details. He also passed on far more details on the woman's backstory. It was time for him to interview Suzanne again.

This interview required great care. Travers could hint that he knew more than he did, to flush out further details. But that would only work if his starting guess was substantially correct. In this case the key question was Suzanne's attitude towards Yvonne.

It occurred to him that one way of putting this was to ask: who made the opening call? Was it Suzanne controlling Yvonne? Or was it Yvonne bullying Suzanne?

Peter still had Suzanne's private phone, taken at her arrest. But he also needed a phone number for Yvonne. Where would that come from?

He rang Maxine in Cleave Camp. 'Maxine, I urgently need to know Yvonne's phone number. Could you possibly get it from your opposite number in Dublin?'

Half an hour later his wife had rung back with Yvonne's number. And also several extra details on her family. Now he had an exercise for his new police recruit, Tommy.

Tommy was bright. He turned up at Peter's office just after lunch, with many sheets of phone call records, some highlighted in red or in green.

'The ones in red were to Suzanne from Yvonne, guv. And the ones in green were the other way round.'

They leafed back through the pages.

The last call between the two was from Suzanne to Yvonne on Jan 9th. Proof, surely, that Suzanne knew something had happened to Yvonne on that date? There'd be no point in ringing her again later – if she knew that she was dead.

But who had made the first call? The two leafed back further. And there it was. In red. A call from Yvonne to Suzanne, in late October. Yvonne was the instigator of the relationship.

Two days later Travers and his sergeant confronted Suzanne in an interview room in Launceston.

The phone data implied Suzanne had been the innocent party in the relationship. But since completing the phone analysis, he recalled an odd fact uncovered by his wife that had never been properly explained.

'Suzanne, did you book in three guests at the Molesworth Arms, ahead of the first space launch?

The question was so unexpected that it caught her off guard.

'Hey, that's right. How did you know?'

'So what were they here for?'

'To help with my protection. Fat chance.'

'Why did you need protection?'

'Huh. Why does any woman need protection?'

'It wasn't, by any chance, from Yvonne Magorran?'

Suzanne tried to deny knowing who Yvonne was. That didn't last long. Then she claimed she was a waitress she'd met in the Trevarrian bar. That didn't hold for long either.

'We've found Yvonne's number in your phone record, you see,' said the inspector. 'There were many calls between the two of you. How did you get her number, Suzanne?'

She was blustering now. 'I can't remember. I met her in the bar and we became friends; so we chatted from time to time.'

Peter frowned. 'That can't be true. The calls go back long before Yvonne was working in the Trevarrian bar. So how did you get hold of it?'

In the end Suzanne had to admit that Yvonne had made the first call, back in October.

'And what was that about?'

'You're being ridiculous, inspector. I can't remember details of a phone call I received six months ago.'

He left that for the moment. 'So was this the first you had heard from Yvonne? Did it come out of the blue? Or was there history behind it?'

This was a new line of questioning. She didn't know which way to jump, did not dare to say anything. Again the inspector moved on.

'You'll know that Yvonne is dead, of course. But you may not know that we found her body, off Bedruthan Steps. We're interested in anyone who was in regular contact with her before January. But you made no more calls at all after Jan 9th – the day of the first launch. Why was that?'

Suzanne mumbled but made no attempt to reply.

'A possible reason, Suzanne, is that you knew she was dead.' He paused then, 'Was that because you had killed her?'

Suzanne had hoped it would never come to this. Was not sure what to say. But Peter wasn't to be thwarted.

'We've a witness that you were at the Trevarrian Inn early on launch night. But then you disappeared. Meanwhile, your car was seen, parked outside the lane, till late in the evening. What were you doing, outside the inn, in the meantime?'

'It's a long time ago, Inspector. Can you remember what you were doing on Jan 9th?'

Peter growled, 'I would if it was the day I'd killed someone. I think it happened in the lane behind the inn. Right below the Cosmic Girl flight path. That's where you and Yvonne stood to fire the laser gun.'

'But that wasn't me,' she gasped. 'Yvonne was the only one that knew how to fire it.'

'But did you like watching her do so?'

There was a pause, but she saw how the evidence was stacking up. 'There were crew members in that plane, inspector – people I knew. Yvonne was going to kill them. I tried to stop her but she fought back. She was trying to kill me. We struggled, then, somehow, I managed to turn the gun on her and she keeled over. It was dreadful.' Suzanne started to cry.

Peter wanted a full confession now she was talking. 'Why not just leave her in the lane?'

Suzanne gritted her teeth. 'I could have scarpered. But I couldn't abandon the laser gun below the flight path. Or Yvonne, for that matter. We were only two hundred yards from where she worked. She was compact. I managed to drag her along to the boot of my car. Then went back for the laser gun.

It was too difficult to move the cables – I guess you found them?'

'Oh yes. Plus the cable socket with your DNA on it. It also had Yvonne's. But you couldn't just leave Yvonne by the road-side. She had to really disappear.'

Suzanne swallowed hard. 'I wanted Yvonne left well away from the Spaceport. I was a Mawgan Porth Mermaid, you see. Swam regularly. I knew about rip tides, how they could make bodies disappear. The girls said the effect was worst around Bedruthan Steps. I decided that was the best place to leave her.'

She paused for a moment, distraught. Then continued.

'It was a hell of a task. Down the cliffs with Yvonne. Then I stripped to my underwear, heaved her onto my body board and swam out to sea, as far as I could manage. After I'd tipped her into the sea, I had to fight my way back. The bloody rip tide nearly got me as well. I was exhausted by the time I was back, completely frozen. It was such a struggle to get dressed. Then I had to climb back up the cliffs. By the time I was back at the car I was utterly shattered.'

The inspector nodded. 'And the laser gun?'

She grunted. 'I didn't want that found, either. I cleaned off the fingerprints, then dropped it down the nearest copper mine. After that I headed for bed. It was three am. But I was too wound up to sleep. No wonder I was in a bad mood for next morning's spaceflight review.'

Suzanne came to a halt. Seemingly with nothing else to say.

There was a long pause. 'It's a good story, Suzanne,' said the inspector. 'The trouble is, it doesn't all hang together.

'Take the Molesworth Three. We've got their pictures from the security system. They're all known to Irish Security and also linked to Yvonne Magorran. You didn't choose them, she foisted them on you. They were here to buy the cables and lay them out along the lane.'

'So let's go through your story. For a start, it's a complex plan to dispose of a dead body. Which, you're asking me to believe, you made up on the spot?

'You'd have needed to park right beside the end of the lane – was that just a coincidence?

'Do you always carry a body board in the depths of winter?

'And how did you know your way, in the dead of night, down the track to Bedruthan Steps? Was that really unrehearsed?

'If you were innocent, you'd be eager to tell me that Yvonne had made the first phone call. You wouldn't struggle to hide it.

'And you knew far too much about John Kennedy's letter. So, putting it all together, I think you went out to the Trevarrian Lane not because of the threat of blackmail from Yvonne but as an eliminator.'

The inspector paused again, gathering his thoughts.

'I don't buy the notion that you accidently electrocuted Yvonne. If something like that had happened, it would have left scorch marks on her body. But no such marks were found.'

'So how was she killed? Well, we know you had a lethal syringe with you which you tried to use on Maxine Travers. That contained a toxin called botulinum. Forensics tell me it has a special property: the trace fades away very quickly. I reckon you also had that with you in the lane – and you used it on Yvonne.

'She thought she was in charge: you'd complied with her bidding, never suspected that you would attack her. Least of all while she was aiming at Cosmic Girl with her laser gun. I wonder. Was the main reason you didn't want her body found quickly to give the toxin time to decay?'

Suzanne did not respond. But she was not rushing to reject his ideas, was offering no contradictory evidence.

'So what was your motive, Suzanne? That took us some

digging out. You told us early on that your mother is dead. But we've checked and found, as you must know, that the death wasn't due to natural causes; she was killed by Irish terrorists.

So after her death, your American dad took you back to the United States. Where the pair of you contacted the Irish mafia, to help identify your mother's killer. And the villain, it turned out eventually, was Yvonne's father. That gave you a very special reason indeed for wanting to take revenge on her.

'So the notion that you killed Yvonne by accident, during a quarrel over an eighty-year-old letter which never arrived, looks, to say the least, implausible.'

The inspector had already got a confession on who had killed Yvonne.

Yvonne hadn't yet admitted to the whole truth. But he'd got more than enough to charge her. It should put the woman away for many years.

EPILOGUE   The Longest Day

June 21st would be the longest day of the year – and longest of all in the Shetlands. The base at SaxaVord was progressing steadily towards a vertical launch in 2025, though there was much still to be done.

Inspector Travers was pleased with his investigation. He'd wrung a confession out of Suzanne Kennedy, admitting to killing and disposing of the Dublin terrorist who had threatened to derail the entire launch plan.

A pathologist was now checking Yvonne's body for any traces of the botulinum which Suzanne had tried to use on Maxine Travers. If any was found, that would be strong evidence that this was the way she had killed Yvonne.

The British and Irish Security Services were studying the terrorist incident in which Yvonne's mother had been killed.

In any case, she had also been charged with assaulting Maxine. She was currently on remand in Launceston prison, would never be returning to the Spaceport.

Newquay Spaceport was basking in its successful launch. Ruth Fisher was finding that life without a Corporate Chair trying to second guess everything was more relaxed and friendly – and no less efficient. The low-key publicity stemming from the Technical Director's secret launch had suited her fine. There were no immediate plans to find a replacement Chair.

The nine satellites launched at the start of June were performing perfectly.

Bridging the Gulf in Dublin, who had sent the final satellite across with Peter Jakes, reported that they were starting to measure the extent and temperature of the Gulf Stream. Readings were being taken on ocean surface temperature many times a day as the satellite circled the globe on its polar orbit.

Over the next few years, they hoped to measure changes in the Gulf Stream's width and relate these to variations in Arctic ice and other factors.

Both Cornwall Council and the Irish Government were particularly interested in the longer-term lessons.

George Gilbert had almost completed her business plan for the Spaceport. It drew substantially on data from the second launch. Her results were positive but realistic. Space flights would never make huge profits but could widen mankind's knowledge. George's short-term contract had been extended to allow her to be part of extended discussions with the UK Government.

Summer term at Fimbarras Academy was drawing to a close for Peter Jakes. His sixth form students were completing their A-level exams, would soon be moving off to university. Peter had submitted his application to be Head Teacher at Wadebridge Academy. Sadly, it had not been successful.

On the other hand, his presentation to the Fowey Writers' Circle, on the life of Sir John Betjeman, had proved a big success. The illustrated tale of the poet's wartime years, using his photographs taken in Dublin, had been riveting. How could such a mild, inoffensive man have such an exciting backstory? Peter was now being urged to convert his ideas into a booklet for wider circulation.

In the spirit of being 'No longer a hermit,' Peter had kept in touch with the team in Dublin at Bridging the Gulf. One day he was astonished to receive an email from them, inviting him to join their team for a year, starting in September.

'Now our satellite is functional,' it said, 'we need someone to coordinate our links with Cornwall Council, looking for new ways that we can work together.'

It was an exciting opportunity. How should he respond?

Meanwhile George Gilbert had also had an invitation, from the SaxaVord Vertical Launch Platform on the Shetlands. Working alongside their strategic planner, Joanna, they needed someone to generate a realistic business plan for discussion with the Scottish government.

It would be a complete change of scene for her too. Very tempting. Should she take it?

Peter and George now needed a serious conversation.

AUTHOR'S NOTES

The abortive space flight from Newquay Airfield on the evening of Jan 9th, 2023, using jumbo jet Cosmic Girl for the first 35,000 feet of ascent, did happen. Everything beyond is fiction.

Putting nine 5-10 kg satellites into a Low Earth Orbit should have come next. Monitoring the Gulf Stream could have been the intention. A recent BBC programme, since much decried, suggested its decline could begin as soon as 2025.

The oddest thing I learned about John Betjeman, from the foreword to his Uncollected Poems, was a letter from an ex-IRA man in Dublin. He had gone on an IRA death list; a gunman had been enlisted to kill him, but he was away on a mission at the time. Subsequently one of the IRA men read his poems and concluded that he could not possibly be a spy.

I made up Betjeman's wartime work in Wadebridge. But he did retire to Trebetherick and is buried at St Enodoc. The John Betjeman Centre in Wadebridge keeps his possessions, including teddy bear Archibald (overleaf). The museum depicts an armoured engine chugging from Wadebridge to Padstow, manned by Polish refugees.

John F Kennedy never flew into Newquay Airfield. But he did give a supportive speech to the Irish in Dublin in 1963. The

A Cornish Conundrum

JFK letter handed over to Betjeman for the Irish is pure fiction, as are all anxieties and actions from the wider Kennedy family.

Whether George Gilbert will go to SaxaVord, or Peter Jakes to Dublin, remains to be seen.

Maxine first appears in Twisted Limelight; her wedding is in Forever Mine. Peter Travers is in Doom Watch, Slate Expectations, Brush with Death and Beyond Reach. Peter Jakes arrives in Well Above Par. Joy Tregorran comes in Crown Dual and Unsettled Score. George Gilbert plays a key role in all the Cornish Conundrums.

I am grateful for wise comments on early drafts: Simon and Karen Porter, Les Williams, Chris Scruby, Mike Pittam, my wife Marion and my daughter Lucy Smith. Angela Bamping was a great copy editor. All remaining errors are mine.

Judith Stanley, Liz Wild and Graham Hindle all appear in the story via a draw at the Caversham Christmas Gala.

If you have enjoyed this book/ebook, please consider a one-line review on Amazon to encourage others to read it. If you have any detailed comments – or ideas for future conundrums – please contact me via the website below.

David Burnell   *website: www.davidburnell.info*
May 2024

Archibald, John Betjeman's long-lasting bear
(Now in the John Betjeman Centre in Wadebridge)

The armoured steam train protecting the Camel estuary
in World War Two
(picture from the Wadebridge Museum)

315

CORNISH CONUNDRUMS 1-11

Printed in Great Britain
by Amazon